ECLIPSE

FRACTURED ORBIT
BOOK 1

HERMAN STEUERNAGEL

THE FOURTH MEDIA PUBLISHING

ECLIPSE

Book One of Fractured Orbit

First Edition

Copyright © 2022, 2023 by Herman Steuernagel

ISBN: 978-1-990505-07-2 (hardback)

ISBN: 978-1-990505-08-9 (paperback)

ISBN: 978-1-990505-05-8 (ebook)

Cover by Covers by Christian

Edited by Novel Approach Manuscript Services

https://www.hermansteuernagel.com

PROLOGUE

Abigail Monroe
The *Black Swan*

ABIGAIL MONROE SCRAMBLED to reach the *Black Swan's* lone escape pod as fire spread across the bridge.

If there was one universal rule she agreed with, it was that no matter which side of the gaming table you find yourself on, it's always the losing side. The only true winner, of course, is the house, and they care little about who wins or loses, as long as the game is played for as long as possible.

She had foolishly believed she had been gambling against another player, risking her life fighting a worthy opponent. But, of course, the Syndicate empire was no ordinary enemy. In this game, they were the house. They controlled the cards, the chips, and the bets. They made the rules. And the rules were made to benefit them. They also believed they controlled the outcome of this game.

Abigail never played by the rules, and she wasn't going to settle for losing.

As she now saw it, she had two options: refuse to play—or burn the house down.

Maybe a little arson would be more to their liking.

Trouble was, she wasn't exactly in a position to put a match to anything at the moment. Somehow, she had already slipped up and it had cost her a ship and her crew.

Abigail's ship, the *Black Swan*, had seen better days. Once a prime shuttlecraft, the shuttle's dark gray interior was now hanging in the balance, sparks flying from its panels. Its main viewport crackled and sparked, though its image remained intact.

The nimble runabout ship was designed for transporting goods with speed and agility, but she hadn't been built to withstand energy weapons. Abigail hadn't even seen who had dealt the deadly blow. If the Syndicate already had a target on her back, their mission was already in jeopardy, and that simply wouldn't do. But whether it was the Syndicate, the Orbital Guard, the Separatists—or even a bounty hunter looking to collect the price placed on her head—it didn't matter. Either way, whoever it was had tracked her down and shot at her. Running from the law was one thing—she had been doing that her entire adult life. Being fired upon by a faceless foe was quite another.

You didn't become one of the most successful pirates in orbit without breaking a few rules and making a few enemies. But there was currently far too much at stake for there to be a target on her back. And whoever was pursuing her knew what they were doing.

To a point.

Abigail's attacker had skillfully hit her fusion reactor. If the shot had been any more precise, she would have been hurtling into the atmosphere in an incandescent fireball instead of being granted a few priceless seconds to get her bearings and jump into an escape pod.

More importantly, her attacker had mistakenly assumed Abigail wouldn't survive the attack. But if there was one thing she would confidently bet on in any given situation, it was that she'd always survive.

Or at least, she had so far. Abigail laughed at the thought. *She wasn't so easy to kill.*

Unfortunately, the same couldn't be said for her three crew members.

They lay dead, sprawled across the ship's floor. The violent jarring of the ship had thrown each of them from their stations when the sparks had started to fly. Their faces had been burned and disfigured, their lungs void of life-giving breath.

A pity, Abigail thought. *They'd been a pretty good crew.*

A whisper at the back of her mind suggested their deaths should have bothered her more. Abigail wasn't heartless, but she had seen her fair share of death. She would have said she'd miss these three, but she had barely known them long enough to remember their names. Fredrick? Chekov? Pria? The words sounded familiar, but the *Black Swan* seemed to pick up new faces every few months. Some were better than others.

The life of an orbital pirate was a deadly one. Few had sufficient mettle. Fewer still survived more than a year. Those that didn't die often disappeared. Whether or not it was by choice . . . well, most were never heard from again, so who was to say?

Abigail swooped her cape over her shoulder and grabbed her staff. The smooth hickory object was more for show than it was for utility, but she never went anywhere without it.

The ship's sole escape pod had been built into the far side of the bridge, its inclusion an afterthought to whichever nitwit engineer had designed the vessel. For one, the gravity plating that lined the bridge didn't extend into the pod. It was meant to be a last-ditch escape mechanism, so that was understandable. What Abigail didn't understand was that it was impossible to fly the *Swan* with fewer than three people, and it possessed the capacity for ten, but the pod was only big enough for one. Two, if you were willing to get intimate with your shipmate.

Abigail shrugged it off. No point in worrying about that now—she had the sole ticket to the finale of this event.

Abigail wasn't sure if it was part of an ancient naval code or merely tradition that stated a captain should go down with her ship. Then again, she *had* never been one for rules or traditions. Since whoever had designed the *Swan* had never intended for more than one person to escape catastrophe, she shrugged off the momentary question of honor. Perhaps it *was* the captain that deserved to fight another day.

Two out of the Loop's eleven FLOW stations hovered majestically on the ship's main screen. Each was a testament to what forced ignorance could achieve.

Future Life Orbital Waypoints. The meaning behind the name had all but disappeared from the vernacular, but the acronym remained. It was a term that had been generated centuries ago that had since lost all meaning. At one point, they were meant to provide salvation to humanity. Now the stations imprisoned a large swath of it.

Abigail almost envied the poor saps on board those stations.

Almost.

But with smoke and flame rapidly filling the bridge of the *Black Swan*, nearly anywhere else seemed appealing. Abigail's life was built on lies, anyway—could it really be any worse if she wasn't aware of the truth? Maybe there was tranquility in not knowing what a shithole the Loop had become. Certainly, it couldn't be any worse than hauling your tired ass into an escape pod to flee an unknown enemy and a ship you'd grown to love.

She choked on the smell of burnt metal and melted plastic. Chaos surrounded her, but time seemed to slow as she surveyed the stations in the distance.

Maybe those on board the stations are better off. Oblivious.

Unlike the rest of those in orbit, who knew the system had gone to hell and either didn't care or had no agency to fix it. Those who were so naïve to believe they had free will. That they were anything more than pawns.

Guess we're all pawns, though, aren't we?

Maybe *she* was the naïve one for believing something could be done about it.

A burst of sparks above her head snapped Abigail from her thoughts, forcing her to focus on the emergency at hand. She faced her bridge one last time.

Abigail didn't fight the smirk that appeared as she pulled the metal door to the escape pod closed and punched in the commands to isolate it from the rest of the ship. She had struck a nerve with someone important, which meant she was on the right track. And she would live to fight another day.

She pushed herself back from the door, fighting the reduced gravity and the queasiness from the sudden shift as she pulled the graphene straps across her body to secure her to the pod's command station.

"Abi?" A man's garbled voice crackled over the pod's speakers as she rerouted systems control to the console. "Abi, what's happening? I've lost your signal."

There he was—the man who had got her into this mess. A man who was the epitome of someone who shouldn't exist within the Loop yet was still one of the sanest voices in the galaxy.

Oddly, if there was one person who could help her to tear the Syndicate apart, it was him.

"Just a minor inconvenience, love. This may not be the best time, but I should probably let you know—I'm going to need a new ship."

"You're kidding, right? You're still going to hit the rendezvous?"

"Uh . . ." Abigail jumped as a panel collapsed, missing her head by mere inches. "I'll have to get back to you on that one, love."

"Damn OG!"

"I don't think the Orbital Guard has this kind of firepower . . . or competency."

Abigail flicked a switch, bringing the pod's power systems online. A few more pushed buttons, and the shuttle shook with the release of its clamps.

"Damn. Who, then?"

"It doesn't matter now. Listen, I'd love to chat about this, but I'm in the middle of getting the hell off this ticking time bomb. The *Swan* won't hold together much longer."

"Things are that bad?"

"What do you think I meant when I said, 'I'm going to need a new ship'?"

"I . . . I don't know, Abi. I've been out of the Loop for so long, I didn't put the pieces together. You said it was an 'inconvenience.'"

"Well, it sure as hell isn't convenient from where I'm standing."

"Shit, Abi. What about your crew?"

"Oh, them? They're dead." She didn't mean for it to sound so cold.

"All three of them?"

"Yes, love. That's what I meant by 'all.' I'm fine, though. Thanks for asking."

"Dead people aren't usually so chatty."

"Well, wish me luck. I don't know who did this to my ship or if they're even still out there."

"Abi, if you get picked up by the OG, you're done for."

Abigail rolled her eyes. "What *exactly* would you like me to do? I can handle the Guard. An exploding ship? Not so much."

"Shit, Abi, we have a rendezvous scheduled. If you miss the pickup . . ."

"And here I was, thinking you were beginning to care about me." Abigail smirked.

"This isn't the time to get cute. If you can't get here, it's going to get a lot harder for me to leave."

"I know what's at stake," she shot back. "Don't forget who's been locked away for seven years and who's been out here flying ships and tracking your sorry ass down. We'll find a way, love."

Abigail entered a few additional commands into the pod's console and felt the single-burn engines igniting below her. The pod would emit an initial burst to put distance between itself and the ship. From there, it would have minimal thrust capabilities. It used old-fashioned rocket fuel, of all things, to power its initial burst. The process was crude and expensive, but it did the trick in an emergency.

At least, I hope it'll do the job.

How long had that fuel been sitting in the pod's tank? Years? Decades?

Once the pod was clear of the *Swan,* solar panels would give Abigail the ability to steer and set course, but the rest would be left up to gravity and momentum. As close as she was to the planet, it wouldn't take long for her to be pulled into the Earth's atmosphere.

As she blasted from the *Black Swan,* the world rumbled beneath her. Abigail thought it was the pod's thrust, but the shaking didn't stop, and soon she was flying end over end, somersaulting into space with far more velocity than her pod should have been physically capable of.

With each rotation, her ship crossed her viewport—or at least, what was left of it. The source of her momentum came painfully into focus.

The *Swan* had exploded.

"That was close," she thought out loud.

A *pop* overhead grabbed her attention. Steam hissed out of a compartment, clinging to the gravity-less walls of the cabin as she spun.

Abigail unbuckled her safety restraints, bracing herself against the freefall of the pod's rotation. She scrambled to grab a cloth and shove it into the leaky compartment. She cursed as her skin connected with the hot metal pipe, and she shook her hand before instinctively sticking the sore finger in her mouth. The release of steam slowed, but it was replaced with the odor of burnt cloth. There was nothing else for her to do except hope the flame-retardant cloth maintained its integrity.

Static filled Abigail's headset and, for a moment, she thought her communications had been knocked out completely.

There was only one way to find out.

"Are you still there, love?" she ventured.

"I'm here. What's happened?"

"New problem: the *Swan*'s toast, and the blast damaged the pod. I don't have a lot of time."

"How can I help?"

"Help? How are you going to help from there? I'll have to figure this one out. Listen, we've kept this channel open for too long. I'll meet you at the rendezvous. Until then, stay alive."

"You t—"

Abigail killed the signal before the man could finish.

He thinks he can help. Abigail rolled her eyes. Men were all alike. It didn't matter if they were in command of a patrol vessel or locked away in a disconnected space station.

"Now I'm in for it," she muttered.

The console's screen was an antique. There was no need to fit the one-use vehicle with a holo-screen, she supposed, but the flat touchscreen display blinked and cut in and out as if impacted by a loose wire.

She entered a few commands and was relieved to discover the system still worked well enough to perform a short-range scan. A nearby ship could be either her savior or her demise, but she was faced with no alternative. Nothing showed up on the scan, though, and she wasn't sure if she should be relieved or disappointed.

"Bloody hit and run!"

She changed the parameters of her scan, expanding the range to the full distance the pod's sensors would allow.

"Abi, darling, you are in luck," she said to herself. "The one ship in the Loop that might be willing to help without flaying your skin."

The ship on the screen in front of her had been on Abigail's metaphorical radar for some time. The odds of it appearing during her moment of greatest need were nothing but providential.

"I could have searched for you for months and turned up empty-handed, and yet here you are . . ."

With a few keystrokes, she sent out a call on a channel she hadn't used in a long time. It was an old pirate frequency that had fallen out of favor when the Syndicate had discovered it a few years back. But it was exactly what was needed to grab the attention of an ex-pirate.

Abigail cleared her throat and narrowed her eyes. "Let's give her a ring, then, shall we?"

CHAPTER ONE

Django Alexander
Eclipse

WHY COULDN'T *things be normal for once?*

Alarms echoed through the dining hall of the space station *Eclipse*, causing Django Alexander's heart to skip several beats at the sudden cacophony of noise—just as it did every time those blasted alarms blared. Django held his breath, waiting for the inevitable message that would follow.

The open space of the dining hall seemed to amplify the noise. Several diners who sat at neighboring tables had covered their ears with their hands, while others continued to eat their flavorless meals with little interest.

Django threw down his fork and it skittered across the table, the bone-rattling noise all around grating on his nerves.

More deaths. More families torn apart.

More change.

Bile rose from the few bites of beans and potatoes Django had swallowed. A glance toward the washrooms ensured he had a clear exit path in case he needed to void his stomach's contents. It likely wouldn't get to that point, but it was wise to have a course mapped out just in case.

In sync with the noise, the panel lighting that lined the perimeter of the room turned from blue to red. Screens flashed in warning before the inevitable message would convey the details of today's emergency: the now-familiar report of a breach in the station's outer hull.

Again.

The increased frequency of the alerts was soul-crushing. Each time they sounded, it meant only one thing—death. Each wail of the sirens represented another breach in the *Eclipse's* hull, which, inevitably meant someone had been sucked into the vacuum of space before the station technicians could fix the problem. As overcrowded as their lower level ring was, no one deserved that.

The *Eclipse* consisted of four torus rings, built before the Climate Wars had destroyed the Earth. Before humanity was forced to evacuate the planet in the hope of saving it.

Four torus rings, separated by the station's core, and a transport shuttle that ran between them, now held all of humanity.

"Those breaches aren't slowing." Eventide Rossi sat across the table from Django, holding a deck of cards in one hand and shuffling through it absently. Her fingers worked through the cards effortlessly, as though each card had a life of its own. She ran her other hand through her hair, confident the shuffling didn't require both hands or her full attention. She had recently cut her hair short and tinged it with blue highlights; it was a style not sported by anyone else on the D-Ring, an influence from the B-Ring that Django found both beautiful and unnecessary.

The alarms dulled, quieting to a tolerable level. The main station lights dimmed, darkening the room and allowing the red flashing emergency lights to take prominence.

Aren't slowing? Django thought. There had been three breaches during the past week alone; a dozen over the past month.

Before that, he could only remember a handful of similar incidents before the start of the year.

Eventide barely looked up as she laid a playing card on the metal table. The jack of diamonds.

"Are you going to be all right?" Eventide asked, pushing back a strand of her blue hair.

Django's stomach roiled, but he thought he had been doing a decent job of keeping it together. Clearly not as good as he'd thought.

The black screen that sat above their table flashed an angry red warning: *HULL BREACH, SECTIONS D-GAMMA-97 TO D-GAMMA-102. EVACUATE IMMEDIATELY.*

The tension in his shoulders released, but the pang in his chest remained. The breach was on the opposite side of the D-Ring to the dining hall; away from where his family was planning his sister Celeste's wedding reception.

Despite the relief, Django didn't reach for his fork again; he'd lost his appetite. Hunger didn't matter, though; the celebration was in a few hours, and there was no point in ruining whatever appetite he might regain.

"Me?" Django asked. He didn't know whether to laugh, cry, or if he should react at all. "At this point? It's just another piece of the station that needs repairing. There'll still be a wedding today, as if it never happened. We carry on as though it's normal."

Or as close to "normal" as we can get. Can we please get back to normal?

"*You're* the one who's going to have to deal with these breaches," he said. "I've been sitting on the edge of my seat for months. If anything, I'm worried about *you*. I still can't believe you chose to spend your days fixing hull breaches when you could have lived the rest of your days in the dirt. Life's a lot simpler that way."

Eventide's face remained expressionless for a moment as she

shuffled the deck again. She placed another card on the table: the jack of clubs.

Django could tell by the way she shook slightly that she was nervous, but moving the cards did a good job of masking her jitters.

"That's the point," she smirked. "There's not enough excitement on the D-Ring. We might not be able to leave the station in our lifetime, but that *doesn't* mean there aren't opportunities elsewhere."

Django sighed. "I just wish it wasn't so dangerous."

Eventide's smile faded, and her hands stopped fidgeting. "For starters, you know as well as I do that when I signed up, hull breaches weren't happening every other day. I thought I'd be adjusting sensors and fixing malfunctioning doorways, not this."

"Does that mean you're reconsidering the position?" Django couldn't help the trace of hope that had bled into his voice.

She smiled. "Anything that's worthwhile carries risk. I'd always hoped I would get to have an adventure. This is probably as close as I'll ever get."

Django sighed, picked up his fork again, and tapped it nervously on the table. "How are the cards falling today? Are you still looking for meaning? Or just keeping yourself distracted?"

"Is there a difference?" Eventide asked as she placed another card on the table. The jack of spades.

"For you? Probably not."

"What's that supposed to mean?" Eventide continued her shuffling, a hint of annoyance in her voice, but the two of them had gone down this road before.

"You know what I mean. You could be down here with us. Things are good here. We work hard; we feed the station; we're sending supplies down to the planet. Is that not enough for you?"

Django regretted the words as soon as they left his mouth. The truth was, he hated the fact that Eventide was moving to the

B-Ring, and he didn't understand why she felt the need to do so. Nobody else in the station's history, as far as he knew, had transferred from D to B, and he didn't know why Eventide needed to be the first.

Things were fine as they were. The four-ringed space station had functioned within this paradigm for over a century. Administrative staff, leadership, and security personnel were stationed in the A-Ring. The B-Ring housed technical staff, engineers, technicians, maintenance workers, and logistics. Most of the station's manufacturing, item repurposing, and artifact recycling took place on the C-Ring. That left the largest torus ring of the station—the D-Ring. The final, donut-shaped level held most of the civilian population, but it was also home to farms, metal reclamation works, and the cargo bays that sent shuttles to and from the surface, carrying trees for reforestation, animal life, and equipment that would be used to purify the tainted consequences of the Climate Wars.

The D-Ring was the lifeblood of the ecosystem's regrowth, and Eventide wanted to leave it to turn bolts, rewire systems, and fix hull breaches.

A flash of annoyance crossed Eventide's face, but it quickly faded as she shrugged off his comments. "We're all made to make a difference—in our own way. I could never be happy here. I was always meant for something more."

Django stopped himself from rolling his eyes. Eventide always talked about purpose. Life on the D-Ring had never been enough.

He'd never be enough.

He swallowed. Her eyes found his and held the same glint they often did when she spoke of better things.

Better than me.

He mentally rebuked himself. There would be time to sulk over Eventide later. Other things were happening today that warranted his attention. Despite the alarms, despite Eventide's decisions, today was his sister's wedding day.

Django scratched at the collar of his dress shirt and wished he'd been able to dress as casually as Eventide for the event.

Instead of traditional formal wear, she sported ripped black pants and a black hoodie unzipped at the front. The purple eyeshadow painted on her eyelids shimmered beneath the station's lighting and complemented the highlights in her hair.

Django wanted to focus on the day's main event—it wasn't every day his older sister got married—but the immediacy of the station's emergency lighting and blaring alarm was distracting, and he couldn't draw his mind away from their pull.

"Are they telling you anything about the breaches in your training?" he asked. "Any idea why they're happening so frequently?"

Eventide shrugged and laid another card on the table. The jack of hearts.

"The instructors don't say much. I don't think our ancestors ever meant for the station to last this long." She sighed, pulled her black-hooded sweater closer around her, suddenly cold, and shook her head as though trying to dismiss a thought.

"What is it?" Django asked perceptively. Eventide lifted her blue eyes to meet his own. "I can tell there's something you're not saying."

"It's probably nothing," she said, shaking her head again. "You know how we send so much of our supplies to the planet's surface? We barely keep enough here to meet our needs. Even through this uptick in station damage. It's as though we're focused more on the Earth's regrowth than our own needs."

"Well, isn't that the point of all this?" Django asked. "Aren't we trying to get out of here as soon as possible?"

"None of us will get out of here if the station falls apart before the surface is ready."

She turned another card. The three of diamonds.

"*Shit*," Eventide said. "A three after three jacks? That's bad luck."

Evie and her superstitions, Django thought. He never understood how markings on cards could signify anything relevant to real life.

"What are you clowns doing?"

Django cringed at the voice before he even saw the man behind it. Faron Lu was another technician-in-training and Eventide's study partner. Unlike Eventide, he had always been a B-Ring resident—and an asshole. At five foot eight, Faron was above average in height, and his entire frame was muscle. The tight black shirts he typically wore left nothing to the imagination, but today he stood over their table, dressed to the nines in a flashy tuxedo that hid his luminescent tattoos and oozed B-Ring self-importance.

"What the hell is *he* doing here?" Django asked.

"Same as always. He's my training partner." Eventide tucked the cards back into her sleeve and pushed a strand of hair behind her ear as she looked up at the man and smiled. "We attend everything together, even family affairs."

Faron grabbed a chair and spun it around so that its back faced the table, then swung a leg over it and sat down in one graceful motion. He crossed his tree trunk arms over its back and leaned forward.

"Don't worry, Jancy, I don't want to be here, either."

Jancy. Faron's nickname for Django burned fury across his skin. Why did Eventide have to bring *him* to the reception? It was bad enough that she wouldn't be *his* date, but did she have to bring her own? Stupid technician protocols kept them together at all times, but they weren't even on duty yet. Why did they have to be joined at the hip?

And why did it have to be *him*?

Django was going to lose the one person who meant the most to him to this next-level ass.

Django's nostrils flared as he tried to control his breathing, his pulse banging in his ears like a drum.

Faron looked around, oblivious to Django's ire, a sneer on his face. He flexed his gloved fingers as his dark eyes narrowed.

"This is one of those events I have to *endure* as part of our training. I suppose we need to fix the problems on the D-Ring as much as anywhere else. Maybe more, judging by the state of things down here. But I'd be happier if we never had to travel here again. Bunch of filthy dirt-ringers."

Django growled.

"Hey, now!" Eventide admonished before Django could step in. "*This* is my home."

"*Was* your home," Faron corrected her. "You've outgrown this place."

"Still, don't talk about my people like that."

Django was about to tear a strip off Faron when the text on the viewscreen disappeared. All chatter in the dining hall immediately stopped as the evacuation notice faded to an image of a dark-haired man Django didn't recognize. The man's hands were clasped and resting on a pristine wooden desk, their positioning causing his suit jacket to crinkle and crease as though it were straining to contain him. He wasn't overweight, but his barrel chest was an oddity on a station that was frequently forced to scale back on rations. On the breast of his jacket glowed *Eclipse*'s emblem: a red and yellow double hexagon surrounding four stacked rings. A sprig of lavender had been pinned to his lapel for decoration.

Which part of the station grows lavender? Django wondered.

Many of the seeds *Eclipse* held in storage weren't currently used, and he had memorized many of them. The station's large inventory of various plants kept the varietals from extinction.

Each species was held in stasis, intended to replenish the Earth's surface at a later date. Once the planet had cooled and its surface was once again agreeable to much of the flora it had once held, humanity could start reintroducing species. For now, it was only hardy tree saplings, fruit trees, vegetables, and grasses that they were trying to restore. Some varietals would take a hundred years to fully develop and fulfill their purpose to absorb the excess carbon dioxide. Once the surface was suitably restored for humanity to return, they'd be able to enjoy the plants that had been preserved and restored.

Django had not seen lavender being grown on the station, though. The flowering plant wasn't something that would survive on the surface for at least another decade or more. On the flip side, he supposed he hadn't been to every field and nursery on the D-Ring; it was likely someone was experimenting with flora he wasn't aware of.

Or perhaps there were labs growing flowers distributed only to the Upper Rings. The man's button-down suit, elegant haircut, and brass pips suggested he was a resident of the A-Ring. Even Faron in his tuxedo wasn't anywhere near as elegantly dressed.

"Commander Benson," Eventide whispered, taking note of the blank look on Django's face. "If it wasn't for Orientation, I wouldn't have a clue who he is, either."

Faron rolled his eyes but didn't comment.

"Attention, D-Ring! This is the station's commander, Roy Benson. Fear and anxiety have been unwelcome companions for many of Eclipse's citizens lately. The recent hull breaches have given each of us pause as we reflect on the loss of life and resources that we have had to endure. It is rare I make an address such as this, but I wanted to take a moment to assure you that the station's commanding officers, administration, and technicians are doing everything we can to address these recent incidents.

"When our ancestors built this station, they hadn't intended for it to be occupied and unsupported for as long as it has been. It was a waypoint to the moon and a gateway to the stars. They couldn't ever have envisioned the struggles we'd have to overcome in sojourning here for generations. As such, over the past few months, a small meteoroid cluster has entered the Earth's orbit and intersected with our path. The breaches we've seen over the past few months have been a result of this new swath of debris. I want to assure you our technicians are doing everything in their power to prevent and repair these breaches, but it is difficult to predict where and when they will occur. We are expecting several more impacts over the next few days, but then we believe the worst of it will have passed as the cluster enters the Earth's atmosphere. If we require further assistance from you, we will keep you informed. Please be patient as our technicians complete the repairs. They are all doing the best they can, but we have limited resources, and it is highly unusual for us to have to deal with so many damaged areas at once."

Without signing off, the screen winked out, leaving a faint silhouette of the commander's figure before the evacuation warning reappeared. The room's lights, however, returned to full strength, leaving only a highlight of the red-lit warnings.

CHAPTER TWO

Django
Eclipse

THE EARTH SAT OUTSIDE of the atrium's viewport, as it always did—or at least, as long as it had during Django's lifetime. But it hadn't always been the gray and blue marble it was now. Ruined. Dead.

Humanity hadn't always been trapped within a single space station, praying that its home wouldn't come apart before they could restore the planet they had abandoned. Before their planet could support life once again.

It wouldn't be within Django's lifetime that humans would be able to set foot on the planet's surface—it'd be another century before that would be possible; until they could undo the damage of their ancestors.

Eclipse was filled with lament at never seeing their home planet, of never feeling the wind on their face or the tide of the ocean at their feet. The nostalgia was a sentiment Django had never understood. He had everything he needed on board the station.

Here, people had a purpose. A direction. A mission to provide humanity with a home once again. Here, at least, everything was contained. The chaos of an enormous planet must have been unmanageable. No wonder their ancestors had failed so spectacularly.

Django took a sip of the concoction in his cup as he surveyed the room. The dank flavor of ale touched his tongue and he struggled to swallow it, but he pushed it down anyway. Dozens of his family members and their friends filled the room with small talk and empty gestures.

The D-Ring's atrium had been purposely designed for such events: a few tables, a bar, and a view. It was used sparingly, and Django wondered if it had been worth spending the credits on a party for his older sister when, in reality, his family could have spent their savings on necessities instead.

Maybe it wouldn't have annoyed him as much if he had any friends to enjoy the evening with. But, as it stood, the only person he was close to was Eventide, and they hardly needed such an occasion to hang out.

At least, they hadn't used to.

Now, even at this event, she was so preoccupied with babysitting Faron that they had barely spoken.

So many of Django's peers used a wedding reception as an excuse to get drunk, but he couldn't be bothered. He had never enjoyed the taste of alcohol, but he sipped at the beverage anyhow, only making enough of a dent to appear as though he was consuming it happily. As long as Django held a drink in his hand, *most* people didn't try to force another on him.

Eventide had given him a wink when she'd told him it was non-alcoholic. He had simply rolled his eyes. She got a kick out of watching him drink the stuff. Each time his nose wrinkled and his face contorted, without fail, she laughed at his reaction. "It's not that bad," he would say as he did his best not to gag.

Eventide sat on the other side of the room. Faron stood beside her like a leech. Django wanted nothing more than to shove the man out of an airlock.

Django's older sister, Celeste, sat on the other side of Eventide, draped in an ancient white dress that threatened to consume her. The dress had been passed down through the centuries from their great-great-great grandmother. It had been mended and altered many times over the years, but the family only broke it out for the weddings of her female descendants. The woman must have been a giant, but she had been the last of their lineage to set foot on the planet's surface. Each generation since was one step closer to returning, and each woman married both her spouse and their hope for the future. The dress would one day return to the planet's surface in fulfillment of their matriarch's legacy.

Despite the dress having seen better days, Celeste looked almost regal within its fabric, beads, and frills. Her brown curled locks flowed over her shoulders more elegantly than Django would ever have believed his sister could have pulled off.

It was a tradition his family had held sacred; a glimmer of hope and stability that had been passed down through the decades.

Unlike Eventide's decision to abandon the role her ancestors had held all this time.

"Surely it can't be all that bad?" Django's Uncle Marvin appeared out of nowhere, two drinks in hand. "You look as though you'd rather be anywhere else. Enjoy yourself, kid! Soon, that'll be *you*, and then you won't have any fun at all!"

Marvin, of course, wasn't Django's real uncle; the man had appeared out of nowhere seven years ago, claiming to be a shuttle pilot. It was rare for any of the pilots to habituate to station life. Nobody else had been close to the planet for centuries, and it was nearly impossible for pilots to acclimate to being confined to a space station after years of flying through orbit. The experience had left Marvin open to wild ideas when the liquor started flowing, but most of the time, he kept them to himself.

In fact, he kept to himself altogether, most of the time.

His uncle stood at least a foot taller than Django's five-foot-three frame. A gargantuan smile split the tightly clipped beard that Django had so often admired.

Marvin wore loose-fitting clothing beneath a green and yellow jacket. Django had always assumed it was a pilot's jacket, simply because he had never seen any other pilot, nor had he seen anyone else wear clothes like those Marvin sported. A small pendant hung from a thin chain around his neck: two small metal circles intertwined.

Django took the second drink with a forced grin, lifting the mugs he held in each hand in a mock salutation.

"I guess I don't see what all the fuss is about," Django said. "It's an outdated tradition."

No point in moaning about Eventide and her new interest.

A small smile crept over Marvin's face. "As you get older, you realize it's important to find reasons to celebrate. Things change before you know it, and one day you'll look back and wonder why you didn't make more of an effort to appreciate what you had, while you had it."

Django absentmindedly took a sip of the drink he held and nearly spat it back out as it hit his tongue. He had forgotten what he was holding, but he forced it down.

"I'm happy with things the way they are," he replied. *Mostly.* "I don't need a party to appreciate that."

Marvin chuckled and raised his glass. "That's the point, lad. Take stock of where you're at now. Enjoy this moment. Life changes fast, and in ways you don't expect. You'll blink, and one day you'll wonder where it all went."

Django was unconvinced, but he lifted his glass to clink with Marvin's.

"Take me, for instance," Marvin continued, unaware that the topic had come to a resolution. "I never expected I'd be living on this godforsaken station for *seven* years. But you know what? That'll change soon. And it's a change I'll welcome. You should consider coming with me, boy. I've always liked having you around."

Marvin eyed the room, eyes wide, as though realizing he'd said something he wasn't supposed to.

Or realizing his piloting days are over.

"But never mind that," Marvin said, raising his glass again. "Enjoy the party."

"Cheers."

"To finding our purpose," Marvin said. "And our place among the stars."

Life changes fast, and in ways you don't expect.

Django supposed there was some truth to what Marvin had said. Eventide was already planning on moving to the B-Ring. Soon, he'd have to move out of his parents' quarters and into his own.

Overall, though, he *was* happy with things the way they were. He still had his two sisters, Celeste and Nova. He had been working fields, tending to both saplings and root vegetables, for four years already; a lifelong career he was passionate about. And though Eventide had moved on to train as a technician on the B-Ring, he cherished their friendship and would still see her as often as he could.

Involuntarily, Django's eye drifted to the viewport behind his uncle. *Our place among the stars?* he mused. *Right where we've always been, in a space station orbiting the Earth, just as we have for centuries.*

"To knowing where we belong," Django countered, bringing the glass back to his lips and bracing himself as he took another sip.

Marvin gripped Django's shoulder and squeezed. "Well, I'm afraid I need to head to the shuttle bay. Just because there's a wedding doesn't mean there aren't still things to do."

Beyond the viewport, Earth floated lifelessly below the station. Maybe it was because he rarely got the chance to look upon the planet's surface, or maybe it was all the talk of finding purpose, but Django suddenly wondered what impact their efforts were having. If the seeds, plants, trees, and animal life, as well as other technological and biological resources they were sending to the planet's surface, were having any impact at all on its ecosystem. Those who had survived the catastrophe and their descendants had worked hard to restore the world humanity had all but destroyed over a century and a half ago. But after a hundred and fifty years of efforts, the Earth below looked to be just as bleak as ever.

"Uncle Marvin," he ventured, before the man could leave. The pilot nodded for Django to continue. "We've been sending goods down to the surface for centuries. Is any progress being made?"

A glimmer of something caught Marvin's eye as he stole a glance out the viewport. It was only for a moment, though, before he looked back to Django.

"You wouldn't think so by looking at it, would you?"

He looked as though he wanted to say more, but instead, he pursed his lips as though he thought better of it and left.

Before Django could give his answer any thought, Eventide caught his eye. She was sitting with a group of women, which also included Celeste. She nodded in his direction and flashed him a smile.

All thoughts of Uncle Marvin vanished as she excused herself from the table and crossed the floor of the atrium.

"Looks like you're enjoying yourself," Eventide said with a grin, nodding to the two glasses in Django's hands.

He blushed, having forgotten his uncle had handed him the second drink. "Err . . . yeah." He scanned for a nearby table or surface to place one of them—or both of them—down, but there was nothing around. "Do you want one?"

Eventide smirked and let out a laugh. "No, thank you. I actually came to tell you that Faron and I need to leave. I'm heading to my parent's quarters before we head back to the B-Ring. We've got to keep studying for this killer exam we have tomorrow, and then we've got intensive training exercises."

"Exercises?" Django inquired. "For what?"

Eventide rolled her eyes. "What do you think the alarms have been for, dumbass? Do you know how many technicians don't live through their first year?"

"Yeah, I'm well aware."

"Come find me tomorrow evening at my new quarters. We're having a real celebration with my colleagues. You could join us."

Django resisted the urge to look down at his oversized hand-me-down dress clothes. The thought of joining Eventide on the B-Ring was terrifying—mostly because he knew he'd stick out like a moldy sack of wheat.

Eventide offered a reassuring smile. "You'll be fine. They're not like most of the Upper-Ringers."

"Just like Faron isn't like the Upper-Ringers?"

"He's not that bad once you get to know him. But he was born into a different life to us. Give him a chance."

Django was unerring. "I still don't know what you see in him."

Eventide rolled her eyes. "I keep telling you, it's not like *that*! We're coworkers—friends, maybe—but there's nothing else between us."

Yeah, right. How long have we been friends, Evie? You don't flash those flirty eyes at me.

Regardless, he could sit at home and pout about it, or he could accept her invite to the party. He didn't *want* to go, but the fear of missing out was too great. If he could be accepted into her B-Ring parties, perhaps he could keep her as part of his life.

Django let out the tension he had been holding in his shoulders. "Okay, I'll come over. If you think your colleagues will be okay with me tagging along."

"They'll be more than okay with it." She gave him a fake punch to the jaw. "Anyway, I really have to split. Don't spend all night sitting in the corner by yourself."

Django didn't mean to be antisocial, but everyone else was so boring. He would have joined the group Eventide and Celeste had been a part of, but he didn't know any of them well enough to make conversation, and they were all at least two years older than him. Eventide's natural ability to make friends was enviable, but he spent twelve hours a day tending to the communal farms, which didn't exactly lend itself well to socializing with others.

Django recognized a few of his coworkers. Two of them stood beside the bar, laughing at a joke shared between them. Neither had a strong work ethic as far as Django was concerned, but they were friendly enough. Maybe he just needed to suck it up.

Django scanned the room, looking for a conversation he could join, even if it were just to eavesdrop enough to seem interested in the evening. He could always add the occasional nod or murmur of agreement.

Instead, his gaze returned to the dead Earth. Because of his workload, Django rarely had time to sit and look out at the stars; to look upon the planet that used to be humanity's home.

Something seemed different with the display tonight, but he couldn't quite put his finger on it, except that the colors weren't quite right. The brown land masses showed hints of green; the dull blue oceans appeared more vibrant, as though the gray clouds above them had thinned. It had been years since he'd last taken more than a passing glance, though. Perhaps the planet wasn't as dead as he'd imagined as a child.

Django jumped, ripped from his thoughts, as a firm hand clasped his shoulder. A deep chuckle greeted him.

"Easy there, big fella," the man said.

Django squinted as he tried to place the man. He tried to recall a time when he had seen anyone as muscular or refined (though annoyingly, Faron came close). Django took two steps backward as the artificial light highlighted the man's broad nose, styled, healthy hair, and strong features. He stammered as realization struck him.

It was only then he realized that the rest of the room had grown silent.

"Commander Benson." Django didn't know if he should bow or shake the man's hand. Instead, he just stood there, his mouth agape.

CHAPTER THREE

Django
Eclipse

THE SPACE STATION commander wrinkled his nose as he surveyed the citizens surrounding him. He lifted a fist and held it over his mouth as he cleared his throat. "I decided to visit the D-Ring after the breach earlier today—it's been too long since I last came down here. I caught word of the celebration tonight and was surprised I hadn't heard about it earlier, though it is hard to keep track of half a million residents."

The commander carried himself as though his presence was nothing out of the ordinary, as if Celeste might have been some respectable dignitary that would warrant the attendance of the leader of the entire space station to her wedding party.

Silence followed as Django struggled to find the words to respond. His mouth moved, but no sound emerged.

He hadn't heard it shatter, but his mother now stood over shards of glass and a puddle of its former contents.

Two station guards stood beside the commander, a few feet away and larger than life. Their white metallic uniforms were radiant compared to the best outfits of the drab crowd around them. Their eyes scanned the room as though anyone might pull out a weapon and open fire on their principal.

People often told Django he looked like his mother, and he imagined that was never as true as it was now. Her mouth hung open, her lips moving as though she knew she should say *something* but was unable to find the words. The rouge on her cheeks appeared gaudy and rural compared to the pomposity of the diplomat in their presence. For all the time and care she had taken to fix up her hair to the most immaculate state it had ever been in her life, it had lost its magic in an instant. The mousy brown mess was coming apart in strands, its color faded, its edges damaged.

Similarly, his father, who had protectively grabbed his wife around the waist, suddenly appeared a little too lean for the clothes he wore. The threads of his suit were faded and sticking haphazardly out of the coat's seams. Even if the suit had been in brand-new condition, it was clearly outdated by a decade or two when compared to the style of a man like Benson, whose mere presence filled the room. His golden cufflinks and silk handkerchief likely cost more credits than the clothes of the rest of the room combined. And though his father's eyes were as wide as his mother's, the tightness of his lips and the protective stance he held suggested he wasn't as enamored with the commander's attendance.

"Commander Benson." Django's mother dipped her head. "You honor us with your presence."

Django nearly scoffed, but he stopped himself from doing so openly. Benson and the rest of the administrative A-Ring hadn't done a damn thing for the lower torus. Django loved his home, but it was hard to ignore the luxuries the commanding officers enjoyed while the farmers, manufacturers, and reclaimers who worked hard to keep everyone fed and comfortable didn't get the same level of treatment in return. He held no ill will toward the commander, but he certainly wasn't *honored* by the man slumming it with them.

"Despite the difficulties *Eclipse* has faced lately," Benson continued, his voice as bold as his fashion sense, "it's apparent the D-Ring has much to celebrate tonight. It is a great day for both this couple and the station." The commander turned his attention to Django, his eyes fixed upon him with dark intent. "Young man."

Django nearly jumped out of his oversized clothes as the commander's attention focused pointedly on him. He wished he was anywhere else; that he had left with Eventide and Faron.

Hell, he wished he had left with his Uncle Marvin. Benson made Django feel like he was at fault just for being in his own skin.

"You are the brother of the bride, are you not? You appear barely old enough to be here. Is this your first?"

Django could feel his face growing hot and turning shades of red. It was bad enough the commander had singled him out in front of everyone, but he'd chosen to highlight his age as well. The minimum age to attend the adult-only reception was eighteen, and he had just reached that milestone the week prior. His younger sister, Nova, on the other hand, had been able to attend the ceremony but didn't have to suffer the doldrums of the reception.

Benson kept talking before Django had a chance to answer. "I also hear there is a cadet from this section making quite a stir on both the D and B decks. A young lady who has decided to become a technician?"

The commander lifted a cone-shaped goblet made of glass to his mouth. The man must have brought along his own beverage, as even his cup seemed strangely out of place. He took a sip of its contents, the hazy red liquid spilling over slightly and dribbling down his chin.

Django grabbed a napkin from a nearby tray, but before he

could offer it, Benson had already wiped it away with the back of his hand.

"Is she here?" Benson asked, turning his focus back to Django. "This . . . Everrule, is it?"

"*Eventide* has retired for the evening," Django said. "She's studying for her exams."

The commander's face dropped slightly, and a hand went to the back of his neck, fingernails scratching at a thumbnail-sized growth. "I see," he said. "And what of you, boy? Do you have plans to traverse the Rings as well?"

Django furrowed his brow; the commander's intonation was insincere, but Django couldn't determine if he was making a joke or offering an insult. Perhaps it was just typical A-Ring condescension.

"No, sir," he replied. "But I'm skilled at what I do."

Ugh! Why not just say I shovel cow shit? The commander of the station doesn't care.

"Django is one of the station's most skilled farmhands." Django's father appeared behind him, a proud hand resting on his shoulder. Django did his best to straighten his posture. He didn't much care for praise, but he was proud of what he did. It didn't matter what any A-Ring asshole thought, not even the station's commander.

"Is that so? A very impressive feat for the young man, I'm sure." Benson gave a dismissive wave, his eyes scanning the room, disinterested.

The rest of the crowd closed in with anticipation. All eyes followed the commander. Jaws that had not yet left the floor struggled to close as they considered what the man might say next.

Benson turned to the wall-height viewports that lined the edge of the room, the Earth reflecting the sun's light and illuminating the room with a dirty brown glow.

"Generations ago, our ancestors came here to ensure we had a future." Although still directed at the viewport, Benson's eyes had glazed over, not focusing on anything in particular.

"They left our planet so we could make a better life for ourselves; so that people like Everrule—people like *you*—could make a difference. To ensure future generations may one day be able to return. In order to do so, we have all made sacrifices; all succumbed to a certain order of things so progress might be made."

Benson turned back to the room and shook his head, as though he had forgotten where he was. "It is a structure that we have lived with for centuries now. If followed, perhaps one day, we can get off this station—or at least that's the hope for our children and grandchildren. We must do whatever we can to maintain that order."

Commander Benson shifted his weight, taking a deep sip of his drink, and then passed the empty goblet to a nearby guard. "I had hoped to meet this Everrule, though. I find her aspirations most . . . *ambitious*."

As much as the man made Django's skin crawl, Eventide would be disappointed if she missed Benson's appearance by mere minutes.

"I'll be right back," Django said, making his way to the room's exit. "Please don't leave just yet."

"Django, don't be rude!" his mother admonished. "You can't leave while the station commander is here."

"No, it's all right, ma'am," Benson droned. "I have to be . . ."

But Django was already out the door. He propelled himself down the hall, his feet barely touching the dust-covered carpet. He didn't have far to go before he reached Eventide's parents' quarters. The exterior comm panel lit up as he approached the doorway and pressed his thumb to the doorbell.

It only took a few moments for his friend to arrive at the door, wearing a perplexed look.

"Tell me you didn't just skip out on your sister's reception?" Eventide said with a smirk and a glint in her eye.

"No," Django said, huffing as he worked to catch his breath. "The Commander. He's here, and he's asking about *you*."

Eventide scrunched her forehead, her blue hair bobbing as she shook her head. "I don't understand. What commander?"

"Roy Benson. Commander of the station. He's been going on about how you've worked your way up to become a technician."

Eventide tilted her head, still skeptical. "I don't know what game you're playing, Django, but . . ." Won over by his determined eyes, she relented. "Okay, we'll scope things out from the lookout tunnels first."

The "lookout tunnels" was their code name for the maintenance walkways that ran through the back halls of much of the section. They had found the passageways as kids and had used them to listen in on the adults and their plans, as well as for spying on their classmates.

"I haven't thought of those in years." Django couldn't help but grin. "Why do you want to look from there?"

"Because I don't trust you," she said, jabbing her forefinger into his chest. "There's something else going on here."

"Yeah, okay. But he seemed like he was ready to leave, so we can't waste any time."

A short series of hallways led them to where they needed to be. A small flight of metal stairs brought the two friends above the main floor and onto a grated byway. Black dwarf walls lined a catwalk overlooking the rooms below.

"What did the commander say about me?" Eventide asked as they closed in on the lounge. "Did he really ask for me by name?"

"Well, kind of." Django smirked. "He called you Everrule."

"Close enough, I guess." Eventide shrugged. "At least he's heard of me."

The two slowed as they approached the grate above the

atrium. The landing on this floor was open to the room twenty feet below. Anyone looking in their direction would easily discover them.

The party attendees had all pulled themselves to one side of the room. There was a silence hanging above them that felt unnatural. If it were possible, there was less noise now than when the commander had first appeared.

"I hope he didn't leave," Django whispered. "I don't see him."

He glanced to Eventide. The girl's mouth hung agape, her hair framing her face in a perfect "O." Django was about to ask what she'd seen, but he followed her gaze to the viewport overlooking the Earth below.

Instead of lackluster browns and grays, the planet below appeared in vibrant shades of blue and green. Other space stations —near replicas of their own—hovered in the Earth's orbit around them and spread out over a distance Django could hardly fathom. Other structures orbited with them: smaller, but closer to the planet's atmosphere.

Across the atrium, nothing moved. Then whispers began to flit among the guests. Django couldn't hear anything being said and considered descending to the main floor to find out, but he couldn't move his legs. He couldn't tear his gaze from the surreal display before him.

Questions buzzed through his mind, but they flew by ethereally, and he was unable to grasp any of them.

Before the conversation grew loud enough for him to make out, a door Django had never seen before slid open in the wall closest to the viewport. Two people, a man and a woman, strolled through, both dressed in iridescent space suits. To complete the look, instead of their helmets, which hung at their sides, they wore sunglasses.

The woman grabbed her glasses and repositioned them to the top of her head as she addressed the room. "Attention, attendees!

There's been a breach in the outer hull. We are evacuating this room."

As she spoke, red alarm lights flashed overhead, though the sirens had yet to sound.

Several attendees moved to exit through the main door, but the entrance didn't slide open for them.

"Not that way," the man barked. He gestured to the hidden doorway they had emerged from. "Through here. We'll ensure you get to safety."

The man ducked through the door and waved for the crowd to follow. The woman circled the group from behind, encouraging them along and ensuring they all filed in.

Django instinctively ducked as the woman performed a final scan of the room.

"We're all clear, sir," the woman's voice echoed. "You can send in the technicians."

"Should we go, too?" Django whispered.

"No, I want to see what's happening," Eventide replied.

"Didn't they say there was a breach in the outer wall?" Django asked. "We should go."

"Relax," said Eventide. "If there was an immediate concern, those patrols would have their helmets on."

"That's security?" he asked. "I've never seen them wear suits like that before."

"Those are pressurized suits in case of a breach. There are a lot of things we don't see on the D-Ring."

Two more men walked in through the same side door, wearing similar suits and each holding a large yellow duffle bag. Though one of the men couldn't have been older than his late twenties, he was balding. The second was younger still, barely older than Eventide. The teen was blond, with a face that held a bit of fat around his jowls.

"Those are technicians," Eventide whispered. "Likely scanning for the source of the breach."

"I dunno," the younger one said, continuing a previous conversation as they entered the room. "These malfunctions are happening more frequently. I'm not saying I believe in conspiracy theories, but there's been a lot of 'coincidences' lately."

"If you start reading into these things, you'll drive yourself crazy," said the older technician, his voice rough like sandpaper. He appeared grizzled, as though he hadn't had a drink of water in days. "That's how kids end up out the airlock. The sooner you realize this is a job like any other, the better. You do what's needed, you go home, you kiss your wife goodnight, and then get up and do it again the next morning. At the end of the day, that's what this life is about."

"But what if these malfunctions aren't random? What if Admin are causing them on purpose?"

"And what if they are, kid?" The balding man grabbed a datapad from his bag. He held it in one hand and tapped it against his palm. "What do you think *you're* going to do about it? Report it? To whom? Listen, if you want to live a long time in this role, you keep your mouth shut and do your job. That's the only advice I've got for you."

The grizzled man opened a panel beside the viewport, revealing a swell of data chips and maintenance indicators.

"What kind of interface is that?" Eventide whispered.

"You don't know?" Django asked. "Isn't this what you're training for?"

Eventide's brow creased. "Nothing like this."

The two men worked for several minutes while Eventide watched, wide-eyed, marveling at the circuitry they slid in and out of the panel. The younger man whispered to himself, but his tone was too quiet for Django to decipher what he was saying.

"Besides," the balding man offered, apparently having thought more about their conversation, "there ain't nobody on D-Deck worth offing. Nothing more than a bunch of farmers and laborers. If Benson had it in for anybody, it'd be an A-lister and they deal with their own up there."

The younger technician let out a sigh as he shrugged. "Fine, you've made your point. I'll keep my mouth shut."

"Attaboy. The longer you remember that, the longer I'll have a partner. Now, do you want to flip the projection? Let's see if we can get this damn thing working again."

Django nearly jumped as the viewports flickered, as though they were giant screens. The viewports flashed white before the space behind them changed. The other space stations that had been in orbit moments ago were now nowhere to be seen, and the Earth was once again dull and drab, lifeless in a sea of endless stars.

Eventide's eyes nearly popped out of her head, but she kept her voice to a whisper. "What the hell is going on?"

The image out of the viewport shimmered as though a screen had been turned on; the dead Earth returned. Dull grays and browns replaced the greens and blues once again.

Do you want to flip the projection?

Did the technician flip it on or off? Why is there a projection at all?

Django's heart stopped as the alarms sounded. They needed to get out of the atrium.

It was hard to hear what the technicians were saying over the noise, but their chatter increased as they checked their datapads. The formal change in their tone suggested they were speaking to someone via comms. Then, scurrying as if in a panic, the two of them put on their helmets, opened the hidden doorway, and left.

Eventide's expression was blank, transfixed on the hidden door.

"Come on," Django urged. "We need to get out of here."

CHAPTER FOUR

Mikka Jenax
The *Redemption*

"THIS IS TAKING TOO LONG. *Why* is this waystation so
backed up?"

Mikka Jenax paced the bridge of the *Redemption*, hands
behind her back. She was brooding, but she didn't care. They had
been waiting for over an hour, stuck in the queue.

The waystation wasn't typically a stopping point for regular
traffic, which was what irked Mikka the most. If this was the way
orbital traffic was going, rum-running through the sector was going
to be a nightmare, but it wasn't as though she had any other career
paths laid out for her.

"A wave of leftover debris from the *Infinity*." Kiara Ryson
strode across the shuttle, assuming her seat in the cockpit. Mikka
shook her head as the woman straightened her faux leather jacket
and pulled her sunglasses down over her face.

"I know that, genius, but the Syndicate's had seven years to
clean this mess. I'm tired of it backing up the transport corridors."

"Just sit back and wait it out. We get paid either way." Kiara's
matching brown boots found their way onto the edge of the

console, and she crossed her legs at the ankles and leaned back. With the woman's short frame, her feet barely reached the panel from the navigation console's seat.

Agitation coursed through Mikka's veins, and she couldn't calm herself enough to sit. Kiara's laid-back attitude was usually a godsend, an anchor in her spaceport, but right now, with their next round of credits on the line, it was infuriating. Mikka adjusted her own gray jacket and ran a hand through her coarse black hair before reaching under the counter of the navigational console and pulling out a bottle of whiskey.

Might as well enjoy some decent alcohol while we're waiting. Stars know, there won't be any once we get to Lunar.

"We'll get paid for this load," she said as she poured, "but we'll be late for the next one. Every hour of delay means credits off our paycheck."

"And what do you propose we do? There's a river of debris between the stations we have to navigate around. I'm not about to blow a hole through our engines for a couple chips."

"I'm not proposing we *do* anything." Mikka swilled the drink in her glass, watching as the artificial gravity pulled the droplets against its side, before draining its contents in a single shot. "I just hate sitting around. I've got bills to pay."

"I do too, but you don't hear me whining."

"Times are tight. My mother's not getting any better."

"*Pfft.*" Kiara waved a hand dismissively. "Times are always tight. You worry too much."

Mikka bit her tongue as she poured another drink. She sipped this one slowly, allowing the woody taste of the alcohol to coat her tongue and throat as it slipped down. The amber liquid still bore the grit and metallic tint that Lunar whiskey always held, but it was a hell of a lot better than anything she'd find on the moon's surface. The whiskey's sharp fire was enough to distract her for a moment, but only barely. They had just picked up a shipment of computer parts and cabbage from Space Dock Eleven—one of their better-paying hauls. But their delivery window was narrow, and the clock was ticking.

If only we could get through this damn debris field.

The space station *Infinity* had been decommissioned seven years ago. A year later, some Syndicate fat cat decided it was time to put an end to the ghost station's misery and pushed it into the Earth's atmosphere, resulting in a series of explosions. Whoever that genius was, they hadn't accounted for the chunks of metal, plastic, and the stars knew what else had been left behind from the explosion that ripped it apart. Instead of spreading, the fragments that were not drawn into the atmosphere clumped together in a hazardous blob. It usually occupied less frequently traveled paths, but over the past month, it had become lodged in the main transport corridor.

"It's crazy we still can't go around. These new space routes are getting on my nerves."

"Easy, Mikka." Kiara lifted both hands in a conciliatory motion. "We'll deliver this shipment, pick up a round of Helium or whatever our next load is, and be on our way again before you know it. You might lose an hour or so of sleep, but no harm done. Chill out now and it won't matter."

"Looks like I don't have a choice, do I?" Mikka slammed her glass down harder than she intended, sending a crack through its side. She grasped her temple between her thumb and forefinger, willing the knots above her brow to melt away. She didn't have time for setbacks, and she was running out of patience. At some point, life had to throw her a bone.

"Is there any chance we can make up for it by taking a double load back?" she asked, hoping the suggestion didn't come across as desperate.

"You're really getting worked up, aren't you?" Kiara commenced picking at the gunk beneath her fingernails with a nail file. "You know the drill—we can only take back what they've loaded up for us."

The *Redemption*'s systems beeped and hummed around them, almost as if the ship was eagerly anticipating being allowed to continue on its way.

From where she was standing, Mikka could see a panel light blinking on the communications terminal, beeping in an irregular pattern.

"You expecting a call?" Kiara asked.

"Are you kidding? Who do I know? It's probably just a patrol announcement."

Kiara grunted, pulling up the details on her own console. "It's no patrol. I don't recognize this frequency."

"Let's see." Mikka pulled up the holo-screen on her own console. The semiopaque projection came to life, hovering above her control pad.

A blinking bar of red lit up, displaying an incoming transmission on a frequency Mikka hadn't seen used in a long time.

"Whoever it is, they're using an old pirate channel," she said. "But it's one that's been abandoned for years. The Orbital Guard cracked its encryption, and it's been useless ever since."

"Pirates?" Kiara's tone grew serious for the first time all morning. "One of your old friends?" She stared at the panel, her eyes furiously darting between the readings as if considering whether there was danger in merely answering the hail. She ran her palms through her cropped purple hair. "What are we going to do?"

"Hang on!" Mikka lifted a hand toward her. "It could just be someone else found the frequency. Maybe it's a wrong number."

"*Hilarious*," Kiara said, her arms crossed.

"A pirate wouldn't use this channel; the encryption has been compromised. If they were after our ship, they'd use a different means of communication." Just the same, only a pirate or the Orbital Guard would have access to the encryption.

The console continued to chirp.

Mikka sighed and leaned over the nearest terminal, tapping the screen. The face of a young woman was projected above her datapad. Her hair was white and cut short, except for a single silver braid that hung down the side of her face. Blue and green beads were tied within it, along with a smaller pull decorated with a few grubby ship parts, metallic shards, and white stones.

Not stones. Bones.

Through the static-filled feed, it was impossible to tell if the bones were human or animal, though Mikka had a pretty good idea.

The woman's eyes— a smoky gray—were as mysterious as the rest of her, as was the scar that curved down through the top and bottom of her left eye socket, as though someone had tried to blind her.

The woman stood, strapped in to hold her from floating around a craft with no gravity. It was hard to tell through the haze of smoke that filled the cabin, but Mikka recognized the markings of the woman's vessel.

An escape pod.

The woman didn't even flinch as sparks and bursts of flame surrounded her. The image flashed in and out, and it was obvious the feed might not last long.

"Thanks for picking up, love. I presume you're Jax Luana?"

Mikka caught her breath.

She scanned the woman's features for a hint of recognition, something that would tie this woman to her old life. Even if the woman's hair or eyes were another color, even if her scar was gone, there wasn't anything about her that struck Mikka as being familiar.

Besides, she was too young to be someone from Mikka's past. She was twenty at most, and no one had dared to call Mikka by the name of Jax Luana in seven years. That would have made the person projected before her thirteen when Mikka had left her old life behind. Even aboard a pirate vessel, thirteen would have been far too young. It was possible she could have come across a youth at a bar or port city, but if that were the case, clearly the encounter wasn't memorable.

Yet somehow this woman recognized *her*.

"I haven't used that name in a long time." Mikka gritted her teeth, attempting to hide her disdain. She absently pulled a knife from her belt, fidgeting with it to both calm her mind and send a message that she was still someone who wasn't to be messed with. "My name is Mikka Jenax. Who are you? How did you gain access to this channel, and why are you calling me?"

The woman glanced over her shoulder as a sharp *pop* sounded from somewhere behind her. Her eyes bulged as, presumably, she located whatever the source of the noise had been. She raised a finger, unclipped her safety restraints, and floated off-camera momentarily.

No gravity plating in those old escape pods. Her ship must have been a relic.

Mikka rolled her eyes at Kiara, but her co-navigator didn't meet her gaze.

"Ah, yes." The woman reappeared, the cape she had been wearing now gone, revealing sweaty but well-toned shoulders. "The name's Abigail. And, well, as much as I'd love to get into specifics—this deathtrap is about to break apart. I'd love it if you could give me a lift."

Mikka groaned. Bringing an unknown woman aboard would be a risk. The woman clearly had a connection to Mikka's past—a past she wanted to avoid. And something didn't smell quite right.

"Not without knowing anything about you. You're calling me on an old, encrypted frequency, referring to me by a name that has been dead for seven years. Can't blame me for being skeptical."

"Let's just say, I'm both a ghost from your past and a damsel in distress. I didn't come looking for you, love, but my circumstances have become quite . . . dire." Another burst of flame erupted behind Abigail's head. "I think we could come to a mutual understanding."

Great. This is just what I need.

"I gave that life up a long time ago," Mikka insisted.

"Well, even if that is the case . . . could you at least save mine? I'm quite happy with the one I've got."

Mikka cursed. "How much time do you have?"

She knew this was a bad idea, but there'd be no more lives lost because of her. Not if she could help it.

"Um . . ." Abigail's eyes darted wildly to the surrounding capsule as she punched a few keystrokes on the pod's display screens. "I'm actually kinda surprised I'm still here. I'm sending you my coordinates. You're not far."

Mikka nodded. "We're on our way. Ping us again if the situation gets worse—but I can't promise there'll be anything we'll be able to do if it does."

"Aye, aye, captain." Abigail gave a two-fingered salute accompanied by an impish grin as the screen faded to black.

CHAPTER FIVE

Mikka
The *Redemption*

"ARE YOU *INSANE?*"

Kiara was on her feet, hands on her hips, marching toward Mikka.

Mikka raised an eyebrow. "Oh? Look who's suddenly interested. You could have spoken up before. You kind of left me hanging there."

"I didn't expect you to be such an idiot! You can't bring a pirate on board! We know nothing about her!"

Kiara turned to the console beside her and pulled up a holographic display. Kiara was a master at navigating the Syndicate network, but she still impressed Mikka with how quickly she had pulled up the profile of the woman on the escape pod.

Mikka's eyes flashed. "Remember whose ship this is. *I* make the calls here."

Kiara ignored her as she scrolled through the entry. "Smuggling. Theft. Conspiracy. Murder! Shit, I'm not ready to die today."

Whatever sense of indifference Kiara had presented a few

minutes ago had now disappeared. Being delayed on a job wasn't something to get worked up about but letting a fugitive on board was another matter.

Understandably so, maybe, but . . .

"I don't care who she is," Mikka said. "I'm not leaving her out there to die. Not when she's asked for our help."

Kiara wasn't ready to back down. "How do you know this isn't a setup to lure us in? A trap to commandeer our ship?"

"She launched herself into a failing escape pod with the sole intent of hijacking a decades-old refurbished orbital trader? Is that what you think? There are easier, more lucrative targets out there."

"Stranger things have happened."

A fair point, but . . . No, Mikka couldn't think of any legitimate reason why anyone would want the *Redemption*.

"I know how her type operate," Mikka continued. "Our current payload isn't worth the effort or the risk."

"She knew you were here," Kiara persisted. "That doesn't raise red flags for you? She's obviously learned enough to make you a target."

And there it was. Kiara wasn't implying the ship was the target.

I am.

The woman's words hung over Mikka like a solar storm. *"I presume you're Jax Luana?"*

Kiara was right: it did raise red flags. Huge, *monumental* red flags.

The only two people in the entire system who knew Mikka used to go by that name were her own mother and Kiara. Not only that, but Mikka had also undergone dozens of surgical procedures to alter her appearance, until she no longer resembled the woman Abigail had named.

Be that as it may, though, her mind was made up.

"I'm not leaving her out there to die," Mikka reaffirmed, punching in the coordinates into the ship's navigation system. "You can cuff her in the cargo hold until we get to Shackleton City if it makes you feel better, but let's get her ass out of that pod before we decide what to do with her."

"Toss her out the airlock—*that*'s what we should do with her," Kiara muttered under her breath.

"We're about ten minutes out," Mikka said, ignoring the remark. "Hopefully, her pod can hold together until then."

"It wouldn't be the worst thing if we didn't make it."

Mikka grabbed the cracked whiskey glass beside her and hurled it across the shuttle. It landed squarely against an empty wall panel, shattering under the force of the impact. A million pieces of broken glass spread out along the hard paneled floor.

Kiara's eyes grew wide with horror.

"What the hell is your problem?" Mikka shouted. "That could have been *me* in that pod! Do you think *I* didn't deserve a second chance? Do you think *I* should have died with my companions? With my friends? Because if you do, you can find another ship."

Kiara didn't respond, instead looking bashfully toward her own console.

"Damn it, Kiara! A life's a life," Mikka said, composing herself. "*Everyone* deserves a shot. If someone hadn't taken a chance on me, I wouldn't be here now. Enough of the bullshit."

"*Fine*." Kiara held her hands up in mock surrender. "But don't say I didn't warn you."

She picked up an energy weapon—her trusty LT800 pistol—from beside her station and attached it to her belt. "And don't think I'm letting her out of my sight. I might help save her life, but I'm not above locking her in the holding cell or calling in a patrol."

"You call in a patrol and you risk exposing me as well," Mikka reminded her. "I'm taking a monumental risk here. Don't forget I have sins I need to atone for, and that pirate's just admitted she knows more than she should. This is still *my* ship, Kiara; I may have agreed to split *our profit for your expertise*, but I'm still the one who calls the shots."

Mikka tapped the projection before her with a few keystrokes. "I'm sending you the coordinates of the pod. The only thing I'm concerned about is making it back in time to hit our window through the debris field. We've got thirty minutes."

"As long as *I'm* not the one who ends up out the airlock," Kiara groused, pulling up her own holographic display. "Just promise me you won't let her talk you into anything stupid."

"I've got a sick mother to worry about. That's enough excitement for me."

The *Redemption* groaned as it propelled into a lower orbit. The crest of the Earth filled the viewport as the ship flew toward Abigail's position.

Abigail wouldn't have to worry about the void of space for long: she would soon enter the Earth's atmosphere, and those pods weren't made to withstand entry. She'd burn up long before she ran out of air.

"We've got to get off the main route," Mikka said. "We're not going to make it in time otherwise."

"Might catch the attention of the OG if we do that," Kiara warned. "If we get pulled over by a patrol, we won't make it, either."

Mikka cursed under her breath. Kiara was right, but she didn't see they had any other choice. Plus, the woman was slowly becoming a thorn in her side, so she didn't want to give her the satisfaction of being right.

"We'll deal with that if it happens."

Kiara shook her head but didn't argue.

It didn't take long before the *Redemption*'s scanners picked up the solitary pod adrift in the lower orbit, just off the main transport corridor. The gray escape vessel floated among a sea of debris, much of it several times larger than the pod itself. If it hadn't been for Abigail's distress call, Mikka would likely have never seen it among the rest of the floating remains, never mind known that there was a person inside.

Her ship didn't just run into trouble, Mikka realized. *It bloody exploded!*

Whatever trouble this pirate had gotten herself into was possibly a bigger deal than Mikka had first realized. Orbital attacks weren't common, especially this close to the planet. If her ship's destruction was simply a matter of Abigail's criminal record, there would have been other ways to handle things.

Mikka tapped her communications terminal. "Abigail, we're descending to your position. Are you still there?"

"I'm here," the pirate's voice chirped. "But I've lost my video feed."

"Is your docking equipment functional?" Mikka asked. "Are you able to connect to our clamps?"

"I don't have any fuel, love. I'm dead in the water. All I've got is enough air to see the end of my days as I incinerate in orbit, and enough power to keep this channel open for a few more minutes."

"All right." Mikka nodded to herself. "Kiara, how close can you get us to the pod without being ripped apart by the surrounding debris?"

Kiara met her gaze. "Are you *doubting* me?"

"I'm just asking!" Mikka shot back.

"We can kiss her on the nose if you want."

"Perfect, but she'll be coming in the other end. Back her up so we can pull that pod into the cargo bay. I'll seal it off manually."

"It's a good thing we loaded our shipment below deck this round."

Mikka hit another few commands on her console. "Abigail, we're going to pull you into our cargo hold. You shouldn't get banged around too much, but you should probably strap yourself in."

"Already buckled—and I've got nowhere else to go, love. Do what you need to do."

The *Redemption* shook again as Kiara decelerated, weaving around some of the larger pieces of debris.

"Hang on," Kiara said. "I'll get us in, but there's a lot of garbage here. It could get bumpy."

As promised, the shuttle rattled and bounced as it slowed. Mikka did her best to hang on as she pulled each of the four toggles that would seal off the ship's bridge from the cargo bay and braced herself for the inevitable turbulence. The pressurized seal allowed them to release objects into the void of space, but they didn't typically try to bring objects in. It was an unusual maneuver, but if anyone could pull it off, it was Kiara.

"I'm opening the cargo door now," Mikka said.

"Reversing engines to overtake the pod," Kiara replied.

There was a faint *whoosh* and a crack formed in the wall behind them. The *Redemption* groaned as she strained beneath the atmospheric pressure. A *thud* and a couple of shudders told Mikka their task had been successful, even before Kiara reported the outcome.

"And she's in. Re-pressurizing the cargo bay."

Mikka let out a sigh of relief. "All right. We've got twelve minutes until the waypoint sends us to the back of the line. I'd rather not miss our window through the debris field. Let's get back and take this shipment home."

"And hope the Guard doesn't want to inspect our ship on the way through."

"They won't. The gates are backed up enough already."

As if in response to her promise, the holo-screens and monitors in the shuttlecraft all shifted. Big, bold text in orange and red lit their screens, and a rendering of Abigail's bust hovered above the panels.

Emergency Bulletin.

Fugitive Wanted. Charges: Theft. Conspiracy. Piracy. Murder.

Abigail Monroe. 10,000 Credit reward.

Mikka caught her breath.

"Spoke too soon. Looks like we won't need to kill her," Kiara remarked. "We can just turn her in."

CHAPTER SIX

Django
Eclipse

THE WALK from the lounge to Django's residence was insufferably long. He kept replaying the scene they had witnessed over and over in his head. Was it an illusion? A prank? His mind struggled to comprehend the images of other stations; of shuttles; of an Earth painted a different color.

Do you want to flip the projection?

Whatever it was, whatever vivid dream had presented itself, Django didn't believe it.

Eventide walked beside him, her eyes glazed, matching his slow cadence as they trudged through the station's halls. If nothing else, her reaction proved it wasn't just his eyes playing tricks on him. Whatever it was, she had seen it, too, and Django assumed that, like him, she hadn't quite digested the apparition enough to put it into words.

The alarms had quieted, though the lights remained an ominous red. Django hadn't bothered to confirm the breach's location on the multiple screens they passed; he didn't have to. All he could do was hope security had escorted his family to safety before the technicians' panic had set in.

His parents would hopefully be waiting for them back at their quarters. Maybe they could explain what was happening. Maybe they could tell him what it was he had seen; how a breach in the hull could cause such an image to be displayed.

The Earth. Alive.

Perhaps it was an old program; a memory of when the station had been built, before the Climate Wars. Before humanity had nearly destroyed itself.

They were only two turns away from his quarters. Other station members passed by, many exhibiting the tired look of just coming off the fields or the assembly lines. Despite their ragged faces, most looked either happy or relieved to be heading home to their families after a long day of work. Like Django had so often been, they seemed indifferent to the red flashing lights and the announcements informing them of the breach. They hadn't been a part of it, and that was all that mattered for today.

Many of the workers who passed them were his peers, but Django hardly recognized any of them. He certainly didn't know any by name. As much as they lived on the same Ring and fulfilled the same purpose, there was hardly time for them to interact with each other outside of their duties. The long hours and laborious shifts didn't allow for much socializing.

He was grateful to have Eventide at his side.

They turned the last corner and almost walked straight into Uncle Marvin. Django jumped as he was ripped from his thoughts. Eventide slowed, but only barely. She didn't even lift her eyes to meet Marvin's.

"You're okay!" Marvin exclaimed, bending down with his arms wide open and wrapping them both in an ungainly embrace. "I thought you were in the lounge when they sealed it. Thank the stars you're all right!"

The pilot's breath stank of alcohol, but not the dank ale served in the atrium; the scent on his breath carried a hint of sweetness to it.

Marvin sniffed a few times as he held them tightly and then pushed them back, holding them each at arm's length as if he were looking at two people he hadn't seen in years, rather than only an hour before. His eyes were wet and puffy.

"Of course, we're okay," Django said. "But we're trying to understand what we saw in the atrium. There was some sort of glitch on the viewports, I think . . ."

Marvin's eyes widened, and he motioned for Django to be quiet. "Stop! Don't say *anything* else."

He peered around, as if expecting someone to be listening over his shoulder.

"Listen." Marvin pulled the two friends in close, hastily lowering his voice. "We can't talk about it here. We'll discuss it later—when we're in your quarters. Until then, it's extremely important that you do not mention what you saw to anybody. Don't even talk about it with each other."

"What about with Mom and Dad?" Django asked. "They would have seen it. They were there, too."

Marvin took a step backward and sighed. He looked down at his hands, as if they might hold the answer. Finding nothing, he looked up, his tear-filled eyes transfixed on Django. "I'm sorry, Django," he said, unable to contain the crack in his voice. "They're dead."

The floor gave way beneath Django's feet. His heart leapt into his throat as the words collided into him like a battering ram to the gut.

Dead?

How could that be possible? He had *seen* them exit the lounge only minutes ago, with the security guards. They would have taken them to safety.

Django's heart sank in his chest. Even though he couldn't comprehend the news, he knew it was true. He could feel his mouth moving, trying to say something, to convey his emotions, but all he wanted to do was collapse on the floor and wish it all away.

And yet, he couldn't show his true feelings. Not in front of Eventide. Not in front of *anyone*. His feelings were inconsequential.

Eventide stood wordlessly beside him, as dumbstruck as he was.

This is a dream. It has to be a dream.

Marvin placed a hand on his shoulder with an ironclad grip. Django winced at the gesture, though his thoughts were so scattered that he didn't know whether he should shrug it away or embrace the man he called 'Uncle.'

"Admin will tell you it was an accident," Marvin whispered. "It wasn't. But react as though it's the truth. You can't tell the guards what you saw. If they ask, lie. Tell them that you left the room to get your friend, and by the time you got back, the door was sealed. If they press you, stick to your story. Both of you. Do you understand?"

Understand? Of course, he didn't understand. An impossible image outside the space station. A breach in the hull. His parents dead, even after security evacuated them to safety. And it wasn't an accident? Nothing was making sense.

His legs threatened to buckle beneath him, but Django forced them to remain firm; forced himself to stay upright.

It wasn't an accident.

Django couldn't form words . . . He didn't have the resolve to argue with his uncle. How could someone have orchestrated a hull breach on purpose? *Who* would have done so? Why?

It didn't matter, though; his uncle had always been prone to mad ramblings and conspiracy, and this was just another of those times. Anger churned within Django's gut. This was no time for madness.

Dozens of workers streamed past, oblivious to Django's suffering. What could he say to such an accusation?

"I'm so sorry," Eventide managed, her first words since leaving the lounge. "Your parents . . . I . . . They were like my parents, too. And Celeste?" She turned to Marvin, her eyes pleading for a different answer than the one she expected to hear.

Marvin simply nodded. Another kick to Django's stomach.

"This . . ." Eventide shook her head and let her words trail off.

Marred with grief, Django wrapped an arm around Eventide's shoulder and brought her in toward him. She pushed him off, though, never having been one for physical affection.

If he could ever have used a little physical comfort, now would have been the time.

"Ah, I see you've broken the news to them," a strong female voice said behind them. "Normally, we would prefer the entire family be present. It makes things more . . . uncomfortable when bad news has to be repeated."

Two officers approached—a man and a woman. The woman had shaved the right half of her head, with straight long hair hanging to her shoulder on the other side. What hair remained was so blonde, it was practically white. Her gaze lingered on Marvin, her mouth twitching as though she didn't know whether to smile or frown.

The uniform of the Station Guard had always struck Django as little more than decorative. The *Eclipse* hadn't seen an armed attack in recent memory, yet their attire suggested the Guard expected an assault at any moment. Hard white panels covered their shoulders, chest, forearms, and hips. Uncle Marvin had once told him that the suits were some sort of graphene and nanotech hybrid, but to Django, that description meant little. He had to assume they were artifacts of the old world, passed down and maintained through the centuries.

The glowing station insignia etched on their left breastplate displayed four stacked blue rings enclosed in a red and yellow double hexagon. A heavy-duty black material, flexible and yet firm and resilient, covered the sections of body the panels didn't, but Django didn't know what kind of material it was; there was nothing else like it on the station. Energy weapons hung from their belts, white-handled pistols finished in a material that resembled the paneled pieces of their uniforms and incorporated a computerized display and flashing lights. Django had never seen an energy weapon up close, so their functionality was a complete mystery to him.

"Apologies, Avery," Marvin said. "I met them in the hall, and I thought it'd be better if they heard the news from me."

The woman was a foot shorter than Marvin, but her presence was so commanding that, except for the second guard beside her, she had a clear two-foot radius around her where passersby refused to tread. Those forced to pass hugged the edges of the hallway to maintain the intangible barrier. Her face was as jagged as one of the D-Ring's farming tillers, pointed and as hard as steel. Her mouth was taut, as though she had just swallowed something sour. Everything about the woman was tense.

Beside her, the second officer stood with his arms on his hips, as though he had been out for a stroll and had stopped for a chat. His stance was relaxed compared to his companion's, but his presence was no less intimidating. He leaned back slightly as he surveyed the hallway, staring down those who passed by as if each person was a suspect in a crime he was attempting to solve. And while his face wasn't exactly set in a scowl, his flat grimace and wrinkled nose made it clear he'd rather have been anywhere else.

The man appeared worn out, as though sleep had evaded him

for several nights. His eyes, though alert, had bags beneath them, and wrinkles at their edges aged him beyond his years. Django was sure neither of the officers was older than twenty-five, but there were too many thoughts swarming about his head for him to focus.

"While I'm on duty, you will address me as Officer Inglewood," Avery chided. "Remember your place."

Marvin blinked a few times, as though taken aback by the admonishment. It surprised Django that his uncle knew this officer by name, but perhaps security had more of a presence in the shuttle bay.

"My apologies, Officer Inglewood," Marvin sheepishly responded. He then cast a glance to the man beside her with a nod. "You and Officer Isaacs honor us with your visit. It has been a rough hour; please forgive my impropriety."

He gave a knowing but apologetic glance at Officer Inglewood, and it seemed to Django as though there might more to the exchange. Though, it was just as likely he imagined the knowing looks.

"Now then." Avery pulled out a datapad, its screen projecting a holographic image above the device rather than the flat screen most of their devices had.

"Earlier this evening, at approximately 7:07 p.m., Earth Standard Time, a meteoroid struck the exterior of the D-Ring near Beta-834B, breaching the station's hull. Oxygen levels within the room had reached critical before we could retrieve its occupants. Our highly qualified technicians quickly repaired the breach, but we regret to report all eighteen occupants perished in the incident. The full list of casualties is available upon request.

"Django Alexander, as you are the eldest surviving member of the Alexander family and recently of age, you inherit the right to take possession of your family's quarters and the contents within. Your mother's research—one Zahra Alexander—is the property of the station and will be assigned to another laboratory assistant. The role your father, Peter Alexander, held as Assistant Directing Arborist will be reassigned, either in part or in whole, to others in the field. If there are any disputes or you feel you are inadequately suited to inherit these commissions, you can file an appeal within the next thirty days."

Dead. They were all dead. Uncle Marvin had been right—at least in part. He couldn't wrap his head around the fact that they were gone.

I saw them leave the room. Why wasn't security able to get them to safety?

He was about to protest, was about to argue that his parents couldn't possibly have been killed, but his uncle's words forced their way into his head, stopping him from voicing his objections.

You can't tell the guards what you saw. If they ask, lie.

Django didn't understand Marvin's motives, but he couldn't process everything fast enough to overrule the command that he'd been given, so he remained silent.

Avery powered down the datapad and tucked it into her belt. A wayward eye veered toward the second officer. Her expression didn't change, but if Django didn't know any better, he would have said she was seeking approval. Avery's gaze then moved from the officer to Uncle Marvin, and, for the first time, her expression changed, softening only slightly; though it didn't reach her lips, which continued to pucker.

She then turned without further word and marched abruptly back down the hall.

Big brown eyes awaited Django and Eventide as they stepped into Django's quarters.

My quarters.

Every step held fresh revelations as his brain worked to process the past hour.

It took all of his focus not to let his lip quiver. He had to show he could push on.

By default, his sister would be his responsibility now. At thirteen, she was not yet old enough to bring in credits to the household, though it would only be another year before she would be allowed to make that transition.

Nova leapt into his arms before he could make it through the entrance. Her brown hair pressed against his chest, matted with grime from the growing pods. Her class must have been doing hands-on training today. Unfortunately, it would be another couple of days before their water rations would allow her a shower.

Django gripped her tightly. Only then did it dawn on him how grateful he was that Nova hadn't been old enough to attend the reception. He squeezed her back, breathing in the familiar scent of dirt and seed. Of family.

"Is it true?" Nova whispered into his chest. Django could feel his dress shirt becoming damp beneath her face.

It wasn't an accident.

The devastation ached in every muscle of his being, but he couldn't let it show. He had to be strong—for Nova, if for no one else.

A small semblance of relief passed through him, with Nova in his arms and Eventide by his side. But the void left by his parents? Django thought he might be sick. Part of him believed they would walk through the door any moment, ruffle his hair, and ask how his day was.

"It is," he replied.

"I should probably let you guys have some space," Eventide said, her hand resting on the edge of the doorway. "Family time, you know?"

Marvin had worked his way inside and had found a seat at the kitchen table. Django could only remember the man visiting them on a handful of occasions. Though he was of above average height, he'd seemed so much more of a giant when Django was younger.

"You're just as much a part of this family as any of us," Marvin said to her. With his elbows resting on the table, he held his face in his palms, rubbing his temples with his fingertips as though they could wipe away the day's tragedy. "Besides, we need to have a talk. Shut the door."

Eventide stepped inside, allowing the door to slide closed behind her.

Django let go of Nova, the scent of dirt and fertilizer drifting away as she moved to the small bench that lined the side of the room.

Marvin looked up and cracked his knuckles, his eyes surveying the three youths before him as though sizing them up for whatever he was about to say.

"Tell me what you saw."

Django swallowed. What was he supposed to say? That he'd seen a world that shouldn't exist? That something they had been working hard to achieve for centuries had already been completed? No matter how he tried to frame the words, none seemed sufficient.

Or believable.

It wasn't real. It couldn't have been.

Eventide shuffled her feet. Nova just looked between the two of them, her eyes still wide.

"Listen," Marvin attempted. "No matter how crazy it seems, you can tell me. I won't laugh."

Django cleared his throat. He could feel the tears welling in his eyes, the emotions of the day wreaking havoc on his nerves, but he fought them back. He had to keep it together.

"I don't know what we saw," he said, gaining composure. "A

prank. An illusion, maybe. Something projected on the viewports, making it appear as if there were other stations, shuttles flying around them, and an Earth capable of life. The best I can come up with, someone wanted to display the planet the way it *used* to be. Before it was destroyed."

"It's no prank," Marvin stated. "Everything you saw is real."

CHAPTER SEVEN

Django
Eclipse

"WE NEED TO LEAVE."

Marvin leaned forward, his hands on his knees. His eyes were wide with either desperation or excitement; Django wasn't sure which—or which would be worse. The pendant his uncle wore—two intertwined circles—had come loose from inside his shirt and was hanging in front of him as he leaned forward, catching and reflecting the light of the quarters.

"*Leave?*" Django asked, confused. "We just got here. And I'm not sure I can handle anything else today."

"No. Leave the station. Nova and Django—start getting your things together. Only what you need for a few days. Eventide, you do the same. Or better yet, don't return to the B-Ring. You can always get new clothes."

Django put his hands up in front of him. "Whoa, whoa, whoa," he said. "What the hell are you talking about?"

"Trust me," Marvin urged. "We can't stay here. And there's more opportunity for us out there than there ever will be in here."

"What else is there?" Django spluttered. "Here, I have a job, my sister . . ." He looked to Eventide. "My closest friend. Anything else I might want . . . I'll never get back." He crossed his arms, sinking back in his chair, until the realization of what Marvin was saying finally dawned on him. "What do you mean, 'leave the station?' Uncle Marvin, whatever that was, whatever we saw, it was just a glitch. There's nothing else out there."

"Just because you want something to be true, doesn't make it so."

"Yeah, I've noticed,' Django shot back. 'What I *want* is for my parents and Celeste to be alive. But guess what? They aren't."

Marvin's nose curled up and his eyes narrowed.

"Admin is *lying* to you, Django. They're keeping us locked away here in a prison when there's so much *more* out there."

It was all too much. He had lived a perfectly happy eighteen years so far. What purpose did tampering with the viewports serve? Why would someone torment *Eclipse*'s residents in this way?

Django pressed on. "What I *want* is to continue my parents' work. To grow food, to feed whoever needs to be fed."

Marvin had always had some crackpot theory about where their goods were being sent. "Why does the Earth need so many chickens and sweet potatoes to be habitable?" he'd often ask. Django knew it had nothing to do with sweet potatoes and everything to do with cross-pollination. But telling that to Marvin never seemed to satisfy his uncle, so he'd learned to keep his mouth shut.

Nova had tears welling in her eyes, looking from Uncle Marvin back to Django, questions forming that she couldn't bring herself to say.

"Listen," Marvin said. "There's something I need to tell you. Something I haven't told anyone . . ." He sighed, his hand moving to his pendant as though it might offer him protection from the words he was about to say. His eyes landed on Django.

Definitely desperation.

"I'm not from the *Eclipse*. I was a pilot, but not the way you think. I managed to escape an accident at another station called *Infinity* but wound up stuck here. Since then, I've been trying to find my way off this head trip without arousing suspicion. It hasn't been easy, but I've finally found a ship willing to take me. They'll take you as well, but we need to be ready to leave when it gets here."

Django's mind reeled. Of all the wild fantasies his uncle could have conjured. He clenched his fists. Was this some sort of joke to him?

"I think it's best you leave now." Django kept his voice low but firm. Even though he felt like an impostor in his own home, whether he liked it or not, he was the man of the house now. It was up to *him* to protect his sister; to ensure it was a safe place for them both.

"I wish there was time to let you grieve," Marvin replied. "Your mother was like a sister to me. But it has taken me this long to find a way out of here. We need to take it—especially now, after this. None of us are safe here. If Admin suspects any of us knows the truth, they'll fake another accident and that will be the end of us, too."

Nova burst into tears. "Not you too, Django!"

"They'll kill anyone who knows the truth. It's the reason I've said nothing about this before now," Marvin continued. "It's why it's been so hard to find someone willing to risk getting me out of here. We were much too close to this accident. They'll get rid of us if they decide we know even a hint of the truth."

"That's enough!" Django barked. Nova's lip still quivered, but she held back from releasing further emotions that sat behind the razor-thin wall she had erected.

Eventide's brown eyes lit up momentarily before continuing to survey Marvin. She had been curiously silent throughout the entire exchange, though Django assumed she was in shock. He knew he was.

"I think we've suffered enough today," Django continued. "Please leave."

Marvin opened his mouth as though he was about to say something further, but Django shot him a warning glare.

Marvin sighed. "Fine, but please consider it. You're the only people I consider family on board this station. I don't want to lose you, too."

He stood to leave, his body sagging as though it carried the entire weight of the day on his shoulders.

The weight of what, though? Marvin didn't seem too concerned with the loss of their parents, only his crackpot scheme to leave the *Eclipse*.

"Wait." Eventide clasped her hands between her legs as she sat, slumped over, gazing at the floor. "Why would we all be in danger?"

Marvin paused, surveying the young woman. A deep breath seemed to loosen some of the tension he held.

"Eventide!" Django hissed. He didn't need to hear any more of his uncle's lunacy.

"Listen," Eventide said. "It won't hurt to know why he thinks we're in trouble."

"Admin is paranoid about anyone finding out the truth," Marvin said without hesitation, eager for the chance to continue. "The three of us know we're not the only ones out here anymore. After seven years of being on board, there is one fact that has always remained true: every person who finds out, every person who lets slip the truth, will eventually be sent out the airlock. It's a cast-iron guarantee that I've seen play out over and over again."

Nova sat huddled in the corner, her eyes locked on her uncle, but there were no more tears. Eventide still stared at her hands, as if she was unsure what to do with them, her cards silent in her pocket.

Django was still staring daggers at his uncle. "What we saw wasn't the truth; it was a glitch! Our leaders wouldn't trap us aboard a space station for a hundred and fifty years for no reason. But if it worries you so much, you can rest assured that nobody outside this room knows what we saw. Let's just keep it that way." Grit and steel came through in his voice, but inside he was shaking. He wasn't daunted by the potential of being murdered for witnessing some glitch in the machine; his anxiety stemmed from being in charge now. He was the one who had to send Nova to bed. He was the one that had to make sure they had enough credits to meet their needs. *He* was the one that had to tell Marvin it was time to go.

Like he'd tell anybody the truth, anyway. Never mind the airlock, he'd be ridiculed to the point of being ostracized. Even if Admin allowed him to maintain his current station in the Agricultural Sector, any hope of a promotion would be firmly out of the question.

Leave the station? *That* was a wild fantasy, and if there was anything certain to get them killed, it would be sticking their noses where they didn't belong. Even a shuttle would eventually have to come back and replenish its supplies, and Django couldn't imagine station security would appreciate them joyriding on a supply ship.

Marvin clasped a hand onto Django's shoulder. "Well, lad, if you change your mind, come find me. As soon as I have a docking time for the expected ship, I'll let you know."

"I DON'T LIKE any of this." Eventide clenched her jaw as she hugged her knees to her chest. Hours had passed since Marvin had left. "But it's all starting to make sense now."

Django had known her his entire life and never once had he seen her so shattered, though he couldn't honestly say he felt any different.

The three of them had gone to Eventide's quarters in the B-Ring for the evening. There were too many memories in Django's quarters. Sleep might not come for any of them that night, but there'd be no chance of it in the room where they had grown up.

At Eventide's invitation, they'd traveled via the InterRing transport to her new residence. The trip had been a blur. It had been Django's first foray into the world of the Upper Rings, but his mind had been so unfocused that he hadn't been unable to take any of it in. He might as well have been walking on the moon's surface for all the difference it would have made.

His throat had been tight all evening. Nearly everyone he knew was now dead—and almost more confronting than accepting that fact was trying to shake off Marvin's words.

Everything you saw was real.

There was no way it could be true. How could the Administration fool so many? Half a million people on board *Eclipse*, and not one of them could figure it out? All the shipments of animals, plants, and raw material that left the station every day, and nobody could put the pieces together?

Extraordinary claims required extraordinary evidence. There were other, more plausible explanations.

Django stared at the wall of Eventide's living room. If it had been any other day, he would have been impressed with the B-Ring accommodation. Not only was Eventide the only occupant living in her quarters, but she also had a separate bedroom, a separate kitchen, and a separate living room. A few decks of cards, a couple of potted plants, and several photos of her family filled the empty spaces between books on the gray metal bookshelves that lined the walls. Textbooks lined the shelves: among schematics of the *Eclipse* was an assortment of reference material covering a wide range of topics, ranging from Engineering, Quantum Physics, Computing Mechanics, and Astronomy. Everything an aspiring technician might need to know at a glance.

The Alexander family had been privileged with their accommodations. Their quarters held the five members of their family in a two-room unit. Django and Nova shared their room with the kitchen and living room, and there was a small closet for the bathroom that housed a toilet. They shared showers with the rest of their section. Unlike many in the D-Ring, Django's father's position had allowed them to have their own unit, and it was a testament to Django's potential future in the Agricultural Sector that he'd be allowed to keep the quarters now that his parents were gone.

Others on the D-Ring shared group accommodations. Dozens of families would sleep on bunks lining large chambers. Those spaces were crowded and dark, yet functional, and the station provided them with food, clothing, and enough rationed water to shower once a week.

Eventide was still only training to become a technician. Her already being provided with quarters so grand was indicative of the importance of the role on the station.

Eventide's words pulled him from his thoughts.

"Wait," Django said. "*What*'s starting to make sense?"

"The technicians. They're always saying things like: 'Things will be different in the field,' and 'Wait until you see what's really involved. It'll *blow* you away.'" Eventide raised her hands, mimicking an explosion.

Django blew air through his lips.

"You think there's a chance that what Marvin was saying is true?"

"I honestly don't know what to think," she responded, burying her face between her knees. "Why train us, for one thing, if there's really something else going on behind the scenes? Why not tell us up front?"

"I just don't believe it. And even if I did, what am I supposed to *do* about it? My parents are dead. Nothing's going to bring them back. I still have a job to do, and Nova still needs to be looked after. I'm not going to risk what little I have left on a wild theory."

He stretched out on Eventide's couch. Gracefully, Eventide had offered to share her bed with Nova, and the crying coming from the next room had at least died down. He wanted to curl into a ball and sleep for a week. His neighbors had even agreed to pitch in on the farm, filling in the gaps where needed to allow him time to mourn.

Eventide stepped into the kitchen, lifted the electric kettle she had put on earlier, and poured two cups of tea.

"Here, this will calm your nerves," she said, pouring the green liquid into a small blue cup.

"My nerves are *fine*," Django snapped.

He immediately regretted the outburst. *Stars, am I really so on edge?*

"Sorry. Maybe I could use the tea, after all."

He held the cup between his thumb and fingers. The porcelain felt delicate, and yet Django didn't think he would have had the strength to break it.

He was supposed to be an adult now: to work the fields on his own; live on his own; to take care of Nova on his own. But he wanted nothing more than to curl up on his mother's lap like he had when he was a child and have her run her fingers through his hair and tell him everything was going to be okay.

The tea was bitter, but Django forced himself to swallow. Eventide laughed as his face twisted at the taste, but it was only momentary. He inhaled deeply and tried to push away everything that had happened.

"I just want to live my life," Django said, his gaze focused on the cup. "I want to know I've made my parents proud, and I want to make sure Nova has every opportunity available to her. I can't worry about what is or isn't outside the station."

"But doesn't it bother you that we could be sending supplies to a world that doesn't need them?" Eventide said. "The produce, the corn, the flowers, the trees, the animals? They were all supposed to be shipped off to make the Earth ready for repopulation. Why are we growing these crops here? Why are we stuck here if there's more out there? We could set foot on Earth again—see the mountains, see the oceans!"

"That's *why* it doesn't make sense! Admin wouldn't have us doing those things for no reason! And even if we left *Eclipse* and found our way to the planet, then what? This is my home, Eventide! *This* is what I've worked my entire life for! We don't have much here, but we have friends and . . ." Django stopped himself short. He had been about to say 'family,' which renewed the pang in his heart. "And we have each other."

A grin crept over Eventide's face. "Of course." She reached for his arm, and all anger melted at his friend's touch. She so rarely offered physical affection that everything else disappeared in one simple action.

His words had been impulsive, but he had meant so much more by them.

We have each other.

Django grinned back at Eventide. Her eyes were soft with compassion, her painted-blue lips plump, inviting him in for the kiss he had always dreamed of. But Django fought the impulse. This wasn't the time to confess what he had really meant; to confess how he truly felt. He couldn't handle being let down yet again today.

To distract himself, he scanned Eventide's spacious quarters around him and couldn't stop his heart from sinking even further.

In his mind, Eventide would always be the girl next door, the girl he had grown up with, but she wasn't that girl anymore. She was now a woman and had risen above their D-Ring life, and he doubted there was a place for him here. Every inch of her quarters was filled with a lavishness that he'd never be able to afford or fit into. Eventide wouldn't have to settle for a teenage farmer from the D-Ring, not when there were guys like Faron in her world. Django clung to his place in her life for now, but he doubted that would always be the case.

"We should probably try and get some sleep," Eventide said, her dark brown eyes locked on his. "I know you've been granted time off from your shifts, but I have my final testing session tomorrow. Plus, it's also my first day on the job."

Final testing.

"Maybe you'll learn how to fix those glitches."

CHAPTER EIGHT

Mikka Jenax
  The *Redemption*

WHATEVER PRECONCEIVED NOTIONS Mikka had about
the type of person Abigail Monroe would be disappeared the
moment the pirate stepped out of the cargo hold and onto the
bridge. The woman was barely five feet tall, but she carried herself
as though she were six. A staff was strapped to her back, carved of
some type of Earth-grown wood Mikka didn't recognize. It was
smooth and varnished, causing it to reflect the blue lights of the
Redemption's display panels. The red jacket that hung from her
shoulders perhaps wasn't meant to reach the knees of a woman of
average height, but on Abigail, it flowed more like a cape. It was
soiled from the smoke of the escape pod, and perhaps whatever
vessel she had vacated, but it still ascribed a ridiculous pomposity
to the woman.

Beneath the robe, a wide strip of fabric covered her chest,
leaving her midsection exposed, along with a gash across the right
side of her belly that had both fresh and dried blood clinging to it.
It didn't look like it had been a deep cut, but more than one trickle

of blood made its way down and over her baggy, dark green cargo pants.

"You're injured," Mikka observed. "Kiara, get some gauze and antiseptic."

"*Please*," Kiara said with an ounce of sass, but she strode over to the access panel anyway, muttering something about being ordered around.

"It's just a scratch," Abigail downplayed. She lifted her hands in protest but winced partway and moved one of her hands to her side. "Really, I'm quite all right."

Mikka snorted. "We'll get that seen to, regardless. There's no point in letting it get infected." She stuck out a hand. "Welcome aboard, Abigail Monroe."

"Oh, *good*. You've learned my surname." The injured fugitive waved a hand. "My reputation precedes me, then. And here I was, beginning to worry you'd never heard of me. But I must insist you call me *Captain* Abigail." She reached out and grabbed Mikka's hand.

"You're no captain on this ship." Kiara shoved the medical supplies into Abigail's arms, with a roll of her eyes. "We *hadn't* heard of you until we saw this." She grabbed the datapad from her belt and held it up so Abigail could see. The wanted message hovered in midair as the display came to life.

"Only ten thousand credits?" Abigail reached for the datapad, but Kiara yanked it back before the newcomer's hands could reach it. "That's practically offensive."

"Are the charges legit?" Mikka asked.

Abigail smirked. "That depends on who you ask. Some of it, sure, but I'll tell you this: I'm no murderer. I only kill in self-defense."

"Those on the other side of the blade might disagree," Kiara said, her hand inching toward the pistol holstered at her hip.

"What happened to your ship?" Mikka probed. "Assuming it was your ship?"

"It *was* my ship," Abigail said, leaning on her staff for support. "Though those Syndicate bastards—assuming that's who it was—didn't agree. Blew her out of orbit without a second thought."

"*Hah!*" Kiara scoffed. "I'm sure they had a good reason."

"If you call picking up a shipment a reason."

"Legitimate or stolen?" Kiara asked, crossing her arms. She leaned her thin frame against the rail of the communications panel.

"Kiara," Mikka said, holding a hand up to her navigator. "You don't like her. We know. Cool it."

The navigator shot an annoyed look at Abigail but bit her tongue.

"No, it's fine," Abigail responded as she flourished her cape. "I suppose I can't vouch for the shipment's origins, but I have reason to believe my contractor is the legitimate owner. And I, for one, am being paid for its transportation. I can't commit to much more than that, though it is a perfectly understandable question given my apparent infractions. In fact, . . ." Abigail took a slow, obvious scan around the *Redemption*. "I was just about to ask the same about *your* ship. I know that Jax here has her own sordid past that perhaps lent itself to its acquisition."

Mikka gritted her teeth. "Like I said, I don't go by that name anymore. And since I'm the only thing stopping you from being handed over to the nearest patrol ship, you might want to remember that. The stars know, I'm a razor's edge from having made up my mind."

Kiara flashed a self-satisfied grin.

"My apologies." The fugitive bowed. "I don't mean to offend. It's one of the names I was instructed to seek, so it might take me a while to adjust. I can't believe my luck, *you* stumbling across my distress call."

Mikka raised an eyebrow. "Instructed by who?"

"I'm not at liberty to say. Not yet, anyway. We'll get to that in time, love."

Mikka had half a million questions, but the most important of them would have to wait.

"What happened to your ship?"

"It's like I said. We were on our way to pick up a shipment from the *Eclipse*—a very lucrative payout, as it happens. We were simply en route to our *legitimate*," Abigail's eyes darted toward Kiara, "pickup and, out of nowhere, a vessel shows up and starts firing on us. Blew the *Black Swan* to pieces. The rest of my crew are dead, and if it wasn't for you, I would've been as well. I would love the chance to make it up to you, if I can."

Mikka studied the woman for a moment.

"As you seem to know," Mikka said, weighing her words cautiously, "I've lived enough of a dubious life to never trust a first impression. But I also know that Syndicate charges are often bull-shit. The truth usually lies somewhere in between. I don't fully believe your story, but the only charge you've denied is murder, so I think I can believe that. It's a rare claim for a pirate, so I'm sure you understand why I'm having trouble with it. That said, we're headed to Shackleton City. The least we can do is give you a ride to Lunar."

Kiara made a strangled noise but didn't voice her obvious objection.

"I appreciate your compassion," Abigail said. "If we could come to an agreement, I think I could also make this arrangement worth your while."

Kiara coughed. After her behavior today, Mikka wanted to strangle her navigator, but, in this case, she echoed her concern.

Mikka shook her head. "You can keep your money or any other 'arrangement' you have in mind. We're obligated to answer distress signals by orbital law, and we're willing to take you with us to Shackleton City, but after that, you're on your own."

"Mikka, I hate to stop this exchange, but if we want to hit our window in the queue, we need to move now."

Abigail smiled. "Well, it sounds like I'll have some time to change your mind. But for now, I wouldn't mind a place to clean up."

Kiara rolled her eyes. "We're a transport shuttle, not a luxury cruise. There's a toilet through the door behind you. It's got a washbasin, but we're only equipped for short-haul flights."

"That'll do, love. I just need someplace to wash off the blood."

The bathroom door slid shut with a *hiss* as Kiara grabbed Mikka's arm.

"You can't seriously be thinking of taking her through the checkpoint? If we're caught harboring a fugitive, that's it. The OG will confiscate your ship and arrest us. I have three kids, Mikka! And you? How are you going to pay for your mother's medical bills if you're locked up?"

Mikka sighed. "What would you have me do? Hand her over to the patrols? They'll sentence her to death."

"She's a *criminal!*"

"I know how these campaigns go, Kiara. I don't believe she's murdered anyone."

"That's not the only charge against her, though, is it? And you've only just met her. Is she really worth risking your ass? Besides, she's a *pirate*." Kiara caught herself short, biting her lip and stepping back. "Sorry, Mikka. I didn't mean . . ."

"I think you said *exactly* what you meant, but I don't blame you. At the end of the day, she's not our responsibility. But I'd rather take the risk of getting her through than turn her over to the Syndicate. We'll drop her off on Lunar, and she can find her own way from there."

Kiara pulled in close and lowered her voice. "All I'm saying is, ten thousand credits will go a long way to paying off some of our debts. You know we could use the help."

Mikka sighed. Ten thousand credits would do more than cover the debts she had. It would help to cover some of her other commitments, and perhaps she could even take on fewer contracts. If she hadn't seen the other side of the situation, it would've been tempting.

"You know the Syndicate are soulless bastards. There's no way I could turn her over in good conscience."

"Well, that's good to hear," Abigail said as the bathroom door hissed open, wiping her hands on the fringes of her cape. "I was beginning to worry you'd forgotten where you came from, love."

Kiara grunted as she stomped over to the navigation panel. "We need to get moving if we're going to hit our waypoint window. Can you at least stay hidden when we go through the checkpoint?"

"Don't worry about me, love. I'm a master of invisibility." Abigail made her way to an open seat and planted herself on its cushioned surface, her staff held in one hand and planted on the ground beside her.

A queen on her throne, golden scepter in hand, Mikka thought. There was something about this woman she didn't like, but she couldn't put her finger on it. Perhaps it was the way she strutted around the *Redemption* like she owned the place. Some pirates believed the Loop owed them something. But there *was* something special about Abigail Monroe; something that both intrigued Mikka and told her to be cautious around her.

"*Damn!*" Kiara leaned over her console, hitting a few buttons on her datapad before looking up at Mikka. "OG's calling. What do you want me to do?"

Mikka sighed, still considering their new passenger. If the patrols even suspected they had Monroe on board, they'd tear her ship apart, panel by panel, and not think twice about it. And they'd leave her with the bill.

Even if they didn't go to such extremes, the delay would surely cause them to miss their window through the waypoint. The profit from their haul would be all but wiped out in penalties and fees.

Abigail sat, unperturbed, inspecting her cuticles.

"I hope saving your ass is worth this." Mikka turned to Kiara. "Answer it."

"Shuttle *Redemption*. License 82Xi-17Delta. This is Orbital Patrol. You've picked up an escape pod that we believe held a wanted fugitive. Please release Abigail Monroe into our custody, and we will let you proceed unobstructed."

Kiara turned to Mikka, her eyes so wide, they were bugging out of her skull.

"This is Mikka Jenax of the *Redemption*. License 82Xi-17Delta. We did collect a pod. It was issuing a distress signal, but it was empty when we arrived. I know nothing of any Abigail Monroe."

There was a pause. Mikka held her breath, hoping that would be the end of it but knowing in her gut that a rum runner's word would never be enough to satisfy them. Not by a long shot.

A few anxious seconds ticked by. Kiara and Mikka exchanged worried glances. Abigail sat in her chair, still examining her fingernails.

"*Redemption,* prepare for boarding and a routine inspection."

Kiara's eyes popped out again, her nostrils flaring.

"Not even a please?" Abigail muttered, earning a death stare from Kiara.

"Uh, sir," Mikka ventured, "we are en route to Lunar and have a scheduled window through the *Infinity* debris field. We're not going to make it if we're delayed."

"I'll send word to the checkpoint to let you through once we're done. Please power down your engines, send over a copy of your ship's manifest and itinerary, and prepare for boarding."

Mikka sighed, but she didn't miss a beat. "Kiara, send over the requested documents. Abigail, come with me."

"Are you locking me in the brig or shoving me out the airlock, love?"

"I might be crazy . . . but neither, actually."

Mikka didn't waste any time as she moved through the shuttle's cargo bay. Thanks to Abigail's pod, the chamber now smelled of electrical smoke. She prayed there was nothing still at risk of catching fire.

"Grab anything you might have left behind in the pod. The boarding party can't know you were ever in there. I assume you were smart enough to have wiped the pod's history?"

"You've done this before, love. I can tell." Abigail stopped in her tracks, put her hands on her hips, and grinned.

"Listen, this isn't a joke. I've worked hard to disappear, and I'm risking it all to save your sorry ass. Now, did you or did you not wipe the pod's records?"

Abigail straightened, her grin fading only slightly. She took a few steps forward and grabbed a flask from her inside jacket pocket. The end of the bottle tipped up, and she gulped before her demeanor shifted. Her eyes focused, and the sway in her step lessened as she closed the gap between them. She leaned in and lowered her voice, her breath heavy with the scent of rum. "Yes, of course I did, love. That's Piracy 101."

Abigail's eyes shifted behind them to the cockpit of the shuttle, and she grabbed Mikka's arm. "How much do you trust your little friend there not to turn me in? I might have done my fair share of misdeeds, but you know how it is out there. I'd like to make it out of here in one piece."

"She's not thrilled about helping you," Mikka confirmed, pulling her arm from Abigail's grasp. "But she's too involved to squeal now. We'll all find ourselves getting acquainted with the inside of a Syndicate cell if she snitches."

Mikka took several steps to the edge of the cargo bay, where a small, dark gray paneled strip lined the outside perimeter of the hold. The color contrast from the standard light gray looked as though it might be decorative, but it was a great space to store smaller items that could be magnetized to the ship's wall to keep them from sliding around. She reached down and pulled up a corner of a loose panel, revealing a small trapdoor with a large circular handle.

"Like I said, love, it looks like you've done this before. Would now be a good time to tell you I'm afraid of the dark?"

Mikka rolled her eyes and grabbed a small blue flashlight from within another hatch along the wall. "You can either deal with the dark or the OG. Get in there, and don't make a sound. Even though the access is hidden, this isn't a secret compartment, so crawl in as far as you can go. The primary space is filled with our Lunar shipment; squeeze past that as best you can. Once you get to the far wall, there are a few hidden compartments you'll be able to crawl into. Don't stop at the first trapdoor, either. There are a few layers in case someone finds the first. Go through several before you seal yourself in. Don't come out until you hear me calling out that it's safe."

Abigail wrinkled her nose. With one last uncertain glance at Mikka, she begrudgingly grabbed the flashlight and climbed into the crawlspace.

CHAPTER NINE

Mikka Jenax
The *Redemption*

"LIKE I SAID, EMPTY POD."

Mikka crossed her arms over her chest as the Orbital Guard officer crawled out of the pear-shaped vessel.

She held her breath and crossed her fingers that Abigail hadn't foolishly left something behind in her rush to get below the floor panels. There couldn't be a shred of evidence of the pirate ever having been on board that pod, or the entire ploy would unravel.

The Orbital Guard.

If anyone ever asked Mikka her thoughts on the law enforcement officials who patrolled the space between Earth and Lunar, she wouldn't hesitate in ranting about how they were nothing but a waste of credits.

Two of the uniformed men had boarded the *Redemption*. The pricks were nothing more than arrogant assholes who couldn't cut it as part of the Syndicate Front, Corpo Patrols, or the United Earth Police Force. Hell, even becoming a PI would have been a better gig. If they ever stopped any of the real criminals, maybe Mikka would feel differently, but as it stood, the Guard spent most of their time handing out bogus tickets for minor infractions and roughing up anyone who looked at them the wrong way. Piracy was a lucrative gig for a reason, and it was mostly because these clowns weren't competent enough to actually do their jobs.

Applicants who cared about security—or what could pass as "security" these days—found opportunities in more regimented organizations. The Orbital Guard was left only with the scraps.

The officer stepping out of the pod was named Hester, and he brushed the soot and dirt from his gray uniform as he rose to his full height. He was only a pimple-faced kid, bright-eyed, and full of his own piss. On first impressions, Mikka was convinced he'd been accepted into the Guard because of some favor to a family member. Even with the unit's low standards, it was hard to believe he had made it through the necessary hurdles to be issued with a badge. Never mind his age, Hester was so slim, he barely fit into his uniform. It hung off his body as if it had been his father's. The clothes were so loose that Mikka wondered briefly if things really had gotten so bad. If the Syndicate was cutting rations to Orbital Patrol, that didn't bode well for the frail stability of the Loop.

Mikka shook off the thought. It was far more likely that Hester was new on the job and had simply inherited some other poor sap's uniform.

"Pod's clean," Hester announced.

Despite her immediate flash of relief, Mikka knew there was no way the kid could have done a thorough job of combing through all the information the pod held. Even if Abigail had wiped the computer, there were likely enough time stamps and navigational blips that would indicate the system had been tampered with. Radiation anomalies could direct an investigator to how long ago the pod had been launched. Even a solid UV sweep of the box would probably tip them off to something being amiss. But Hester was too inexperienced and his superior accompanying him too lazy for them to rub two brain cells together long enough to find something. But such details were what had kept Mikka out of the Syndicate's grasp for so long.

She hadn't become the most wanted pirate in the Loop for nothing.

"Don't take everything at face value." Hester's boss, Argus, was much more irritating. He was clearly a man who had been in the field for too long and had already checked out, Hester's complete opposite. He was overweight, pushing fifty, his hair graying and retreating from his forehead. The pupil of his left eye was clouded, and the color of the iris in his right had faded. Whether the discoloration was due to age or being exposed to more cosmic radiation than his body could handle was impossible to say. He grinned, revealing stained and crooked teeth. Mikka *knew* Guard members were provided with dental services, a rarity for people who lived away from the planet's surface, but Argus, apparently, didn't take advantage of that luxury perk. Then again, if cosmic radiation was an issue for him, it was possible it had microwaved his brain.

Argus pulled his belt up to ensure his pants were containing his gut, but the taut leather could only do so much, and rolls of fat flopped over its sides. Heat radiated off the officer's oversized body as he stepped closer to Mikka. She shuddered as she caught a whiff of something that smelled like the scum scraped off the bottom of a space station's cargo hold. Those teeth didn't only look disgusting; they also smelled the part.

"Monroe is crafty," Argus continued. "I wouldn't put it past her to be hiding here somewhere."

"Like I said," Mikka asserted through gritted teeth, "the pod was empty when we picked it up."

"She's sly enough to have boarded your ship without you even knowing."

Is that what you tell your sergeant to cover your ass for not catching her?

"What do you think happened, Officer? She opened a viewport and crawled in? I hope one of our sensors would have detected a change in pressure."

"On this old scrapheap?" Argus cast an unimpressed eye around the hold. "If Monroe isn't on board, you won't mind if we perform a quick inspection of your ship."

Before Mikka could respond, the man snapped his fingers at the kid, who was frantically typing on his datapad. "Hester, circle the ship, and make sure not to miss any nooks and crannies."

"Be my guest," Mikka muttered. She resisted the urge to glance toward the trapdoor in the cargo room floor, cut into the darker paneled flooring. Instead, she looked to Kiara, leaning against the entrance to the bridge with her arms crossed and her face white, her bottom lip curled under her front teeth.

The woman wouldn't intentionally give them away—or at least, Mikka hoped she wouldn't—but it was possible her navigator could betray them with involuntary cues. Mikka cringed. Right now, Kiara looked as guilty as hell. The woman was actually twitching.

All Mikka could do was watch as the two officers turned the *Redemption* upside down. She glanced at her watch several times throughout the search; the waypoint might extend the courtesy of keeping their approved passage window open if the OG requested it, but that didn't mean they wouldn't get back to the moon base far later than planned.

Too late to get full payment for their shipment.

Argus walked the perimeter of the cargo hold. The transport class shuttle wasn't anything special, and he had likely come across a hundred similar vessels over the years. The only thing that made the *Redemption* stand out was how good a shape it was in, regardless of the officer's earlier slur. Mikka had been meticulous in its restoration, whereas most transport captains would have given up on repairs years ago. Still, the officers' presence was unnerving, and her nerves felt as though they had endured more than they could take for one day already.

Mikka held back a gasp as Argus tapped the panel above the storage unit entry with his foot. The metal plating pinged as it revealed its hollow interior.

She chuckled silently at her own reaction. It really had been years since she'd gone through an inspection. As she'd told Abigail, it wasn't a secret compartment; the space was standard on the Delta Class shuttlecraft, but its main access was beneath the vessel. It made loading and unloading more expedient at port. It was truly only one of two places they could have hidden a stowaway—which, of course, made it the best place to put someone.

"Now, lovelies, we're not going to find anything if we go snooping around your subfloor holdings, are we?"

"That's our excess storage," Kiara said. "You won't find anything but computer parts, beets, cabbage, and a few space rats down there."

Space rats? Easy, Kiara. Overexplaining won't do us any favors.

"You'll have to see for yourself," Mikka offered.

Argus didn't acknowledge the comment. Instead, his focus was on Hester, who was standing on a ladder with his head buried in an overhead bulkhead, ten feet in the air.

"Hester," he called out. "There's a storage area under the floor. Come open this hatch."

Hester didn't waste any time in scurrying down the ladder and across the cargo bay to reach the trap door. The kid was all too eager to follow his commander's bidding.

Admittedly, it had been a while, but this was old hat for Mikka —inspections, the spectacle of pulling chips out of consoles and wires out of walls. The only offense the Orbital Guard held was intimidation, and though they didn't know it, Mikka wasn't worried by a brief stop and a half-assed inspection. Nevertheless, she was eager to be on her way.

For Kiara, on the other hand, this was likely new ground. Mikka noticed her navigator catch her breath out of the corner of her eye—she wasn't so adept at hiding her reactions. It wasn't surprising—Kiara was someone who had spent her entire life keeping her hands clean.

Mikka would have lifted a hand to her forehead if it wouldn't give her companion away entirely. Watching them work, though, she suspected the patrol was too blind to catch the subtlety of Kiara's actions.

The entire setup was for show. In reality, there were only a few places where a stowaway could hide in an empty cargo shuttle, the subdeck storage area being one. Making a big deal out of the search was an attempt to see how nervous the women became as they crawled inside. The success or failure of the ship's crew in hiding their emotions would be the indicator as to how deep and how extensive they searched below. If Abigail was as cunning as she claimed, though, she'd be hiding behind the false wall Mikka had installed in the back of the container, built for occasions like these or rare instances when she carried a small, priceless artifact on board. There were pirates out there, after all.

Hester grinned as he whipped a flashlight off his belt and slid down the hole.

Argus chuckled and stepped away from the trapdoor as he watched the kid disappear. His sights were now set on Mikka. There was an unjustified cockiness to his swagger, as though the guard believed he had somehow pulled a fast one on them; that he had found them out or somehow believed he held the upper hand.

For all his posturing, Argus was barely taller than Mikka, and as he stepped closer to her, she was forced to stare into the man's cloudy eye. Better than the rotting food in his teeth, she supposed.

"Unless Hester finds something," he said, "I believe you'll be free to go."

The tension in Kiara's shoulders visibly relaxed, but Mikka held her rigid posture. She wasn't sure what the man's angle was, so she held her tongue. She didn't want to provide any ammunition he might use against her, however innocent a comment it might seem.

"Of course," he continued, "there is still the matter of the pod. There will be a ten thousand credit fine for the possession of unauthorized cargo."

"*What!*" Kiara gasped. "We were answering a distress call! We would have been fined for ignoring it!"

"So you claim," Argus said, his bottom lip jutting out, and Mikka couldn't decide if he was thinking or simply pouting. "But . . . we couldn't find any trace of a distress call on any authorized channels. And there was nobody inside. From our perspective, you saw an opportunity for some scrap metal and helped yourselves. Not a huge offense, in the scheme of things." He actually had the gall to wink at her.

Mikka shuddered involuntarily.

Argus tightened his lips and continued. "But you *did* take on the pod. Unfortunately for you, this isn't just a simple matter of unauthorized transport. This pod is evidence against the fugitive Abigail Monroe, and thus, the property of the Syndicate. Don't look so glum; there won't be any criminal charges. It's just an unauthorized transport fee. I *could* be charging you with obstruction of justice."

"How the hell do you expect us to come up with ten thousand credits?" Kiara burst out. "That's our entire haul for six months!"

"Not my problem," Argus flatly replied. He paced and then paused. He took three steps in Mikka's direction, his lips curling upward.

"Of course, perhaps we can make *alternative* arrangements.

We could make this all disappear . . ." He lifted a hand toward Mikka's cheek.

"If you want to keep that hand, I'd suggest you keep it to yourself." Mikka held her ground, her voice like steel, and her eyes firmly locked onto the lecherous officer's good eye. Sweat glazed his forehead as his expression soured, and his arm paused in midair as he weighed the reproach.

After a long moment, Argus retracted his hand. His brow furrowed and his shoulders tightened as thinly contained fury replaced his embarrassment.

"Very well." Argus pulled his datapad from his belt and made a few keystrokes on its surface. "You have ten days to pay your fine at any Orbital Guard office. If no payment is made within that time, we'll issue a reclamation order to seize this vessel." His eyes scanned around the shuttle as though he hadn't taken enough of a good look before. "I'm sure the value of the *Redemption* will cover the amount owed, if necessary."

Mikka had to clench her fists in order to keep herself from doing something she'd regret. It wouldn't do anybody any good if she ended up being arrested for assaulting an officer, no matter how much he deserved it.

"All clear down here," Hester chirped as he pulled himself out of the crawlspace. "The captain's right; she keeps her ship *clean*. No space rats; not even cobwebs. Just the smell of cabbage from her cargo."

"She'll fetch a fair price," Argus muttered. Mikka couldn't tell if he was trying to rub salt in the wound, or if he was truly displeased that the cargo space had recently been scrubbed.

"You can dump the pod once we disengage. We'll tow it in from there."

Ten thousand credits.

The money was an issue, but it wasn't the thing that bothered her most about the encounter. It was the sleazy solicitation; the insinuation that she could sell her body to satisfy this man's ego. That she provided nothing more of worth.

But Mikka had long since handled her own and stood up for herself when nobody else would.

This sycophant was clearly not used to being told no. Bruising his ego was immensely satisfying. Mikka could see him sizing her up, debating whether she'd best him in a fight.

She'd gladly take him on with one hand tied behind her back.

CHAPTER TEN

Django
Eclipse

DURING DAYTIME HOURS, the B-Ring sparkled.

When Django, Nova, and Eventide had made their journey to Eventide's quarters the night before, everything had been cast in the haze of his family's death. He had barely noticed how new everything seemed here; how polished the paneling was. The metal rails were similar to those in the D-Ring, except that, in the lower decks, they were dingy, missing bolts, and bore spots of rust and decay. Here, they were sparkling clean, as if they had been installed yesterday instead of centuries ago.

The carpets were a rich burgundy, with only faint signs of wear, as if people hadn't been traversing over them for all that time. In contrast, the D-Ring carpets were barely holding together and, in some places, were little more than sparse threads clinging to the edges of the hallways. If they had once been such a rich deep red color, it had been lost long ago under layers of gray soot and soil.

Despite having made use of Eventide's ensuite shower,

Django could feel the grime and dirt of home still clinging to him, a constant reminder that he didn't belong here.

"It's nice here," Nova chimed beside him. "Everyone looks so happy."

Did they? Django had hardly noticed. The hallway was surprisingly empty for such an early hour. He looked at the few groggy faces that passed by and wondered what Nova was seeing. Everyone looked irritated, especially when they caught sight of Django and his sister.

He instinctively pulled Nova closer to him. "Are you sure?" he asked.

"Yes, it's so lovely here! And quiet! There isn't as much noise as there is on our level."

A pair of station officers conversing idly suddenly caught sight of them. Both noses crinkled in unison, a collective snarl, as the two D-Ring youths approached. They were certainly not the happy, friendly people Nova was perceiving. It *was* quiet, though. He'd give her that.

Beeps and hums from the station's computer panels were eerily invasive, as though each was an alert to Django's presence. Instead of screens, holo-projections informed the residents of the daily bulletins here. The three-dimensional images were cleaner and crisper than any of the flat displays found on the Rings below.

"Are you lost, kids?" one officer, a man not much older than Django, called out. "The farms aren't on this level." Both of them laughed as though it were a joke he should have understood.

Django looked down at his clothes. They were brown and perhaps a little ragged, but they were no different from anything else worn in the D-Ring. Certainly, officers in charge of station security understood the role the D-Ring played in keeping the station fed; their role in restoring the planet below them.

Everything you saw is real.

Just as he did Uncle Marvin's words, Django dismissed the

officers' jeers. It didn't matter what a few guards thought. Or his crazy uncle, for that matter. Why couldn't people just leave him be?

A cold draft flowed through the hall, with an icy bite to its hollow shell. The few people they passed were strangers to Django—not a friend to be seen. Each person was going about their day without concern for an accident two Rings away.

Two worlds away.

The B-Ring was a surreal copy of the one Django knew all too well. It was a mirror image of a different, more shiny reality, where the tech and equipment were newer, cleaner, and brighter, but the people were colder, meaner, and more judgmental.

Two hallway doors slid open as they passed. The handful of residents nearby stopped and backed away. Django froze, unsure of what the commotion was about.

Three guards stepped into the hall, side by side, energy pistols in hand. Their white ceramic-paneled outfits perfectly complimented the blue lights that surrounded them.

Station Guards.

"Out of the way!" one guard called out. "Make way for Commander Benson."

Mention of the commander's name sent a shiver through Django, causing memories of the previous night to resurface. The wedding. The drinks. The viewport malfunction.

The last time he'd seen his family.

Benson had been there, and only now did Django connect the dots that the man had also escaped the hull breach.

He must have left before Eventide and I returned.

Django took a step back toward the wall as the guard passed by, followed by the commander. The guards formed a loose triangle around their protectorate. A determined assassin might have been able to break through their formation, but not without a fatal cost. Mostly, the guards were clearing a path for the station's leader, keeping everyone else at arm's length.

Their uniforms matched the ones Avery and Isaacs wore, with the red and yellow intertwined hexagonal emblem emblazoned on their chests. Four blue rings of the *Eclipse* glowed within. And though each torus differed in size in reality, on the emblem each circle was equal in diameter; each bearing equal importance in the eyes of their ancestors. A sentiment that had faded in time.

Benson's gaze was unfocused, though his brow furrowed, and his stride remained determined.

His eyes met Django's and Benson jumped, as though startled by his presence. With a raised eyebrow, an unspoken question formed on the commander's lips. There was no mistaking his recognition of the oh-so-proud young farmer from the night before.

It was only as Django studied the commander that he realized the pomp and commanding presence of yesterday had now faded. His face was a little paler, his shoulders slumped. Bags hung beneath the man's eyes, shadows creeping up and around the sockets, dark and sunken as though he was plagued by sleeplessness. His salt-and-pepper hair, while not messy, had lost some of its shine, and instead of reflecting the lights of the hall, the rays seemed to be absorbed and darkened by it. The white of his hair had turned a pale shade of blue, the darker grays made darker, as though they existed in shadow. Stubble crawled up his cheeks, his beard spreading upward in an attempt to swallow the rest of his face.

Benson's gaze was weary, but there was more than fatigue behind his glance. Something else lingered there. Surprise? Annoyance? Disgust?

For a second, Django thought the man was going to speak to him—to perhaps offer him a word of condolence or relief. A rebuke, maybe.

It wasn't as though the man wouldn't have been aware of the accident. Benson couldn't have missed it by more than a few minutes—*moments*, maybe—a tragedy linking Django with the commander.

Something in the way Benson's eyes flickered warned Django that the commander didn't see the parallel in quite the same light.

If Benson had something to say, he thought better of it and carried on.

Twice in as many days, Django had seen the commander venture from the administrative A-Ring. That was two more times than in the eighteen years prior. However, as quickly as he had arrived, Benson was gone, marching down the hall of the B-Ring to some unseen destination. Perhaps to a meeting with the technicians, or perhaps providing a similar service to the B-Ring as he had to the D-Ring the day before.

"You got a problem, dirt ringer?"

A blond-haired guard, an energy weapon in hand, stepped in front of them. He stood inches from Django's face, hints of garlic and coffee sullying the man's putrid breath.

Django steered Nova to stand behind him.

"No problem, sir. Just making our way back home."

"You should have stayed there to begin with," the man spat. "Your kind doesn't have any right to be on this deck."

The emblem on your chest would suggest otherwise.

Django kept his thoughts to himself. He had no desire to argue; he just wanted to go home.

"Did you hear me, dirt ringer? While you're at it, you can take that bitch of a technician with you. We don't want her here, either —spreading her legs for anyone who asks."

There were no thoughts that followed, only reaction. Django felt his fist connect with the officer's face, his shoulder to his chest, and his body slamming him to the floor. Waves of flesh rippled against his fists as he pounded repeatedly until two sets of firm hands pulled him away.

A handful of his colleagues rushed to help the officer before Django could even comprehend he wasn't still throwing fists.

A whir of activity followed, his own pulse drowning out much of the frantic conversation.

He looked to his own knuckles, stained red.

Is that my blood? Or his?

We don't want her here, either.

"Get him to the infirmary . . ."

"Should we arrest the kid?"

". . . Jameson's own fault. He was being a prick, like usual . . ."

". . . can't just let a dirt-ringer attack an officer . . ."

"Let him go. It's not worth the paperwork."

"You'd better watch your back, kid. Don't even *think* of showing your face here again."

BLOODY KNUCKLES.

They were all Django could focus on. He had never punched anyone before, and he hadn't expected it would hurt so much.

The red smears on his knuckles, now darker, drying, and congealing, contrasted with the white of the tram.

Like everything else on the B-Ring, the shuttle that traveled between Rings was immaculate. The tram's white metal seats were topped with blue cushions, the car's ceiling adorned with blue lighting and lined overhead with holo-screens. News anchors discussed station updates, but the volume was either off or turned down low so it couldn't be heard over the whirring and grinding of the shuttle as it traversed its route.

The shuttle contained only a few passengers; those who had a reason to travel between Rings. Visiting friends was not a common occurrence, especially between the B and D decks. A handful of technicians, guards, and other officials were spread throughout the car, but it was clear to Django that he and Nova were the only D-Ringers on board. Even here, all eyes were on them. The weight of their fellow passengers' stares prickled the back of Django's neck as he did his best to divert them from his sister.

Much like the fight, Django barely remembered the journey onto the shuttle. One moment, he was being stared down by a few dozen B-Ring residents; the next, he was being stared at by a dozen others on the InterRing shuttle.

He supposed he should consider himself lucky for not ending up in a holding cell.

Or worse.

Not yet, anyway.

If Nova noticed the unnatural attention they were attracting, she didn't say anything. She was too preoccupied, her gaze darting back and forth from one part of the train to the next as if trying to take it all in, much more enamored with the luxury of the tech than the people it contained.

His mind wandered, Marvin's intent echoing in his thoughts. *Leave the station?* Django scoffed out loud at the thought. *We can barely pass for leaving the D-Ring.*

Django let out a yawn. He had barely slept at Eventide's; the death of his family and Uncle Marvin's words had plagued his thoughts all night. It didn't seem real. *Nothing* about the past twenty-four hours seemed real. Yet here he was, on a shuttle, returning from a Ring he had never been to before, traveling back to an empty home.

With knuckles covered in blood.

I punched a guard.

The lump in his throat didn't want to go away. Django didn't know who he was anymore.

The cursed conspiracies that Marvin had touted had plagued

his thoughts equally as much as Django's grief. Could he really believe there was any alternative to the *Eclipse*?

And even if he imagined for a moment that there was, that the glitch he had seen in the atrium *had* been real, Django didn't see why they should leave. He didn't know what was out there. How did he know if they'd survive in whatever world was being hidden from them?

Perhaps they were being kept away for their own protection? During the brief glitch, Django hadn't seen anything that convinced him it was better on the outside than he had it. Sure, the D-Ring might not have the amenities of the B deck, but they always had enough food to get by, and protection from the vacuum, radiation, and cosmic debris of the space around them. Earth might be greener than Admin were telling them, but that also didn't necessarily mean it was ready for habitation.

Without warning, the lights of the shuttle darkened, and the station alarms sounded.

Another hull breach.

Was it because of him? Because of his altercation with the guard? Was this Benson taking his shot against him?

Marvin was getting into his head. Django dismissed the irrational thoughts and moved to wrap a comforting arm around Nova, but she shrugged it off, content to sit on her own and stare at the floor of the cabin.

Several passengers braced themselves as the deafening noise filled the car. As they did anywhere else on the station, the lights filling the space turned from blue to red as the shuttle slowed to a halt.

An informational alert flashed on the holo-screens, and Django fought to keep his heart rate under control. Nova sat still beside him, indifferent.

Commander Benson said there'd be more impacts as Eclipse *passes through the meteoroid field.*

The thought was hardly reassuring.

Django watched avidly as the familiar notification flashed across the shuttle's screens.

WARNING: HULL BREACH, D-RING DELTA-012. PLEASE EVACUATE THE AREA IMMEDIATELY. TECHNICIANS ARE EN ROUTE.

Delta-012 was close to the cargo bay, nowhere near their residence and nowhere near the transport shuttle.

Django breathed a sigh of relief.

Just a coincidence.

In a matter of minutes, the alarms quieted, and the tram began moving again.

Perhaps nothing else will go wrong today.

CHAPTER ELEVEN

Django
Eclipse

THE SWEET SMELL of the D-Ring hit Django's senses before the transport's door even opened. For the first time in what felt like ages, he allowed a small smile to creep over his face as he inhaled the smell of dirt, machinery, and hard work. The D-Ring might not have been as spacious or sterile as the B-Ring, but it was home, and its familiarity allowed every muscle in his body to relax.

The smell was overwhelming after spending a night in the Upper Ring with a persistent smell of bleach and disinfectant. The familiar scent was all he had ever known, but Django suddenly realized why the B-Ring residents looked at him with such critical stares: the odor was comparatively sour and moldy. If even a faint waft had clung to him, he must have been the most offensive thing on the entire upper torus.

A smile touched his lips.

It was *his* odor. The smell of waking up in the morning to laundry and baking. The scent of burning metal and plastics as equipment was maintained and restored. The scent of livestock and fertilizer, ash, and hope. It was the scent of life. It was all here.

And what those on the Upper Rings didn't understand was that this was where everything in their world came from. This was humanity's true form: hard work, dedication, and working together to build humanity.

And Django wouldn't want it any other way.

His hand gripped Nova's, and she looked up at him with tired eyes and a distant frown. Nova, Marvin, and Eventide were the only family he had left. It wasn't much, but it was more than many had.

The walk home was comforting compared to their march through the B-Ring, and it didn't take long for the siblings to reach their quarters.

"*She's* here again," Nova said before Django even saw the woman standing at their door. "The one who came to tell you Mom and Dad had died."

Django hadn't realized Nova had been aware of Avery's presence a day earlier. It had been the first time Django had ever seen the officer, and if he was honest, he would be fine if it had been the last. He wiped his palms off on his shirt before he realized they were sweating. All he knew was, the last time she was at his door, she had been the bearer of bad news.

Avery held her datapad once again, her white-paneled uniform now a sharp reminder of the B-Ring. Pristine, shiny, and carrying the faint scent of bleach. An overt reminder of who held the power on the station.

But the confidence of power didn't translate to her face. Just like Commander Benson, Avery appeared fraught. She couldn't have turned thirty yet, but the creases at the corners of her eyes betrayed the appearance of youth, and the lines on her forehead made it clear the woman had spent more of her life scowling than she had smiling. Her face was still fierce, her eyes intense, but there was a tiredness that hadn't been visible yesterday. It was as though nobody in the entire station had slept the night before.

What hadn't changed was that Avery's features were still hard, stern, as though she would enter into battle at any moment.

"Can I help you, Officer?" Django asked. "Did you forget something yesterday?"

Avery's shoulders slumped, and she lowered the datapad. Her pale green eyes found his, and under her intense stare, he realized she wasn't there for a follow-up. She held up a chain with a pendant attached. Two metal circles intertwined.

Django suddenly couldn't breathe, as though all the air had been sucked out of the station, as though, this time, the breach in the station's hull was on top of him and he was being pulled into the vacuum of space.

Close to the cargo bays.

Avery stood quiet for several long moments. "I'm sorry," was all she could muster.

"Uncle Marvin?" Django asked, though he didn't have to. There was only one reason this woman would be at his door, only one reason she'd be holding Marvin's beloved pendant.

Avery's demeanor was at odds with the person Django had encountered yesterday. The coldness was gone, replaced by a level of shock and sadness in her eyes, as though she hadn't delivered this same message to dozens of families over the last few months.

Avery nodded.

Nova released her grip on Django's hand. "He's dead, isn't he?" The pieces apparently came together slower for his sister, but she still came to the same conclusion.

Avery nodded again, her eyes moist. But if there were tears to be shed, she held them back. She cleared her throat and lifted her datapad again, as though she was going to read the report from it after all. But after a cursory glance, she lowered it, instead holding Django's gaze. "The breach was in an auxiliary room adjacent to the shuttle bay. It occurred during the early morning hours; Marvin was the first to arrive for his shift and was the only casualty. The technicians managed to seal off the breach, but it was too late for your uncle."

Nova shuddered, and Django expected her to finally take hold of him; to seek some support from her older brother. But she didn't; instead, she stepped back and stood straighter.

Django could feel Nova's eyes on him, but he couldn't bring himself to meet her gaze. He didn't want to see further devastation on her face.

"It's just like he said would happen." Nova's voice was calm and assured, not at all the scared little girl her brother had been expecting.

Django froze. Frantically, he reached for and squeezed Nova's hand, praying she would interpret his gesture to stop talking. It would be even better if she would say something to cover her tracks; something that would make the comment seem ordinary. Like his sister didn't suspect their family had been murdered.

It's not true.

But such accusations wouldn't be taken kindly.

With Marvin dead, Nova's words struck Django in the gut. She wasn't wrong, and he had predicted he was at risk. That they *all* were at risk.

But it couldn't have been more than a coincidence.

If there was a shred of a chance that what Marvin had said was true, then the officer before them now probably suspected his sister knew something she shouldn't. Perhaps she had been waiting for them to reveal what Django had witnessed. Perhaps this was all she needed to make *them* disappear, too.

Perhaps she didn't need a reason at all.

Regardless, Nova needed to stop before she dug them in any deeper. Great stars, Django hoped Avery hadn't noticed the slip. He prayed to any entity that would listen that his sister would leave it at that, and the patrol officer would leave without incident. If she stopped talking now, he could probably explain it away.

Every muscle in his body constricted.

"Isn't it, Django?" she continued. "He said we would be next if . . ."

"That's *enough*, Nova!" Django interjected, gripping her shoulder hard. "I'm sorry about her," he said to Avery. "She didn't sleep well. She's been talking nonsense all morning."

"*Ow!*" Nova said, squirming out of Django's grip. "Stop it! You're hurting me!"

Django dropped his hand as his sister broke free. Nova shot daggers at him, clearly annoyed and confused.

Catch on! He pleaded through silent stares.

Avery raised an eyebrow, intently focused on Nova, as though unsure of how to respond.

Nova snarled at Django but was too stunned to say anything further.

"It's been an unfortunate two days for you," Avery responded. "Irrational outbursts are to be expected."

Nova's eyes were wide as she looked from the officer to Django. Django could tell his sister had missed the point, but she was beyond his reach as her mouth opened again.

"I'm not . . ."

It was Avery who lifted a finger at Nova this time, stopping the girl in her determined attempts to convey the pieces of the puzzle she had put together. Nova's eyes continued to widen as she looked at Avery, and Django could tell when the second part of Marvin's message finally clicked in her head.

Don't let anyone else know what you've seen.

"You would do well to control your tongue, young lady," Avery warned, not lowering her finger but taking a step closer toward the girl, who, for the first time in two days, now gripped her brother's arm. "Grief wouldn't be a sufficient excuse for others in my position." She lowered her finger and bent from her waist, bringing her face uncomfortably close to Nova's. "Be *careful*."

Avery then turned to Django. Her uniform creaked and cracked as she shuffled her weight, but she took the time to look Django dead in the eye for more than a moment. Django held his breath, unsure if he was going to be the one blamed for his sister's comments.

Django's mind raced with things to say. *Should* he say anything? A word of thanks? A question of intent? How much had the officer gleaned from Nova's comments?

Avery quickly cast a glance over each shoulder as she straightened.

"I'm sorry for your loss," she reiterated. "Whatever you decide, don't wait until it's too late."

Too late for what?

Avery deactivated her datapad and turned to march down the hallway.

That wasn't how Django wanted this conversation to end. He wanted to ask the officer something, *anything*. There were a hundred questions roaming through his head. Her cryptic message couldn't be anything but a remark about seizing the moment, could it? Or was it a nod to Marvin's words? He had to say *something*, but it couldn't be too obvious.

"Officer Inglewood!" Django called. The woman paused in her stride, but she didn't turn around. He realized he didn't have a plan, so he just kept talking. "I'm a farmer. This is all I've ever known."

Avery let out a sigh, then turned to face Django and his sister. "People always believe the role they play is consequential. The truth is, few will ever make a memorable difference. Few will seize the opportunity to become what they *could* have been. None of us are special, but our *actions* can be. Consider what price you're willing to pay to continue living your ordinary life, and who else is suffering because of the choices you refused to make."

Avery turned as though about to continue her march and then paused.

"I almost forgot." She reached into a pouch that hung on the side of her belt, pulled out a small envelope, and handed it to Django. "Your uncle left this for you. Don't open it until you are in your quarters. Whatever you decide, you're lucky *I'm* the one who found it."

CHAPTER TWELVE

Mikka
The *Redemption*

MIKKA TAPPED the shuttle's controls, helping Kiara to steady the *Redemption* in Lunar's orbit. A dozen other ships circled the moon with them, waiting for the authorization to dock. Like the *Redemption*, nearly half of the ships were also bound for Shackleton City.

Ships flew in and out of the docking station, allowed to pass through the city's single transport force field with ease. It was both a simple and a complex solution to enable ships to pass: simple, because it did away with the necessity for airlocks and decompression chambers; complex, because Mikka had no clue how the system actually worked. The opening allowed ships and solid mass to pass through while preserving Lunar's artificial atmosphere and air and keeping out debris, radiation, and deadly temperatures.

The ease of navigation didn't negate the need for ships to obtain clearance. The procedure was a bane to pirates, though not an impossible one to circumvent. Shackleton City wasn't the only place to land a ship on the moon, after all.

The *Redemption* had been in a holding pattern for nearly an hour, but Mikka didn't mind. She had been relieved they had made it through the waypoint at all. Despite her rejection of the OG inspector's advances, their place in the queue had been held. Argus must have arranged that *before* he'd boarded their ship and then forgot to cancel it—or it was simply too much work for the prick to bother.

Either way, though it was a small win, at least *something* had gone right. They had missed their original scheduled pickup, meaning their profits had all but evaporated, but Kiara had been right: there *would* be others. Though Mikka wondered how much that mattered now.

Ten thousand credits.

No delivery could fill that gap. A dozen extra contracts wouldn't satisfy it. It would take years for her to come up with that kind of money. The *Redemption* itself was barely worth that much. And if she sold the ship . . . Well, she'd be left with nothing. No way to pay her bills unless she took her chances working the ice fields. And even that wouldn't cover everything.

The *Redemption* meant everything to her. Even though Mikka couldn't provide her mother with all of the amenities she wanted to, the ship allowed her to provide *something*.

No ship meant no credits.

But if she didn't sell the ship, the Syndicate would repo it anyway.

Ten days. Either way, I lose.

Kiara had been surprisingly quiet about the encounter. She hadn't exactly been sympathetic once the Guard had left, but solace weighed in her eyes. Perhaps Kiara wasn't as much of a bitch as her captain expected. Mikka underestimated people; a product of being burned far more than once.

Mikka's blood hadn't stopped boiling since the encounter, her mind circling back, again and again, to Argus's lame attempt to force himself upon her.

We could make this all go away.

Asshole.

How many women had he pulled that shit on? How many felt as though they had no choice but to agree in order to be released from a bullshit fee? Mikka couldn't erase the sickly feeling on her skin, nor could she ignore the burning fury in her gut every time she thought about the amount she now owed to the Syndicate.

Ten thousand credits.

She had worked so hard to escape her past.

It had all been for nothing.

Abigail stood to the side of the bridge. She had been uncharacteristically mute since being released from the storage hold. Opting to stand, she rested on her wooden staff, her pale eyes content to watch the viewscreen as they approached Lunar.

It would be easy enough for Mikka to blame the woman for getting her into this mess, to fault her for the OG coming aboard in the first place. But it wasn't Abigail's fault.

Mikka had never felt better about hiding the pirate.

The ship's panels lit up, flashes of red and yellow alternating as they approached the airspace above Shackleton City.

"We're in the queue to land," Kiara advised. She tapped her earpiece and tapped a few commands into her console. "We'll be ready to descend as soon as we're given the green light."

"Great," Mikka replied.

"What do we do about *her*?" Kiara asked.

"Don't worry about me, love," Abigail replied. "Getting through that shield is the easy bit."

"Believe me, I'm not worried." Kiara snorted as she turned to back to Mikka. "Do we turn her in once we dock? Or do we let the LPF know now?"

"Nobody is turning anyone in."

"Mikka, you do realize your new friend here is worth the same amount as our fine for hauling her piece of shit coffin?"

"Hey, now." Abigail held up her hands. "Coffins are for the dead. That rust bucket saved my life."

"You know I wasn't a fan of picking this pirate up to begin with," Kiara continued, "but now she's landed you in hot plasma. Fair's fair—turn her in and carry on."

Mikka sighed and pushed a stray strand of hair from her face. She understood far too well where Kiara was coming from: every person for themselves. It was how the whole goddamn Loop operated. It was how Lunar operated. From the few contacts she had, Mars was no better. Perhaps Earth—opulent, rejuvenated—was spared the sentiment, but it was only because its inhabitants functioned off the backs of the rest of them.

"'Fair?'" Mikka said. "You think what happened out there was *fair?*"

"Look," Kiara said, "I know you have a past, but . . ."

"Don't pretend you know anything about me."

"She deserves to go to jail."

"We all deserve a whole lot different from what we've got, but guess what? That's not how I operate on my ship. I'm going to get Abigail to port. I'll find a way to deal with the Syndicate fine."

"Mikka, you're going to lose your ship! Listen, whatever mistakes you've made, surely it isn't worth throwing everything away? Turn her in, and we'll live to fight another day."

"In exchange for what? My principles? My humanity? Because if I turn this woman in, that's what I've done. I've fallen into their system. You saw what that prick wanted to do to me to get out of that fine. What do you think they're gonna do to a *wanted pirate? That's* the Syndicate's game—turn us against each other so we don't have the strength left to turn against *them.* I'm done fighting, but I sure as hell won't succumb to it, either. You think she deserved to be handed over to that bastard? That's the thing most people don't get about those who have tried to forge their own way. The Syndicate calls them pirates; most of them are just trying to get by. Most of them are left with a rap sheet as long as their arm because they dare to stand up against their order. Because they dare to *fight*."

"Never give up fighting, love." Abigail had pulled out an apple from somewhere within her cape and had bitten into it, continuing to talk as she chewed. "The Syndicate has held us down, but they can't take us out—or something like that."

"I can't worry about fighting the Syndicate. I have my own problems to deal with. But that doesn't mean I'll bend over for them either." Mikka replied. "We won't turn you in, but once we dock, you're on your own. Just don't get caught until you're well clear of us. I might be willing to get you there, but don't add harboring a stowaway to my growing list of offenses."

"I reckon that'd be the least of what's on your record."

Mikka flashed her a warning glare. "Like I've said, that life is behind me. You'd do well not to forget that."

"You were once the most notorious pirate in the Loop, Jax," Abigail continued, ignoring Mikka's warning. "What sort of problems," she took a bite of her apple, "could have tamed *you*, love?"

"That's none of your business."

Abigail smiled. "There are rumors, you know? Rumors you turned on your crew. Left them for dead on Space Dock Nineteen while you disappeared into the cosmos."

Mikka resisted the urge to throw the nearest object directly at Abigail's head. The woman was nothing if not infuriating.

"You're walking an extremely thin line, pirate. It'd be in your best interest not to piss off the one person trying to stand up for you, or I might just cave in to Kiara's suggestion to trade you in. At the end of the day, I'd rather not lose my ship."

Abigail held up her palms in mock surrender, her mouth open, mid-chew, the motion revealing a long scar that crossed her left palm. The scar had healed long ago, but its jagged edge had never fully faded. The life of a pirate was rife with scars, both physical and emotional, and Mikka ignored the sudden itch on her back; one more thing connecting her to the woman before her.

"I meant nothing by it, love. Your reasons are your own."

"We're cleared to dock," Kiara called from the front of the bridge. "Your friend better hide."

"I'll make myself scarce." Abigail's focus never left Mikka. "But I might have an offer that would interest you. A straightforward gig with a killer payoff. The stars know, you could use the extra credits. And it just so happens, I find myself in need of a ship."

Abigail's eyes wandered around the bridge as though making a final assessment before retiring.

Like hell was Mikka going to throw her lot in with Monroe after all the grief the woman had caused up to now. "I can't help you. I'll figure something out," she growled back.

Abigail nodded without changing her expression, as though she'd expected nothing less. "I'll be at the Velvet Underground tonight if you change your mind. Hell, I'll probably be there tomorrow, too. It's not like I've got anywhere else to be for the foreseeable future."

"Don't hold your breath waiting for me," Mikka replied.

"Velvet Underground?" Kiara said. "I'm disappointed, pirate. That's a well-known anti-Syndicate joint. Not exactly discreet."

"Sometimes the easiest place to hide is in plain sight. Keep in mind, though—if you arrive and there's a whiff of the Front, I sure as hell won't be there. I'll come back the next day."

"Like she said," Kiara muttered, still focused on the holo-screens on her console and punching in the docking coordinates, "don't hold your breath."

"I know I'm not quite your vibe, love, but you're welcome to come, too. I could use an expert navigator—though that's not going to be so important if we don't have a ship."

"In your dreams, pirate."

An amused smile lit up Abigail's face. "We'll see, love. At the very least, you can't blame a lady for trying."

MIKKA ADJUSTED the straps on her backpack as she stepped off the *Redemption*. She couldn't help but cast a glance back at the unassuming shuttle. For seven years, more than any person, the *Redemption* had been there for her. Its role in her life was right there in her name. The moment she'd turned a new leaf and dedicated herself to helping her ailing mother, the ship had been there, a shining path forward through a sea of darkness.

She adjusted the weight on her shoulders. The bag contained only what she'd need for the next forty-eight hours, plus enough Corielus seed to get her mother by for a little while longer. The meager remainder of her possessions were still on board the ship.

Black metallic cargo boxes, passengers, and dock workers all passed by in a blur, nothing but colors and vague shapes. Mikka hated being on Lunar's surface. Everything smelled of burnt cheese and desperation. The artificial gravity never felt quite right, and everyone was either dying to be a Terran or simply dying.

Pairs of white and orange banners and flags flew everywhere— on the walls or lined up against the grated walkways. Orange banners marked the metropolis of Shackleton City, flaunting its proud heritage of being Lunar's first settlement, long before the Climate Wars were in full force. Those days had been marked with hope and pride at what human ingenuity could achieve, and they had set the stage for what would end up being the greatest exodus the human species had ever seen. Shackleton's flags comprised a bright orange background, a circle of blue containing four lines that met at a point to the right-hand side—a representation of an antique rocket—and beside it, five circles that represented the greater area of Shackleton. Ironically, the settlement had been established in the smallest of five craters that bore the namesake, but in those early days, early space colonists, from an Earth country that no longer existed, viewed the South Pole location as the easiest to terraform and colonize. Later, Faustini, de Gerlache, Shoemaker, and Haworth would be developed as well, but since they were all connected through the hollow lava tubes below the surface, they all became districts of the larger Shackleton colony.

The white banners were a later installation, designed by the Syndicate to represent the Lunar colonies as a whole. A blue half circle surrounded by two intertwined hexagons—one yellow and one red, the signature of the Syndicate—represented the Earth, with the gray ball of Lunar resting against the top half. The illustration acted as a reminder that the entire Loop was within the Syndicate's control.

The Shackleton City port itself buzzed with activity: workers loading and unloading shuttles as they arrived and departed, and weary-eyed travelers milling around. Dozens of destitute drifters who had crept up from the Tubes below huddled by the terminal walls, hoping to be granted the scraps of excess cargo. The LPF—Lunar Police Force—used to enforce keeping them below the surface, but of late, there had been too many of them to contain. The threat of force wasn't enough to hold some back any longer; they had nothing left to lose.

It was especially hard to ignore the down-and-outs today. If it hadn't been for Mikka's shipping contracts, her mother would have been in the same place—or more likely, dead.

Mikka wasn't sure which was more disturbing: the people dying portside, or those already dead who hung above it.

The skeletons of three dead pirates hung in cages above the terminal's main square, their mangled corpses left on display as a warning to pirates. A warning to those who would dare work against the Syndicate's monopolistic stranglehold on government, security, and commerce. It was an ancient warning, and it was as effective now as it was hundreds of years ago.

Gibbeted long ago, the poor souls were said to have been caged before the airlock opened. The sight chilled Mikka to her core every time she saw it. What had their stories been? Had they been like her? Desperate to get out of the impoverished Tubes? Desperate to help a family member? Desperate to have a life that wasn't under the thumb of the Syndicate?

Footsteps—light, yet determined—approached along the metal ramp behind her. Mikka didn't have to look to know they belonged to Kiara.

"Do you have any plans of what to do now?" the navigator asked, tightening the straps on her own backpack.

"Get this batch of Corielus seed to Mom."

Kiara nodded. "Is it true it doesn't work as well for lunar sickness as it used to?"

"The only thing that's changed is we lost *Infinity*. That station grew the best Corielus in orbit. Nothing else even comes close. There had actually been signs Mom was slowly getting better back then. Any other strain only dulls the pain."

Mikka shook her head and redistributed the weight of her bag again. It wasn't a heavy pack. There was enough of the seed to last her mother a month, and fortunately, it didn't take up much space. She had been lucky the OG hadn't confiscated the seed along with the pod.

Small victories.

The seed would stay on the *Redemption* until she either departed for their next contract or Mikka was forced to part ways with her ship. She couldn't take it all to her mother or she'd risk it all going missing, too. She could handle looters walking off with just about anything else, but not the only thing that offered her mother a better quality of life. Here, the Port Authority would at least keep the ship under surveillance. It was about the safest place on the moon—or at least, the safest place Mikka had access to.

"I'm sorry to hear that." It was about as close as Kiara came to being compassionate, though the warmth chilled as quickly as it had appeared. "You know that wasn't what I meant, though. What are you going to do about the fine?"

"Damned if I know," Mikka replied. "I'm hoping the right opportunity will present itself."

Kiara nodded. "For what it's worth, I know why you couldn't hand over the pirate. I can't say I would've done the same if it were up to me, but I respect that you stuck to your principles."

"You know," Mikka said, "I don't blame you for wanting to turn her in. This shit's hard. Look around us. The Syndicate needlessly makes life difficult, and the OG pissants only make it worse. But if we don't stand up for each other, nobody else is going to, either."

"If you pirates don't stand up for each other, you mean?"

Mikka gave a sidelong look to Kiara. *Does she truly not get it?*

"*People*, my friend. If we as people don't stand up for each other. You know what? Never mind. Thanks for keeping quiet about the whole thing. I'd hate if I landed you in shit because of it." Mikka met Kiara's eyes to evidence her sincerity. "We're scheduled to make another run in two days. I'll meet you here if you're still interested in the work."

"Still gotta eat," Kiara said, adjusting her backpack again, sliding an arm through its strap to secure it. "Just please, no more pirates."

Mikka chuckled. "That's one thing you don't have to worry about."

CHAPTER THIRTEEN

Mikka

Shackleton City Tubes

EVERY TIME MIKKA descended into the belly of Lunar's underground, she became increasingly aware of how much it smelled of piss and cabbage. She would gladly have taken the burnt cheese stench of the city's port over the nostril-burning aroma that permanently lingered in the Tubes. Most of Shackleton City's Tube residents lived with the odor every day. Many would have been unaware that there *could* be any other smell to permeate the air, as most residents never left the confines of the underground. She supposed they got used to it, eventually.

Mikka had, at one point in her life.

Though she had lived in a better region than this one, memories of skulking the alleys, struggling to find a morsel of something edible, came flooding back each time she visited. Of course, there had been no food. Nearly every other kid underground was doing the same thing, and there simply wasn't enough garbage to go around. Some were fortunate enough to have a parent working the mines; if you could call it fortunate. They'd likely never see that parent again, and if they did, they were a shell of the human they'd once been, but their families would have enough credits to eat for a while. The same could not be said for those *sent* to the mines; manual labor as part of a prison sentence didn't offer the same benefits, and convicts rarely survived more than a couple of years under the oppressive toil of their work and limited rations.

Mikka had never met her father; he had died in a mining accident before she was old enough to remember him. A faulty component in a drill rig had burned him to a crisp before he even knew what was happening. It was slight consolation to the daughter who never knew him.

She had been forced to turn to thievery just to feed herself and her mother, and that was before the lunar sickness had taken hold.

Mikka held her breath as she walked through the sludge. If only she had more credits, then she could afford an apartment for her mother in a more appealing, less smelly part of the city. That was the dream, at least. The Upper Tubes would be better, but she longed to house her mother on the Rim. Ambition aside, nobody from the underground ever made the leap to bringing in those kinds of credits—not legally, at least. It was a dream that seemed to be getting further away by the day. As it was, Mikka was lucky she could scrape together enough to afford a unit in the Lower Tubes.

Those even less fortunate stretched out along the sides of buildings bored out of the igneous rock. The main throughways were a hundred meters across, though their width varied depending on where you were within them. Some said that the original colonists had widened them, but it hardly mattered now. If only they'd known what a cesspit their first settlements would become.

Lunar sickness only amplified the suffering. Nobody knew what caused it, and the illness struck at random, but it primarily affected the disadvantaged below Lunar's surface. It was an affliction that had been traced as far back as the Syndicate assuming control of the Lunar colonies, but no progress had been made in its treatment in the decades since.

Nine years ago, it struck her mother.

Having sworn off her old life, Mikka went two years without knowing her mother had succumbed to the illness. For two years, she had just lain on the street, waiting to die.

It was only after Mikka had nearly lost everything due to a botched heist that she'd heard the news. In that moment, she had sworn off piracy. In some ways, it was a life that had made her comfortable, but it had also stolen much of her soul.

By the time she'd been able to scrape together any funds to help, Mikka could only afford a flat in the Lower Tubes, the poorest and least maintained district of Shackleton City. If she had only paid more attention to her mother's welfare, she could have saved more of the funds she had obtained through her nefarious exploits.

Groans from vagrants huddled in dark corners haunted the tunnels, alerting passersby that the sickness had indeed taken root here. Children scurried around their afflicted parents, some not much older than toddlers, wide-eyed and fierce. All they had ever known was a life of survival. Many would find their way to the surface out of desperation. Some would make it back with a handful of goods.

Others wouldn't be so fortunate.

The pain was more than the afflicted were able to bear but were still forced to endure—at least, for the short time they'd survive. Then they'd lose all faculty, and the madness would take hold.

Within Mikka's backpack was the only thing that lessened the suffering. For whatever reason, Corielus seed numbed the body to the worst of the agonizing effects of the disease. Naturally, in view of this, it wasn't cheap. And it wasn't a cure; it held back the madness and made living a little more bearable, but it couldn't fully eradicate the affliction.

The streets and alleys were dim, the gray regolith making everything appear pale and sickly. Despite most of the dust being controlled within the colony's confines on the surface, it wasn't effectively filtered out of the air systems within the Tubes.

The dust itself was toxic. Lunar sickness and starvation aside, a life in the Tubes wasn't much better than a death sentence; it was just a matter of how and when. Many didn't make it to their eighteenth birthday.

Coughing fits echoed as men, women, and children alike struggled to breathe from within makeshift encampments that filled any side alley and empty space they could find.

Mikka cleared her throat. Just thinking about the dry dust made her insides itch, but she refrained from quenching the sensation through fear of exposing any of the water she carried in her pack to toxic contaminants. Besides, her mother needed the water more than she did. And, more than that, the wide-eyed stares around her threatened to muster up the strength to tackle her for the coveted liquid.

Mikka couldn't help but shake her head. The Shackleton crater was practically the largest source of water on Lunar's surface. These people couldn't live closer to it if they tried and yet they were so restricted in their access to it that they might as well have been trying to get it from Earth.

Thin strips of yellow LED lighting lined the walls along the streets, but their luminescence was barely enough to reveal the twists and turns of the myriad alleyways and avenues.

A small bend in the road and a chipped gate marked the entrance to her mother's apartment. Cold steel bars separated the road from the complex. The gate was meant to dissuade thieves and only worked some of the time. Which was to say, they might as well not have been there at all. When thieves were desperate, it was amazing the obstacles they could overcome. And in the Tubes, *everyone* was desperate.

Mikka raised her forearm, holding it to the access pad at the gate, which scanned her implant and then beeped in response. The lock on the gate disengaged and the gate swung outward, allowing Mikka to slide through the opening before it clicked shut behind her.

Four housing units had been chiseled into the moon rock decades ago, creating prime real estate in a section that had more people than places to live. A faded, hard-packed path, edged with black rocks and haphazardly placed yellow landscaping tile, cut between the units and branched into smaller walkways that led to each home. Three pairs of shoes lay sprawled out in front of the first unit, as though their owners were in such a panic to get indoors that they'd had no time to place them in an orderly fashion.

A small face peered out of the second unit's main window. Mikka had always felt the windows held little value. If they'd ever held glass, it had long since broken or been removed. Now the only thing that stood between these units and the outside was a thin curtain. Nobody currently had either the will or the resources to install anything more permanent.

The lights flickered on the top edge of the ceiling. Mikka would have to talk to Thames, the building manager, about getting the lights looked at, though he'd never actually be bothered enough to do anything about them.

She reached the door of her mother's unit and stopped short. It had been left ajar. Shadows could have hidden much, but she couldn't make out anything else out of the ordinary.

Her watch read 6:45 p.m. It was too early for Tabitha to have arrived. The caregiver was the one other small luxury Mikka managed to provide. The young woman stopped by her mother's residence twice a day for about an hour—from 9:00 to 10:00 A.M, and then again from 7:00 until 8:00 p.m. She was always punctual, but the woman would never have come to the Tubes fifteen minutes early.

As much as Tabitha had earned Mikka's trust, she was still a resident of the Upper Rim and wouldn't spend any more time in the underground than she had to.

And it would have been strange for Tabitha to be careless enough to leave the door open when she left after her morning shift. The woman was meticulous. It was one of her finer qualities.

Mikka wondered for a moment if her mother could have possibly opened the door, trying to get outside, but she cast the thought aside almost instantly. Her mother had been all but bedridden ever since the lunar sickness had taken her nearly a decade ago. On a good day, she would make it to the bathroom unaided, and perhaps to the sitting room. There had been days years ago, after she'd consistently received treatment with Corielus seed harvested aboard the *Infinity*, when she could have made it to the door and beyond. But after the station's accident, and the highly potent strain of Corielus crop became nearly impossible to find or replicate, Mikka's mother had quickly regressed to the incapacitated state she was in now. Nothing short of a miracle would give her the strength to open the door on her own.

Which meant only one thing.

Someone had broken in.

Mikka pulled out her Pulsar SC11 pistol, her heart racing as she held the weapon in front of her. The door, solid metal and covered in regolith dust, creaked as she pushed it with her boot, hands readied on her weapon in case the intruder was still inside.

Shadows and unfocused shapes filled her mother's home. Precarious seconds ticked by as Mikka allowed her eyes to adjust to the dark chamber. As dim as the courtyard had been, the unit's interior was pitch-black. Her heart pounded against her chest as she fumbled for the light switch. It took several attempts to flick them on before she realized the lights weren't operable. Power fluctuations were nothing new to the Tubes; despite the wealth of solar panels on the upper rim of the Shackleton crater, the amount of electrical current streamed underground would have been laughable if it wasn't tragic. Survivable oxygen levels and gravity were about all any of the residents of the Tubes could count on, and even then, Mikka had her doubts.

But there was also the possibility the intruder had done something to the lights; that this was all intentional.

She took a hand from her weapon and swung her backpack around, enough to reach inside, trying to remain aware of her surroundings as she did so, which was no simple task. She muttered a muted prayer of thanks to the universe that she always carried a flashlight.

Small victories.

Space was dark, as her mother used to say, and it was best to carry your own light around. Aboard the *Redemption*, the flashlight came in handy if she had to figure out wiring issues deep within the consoles.

Mikka clicked the button on the device. Only a few square inches of the home were illuminated, but the glow was good enough.

Shit.

The metal kitchen table and chairs lay on their sides, the cabinets left wide open—some hanging off their hinges. Broken glass and ceramic lay everywhere, and despite Mikka's mother not having much, the intruder had otherwise stripped the room clean. Even the two lounge chairs and sofa that had been present in the small sitting room were now missing. Decades-old needlework her mother used to create was strewn over the floor as if the intruder had hoped to find treasure buried among the patterns and scraps of fabric.

Mikka wanted to call out for her mother, but unsure if the offender was still in the house, she bit her tongue and pushed on. Any such plea would be pointless, as her mother couldn't answer. Instead, she held her breath and pulled the flashlight down to her side until she reached the threshold of the bedroom.

Silence filled the tight quarters. Mikka's breathing and heavy heartbeat were the only sounds that filled her ears.

Steady.

She flipped the flashlight into the room and relaxed her gaze to take it in with a quick scan.

A pool of red was all she needed to send her pulse racing, but it was the frail, unconscious woman sprawled out on the floor that caught her breath.

"*Mom!*"

All worry of an intruder immediately vanished. Mikka holstered her weapon and dropped the flashlight as she raced to the body that lay next to the now empty bed.

Blood ran down the woman's face, staining the nightgown she wore.

"Mom! Mom! Are you okay?"

Her mother's eyes rolled back as Mikka deliberated picking her up off the floor. The woman groaned, which was more of a response than Mikka could have hoped for, allowing her to breathe a small sigh of relief. But before she moved her mother, she needed to ensure she wasn't going to aggravate any injuries in the process.

A dark mark, black and blue, stained her mother's forehead from where it had smacked into the floor. A trickle of blood streamed from the cut, but it was only superficial.

Mikka cursed. A concussion would be a real possibility, but it wasn't the greatest danger to her mother in her current condition.

Mikka wasn't a doctor, but she did her best to determine

whether any bones had been broken, running her hands across her mother's arms, legs, and ribs.

She's so thin, Mikka observed. *I hope Tabitha's been making her eat.*

Convinced that her mother's bones were intact, Mikka picked up the flashlight again and completed a quick visual scan. A few bruises, plus the still bleeding scrape on her temple, but otherwise, no real harm done.

"Who would have done this?" she thought out loud.

Mikka lifted her mother's limp frame and placed her on the bed, stripped of its blankets. The woman let out a bone-shattering wail, the sudden movement causing Mikka to jump back.

Definitely alive.

"The pain!" the frail woman cried. "Please, I'm in so much pain!"

"*Shit*, Mom."

She . . . talked.

There was no time to process the sudden coherence. Mikka yanked the backpack from her back, reached inside, and grabbed the small bag that sat on top of its contents. The backpack contained enough seed to last her mother a month, but only this dose mattered now.

Mikka opened the package and guessed at a rough amount that would be equivalent to a single dose. Her mom's cool skin and damp hair rested in the crook of her arm as she positioned herself beside her for support. Mikka worked the seeds, each the size of a grain of rice, into her mother's cracked, dry lips, pulled the canteen from its hidden compartment in her backpack, and allowed her mother to sip from the bottle's wide mouth.

"There you go, Mom. This should help."

Vacant. Unfocused. Eyes glossed over. Staring at nothing but the void.

She has no idea who I am anymore.

The lunar sickness had stolen so much. The mother she had known from her youth, who had taught her to never give up, to never back down, could now barely muster the strength to stay hydrated. It wouldn't be long before even the Corielus seed wasn't enough.

And it's my fault you're down here. It's my fault you don't have the help you need.

There had to be something more that she could do. Without a steady supply of Corielus coming in, her mother would simply fade away.

Mikka wiped away dampness from her cheek as she dribbled more of her canteen's contents into her mom's mouth, her white tongue licking at the drops, eager for the moisture.

Ten thousand credits.

It was bad enough she couldn't provide anything better than a Lower Tube apartment that was frequently robbed, but now Mikka didn't know how she was going to provide water, medicine, or even the money for rent or to pay Tabitha.

She had forgotten how terrible life was for her mother every time she left the Tubes. Every time she came back, her heart broke. Every time, she wondered how she could provide her mother with the help she so desperately needed.

Mikka swallowed back tears as she mourned for the life she had promised she'd provide for her mother. An Upper Rim apartment. Medicine. Care. A life.

Her mother's eyes closed as the nutrients from the seed went to work. The medicine would dissolve in her mouth, seeping into her bloodstream sublingually. It acted fast; one small mercy. Hopefully, the dose would get her through most of the night.

Mikka deflated as she rested her mother's frame back down on the bed.

Barely an existence.

There had to be another way—and Mikka swore she'd work her ass off to find it.

A straightforward gig with a killer payoff. The stars know you could use the extra credits.

Did she dare turn back to the life she'd sworn off? Could she face that world again?

There are rumors, you know.

A knock at the door yanked Mikka from her thoughts. She stood, expecting the visitor to be Tabitha, arriving for her shift.

But the tall figure in the doorway of her mother's bedroom wasn't Tabitha.

CHAPTER FOURTEEN

Django
Eclipse

"I'M sorry I almost got us in trouble."

Nova hadn't moved from the bunk bed since they'd arrived at their quarters. They had left the curtain that would normally be closed for privacy open to the living room so she could feel close to her brother.

Django wasn't ready to go to bed, either. If the removal of a thin piece of fabric would offer Nova any amount of reassurance, he wouldn't object.

Django supposed his parents' room was now his, but it didn't feel right to sleep in their bed. It still belonged to his parents. In his mind, it likely always would.

Sleeping in the room was one thing, but earlier in the day, he had decided he would go through their things and clear out some of their possessions. If it was a process he could do now while he wasn't in the fields, perhaps it wouldn't feel like such a monumental chore later.

They didn't have much. Compared to Eventide's quarters, the room wasn't much more than a closet, so the act comprised stripping the bed and preparing their clothes to be repurposed. Old papers, gifts, and cards from special events sat neatly in boxes, tucked away in the few storage spaces their accommodations offered. Storage drives sat unused for decades—centuries, even— heirlooms and records of their ancestors from before they'd left the planet, waiting to be brought home.

Django could still smell the dirt and metal on the cushions, years of farm and laboratory chemicals brought in and caked into the materials. Their essence had never fully been washed out, no matter how many of their precious credits had been spent trying to clean them.

The intertwining scents of lab and field—two aromas of their hard work mixed in a fragrant concoction of his childhood.

Regardless of what Administration said, that bedroom still held part of his parents—the memories of the love that each parent brought home.

But Django hadn't been prepared for what he'd found. He had reached beneath his parents' bed, intent on one last sweep before retiring to the couch, and his hand had hit something hard. His hands gripping the object, hesitant yet excited at what they had found, he'd pulled out a black metal box.

He couldn't remember ever seeing the item before. The case's shape reminded him of one that belonged to an old, rectangular musical instrument. A small brass latch sealed the case, and without hesitation, he'd flipped it open, eager to discover its contents.

His eagerness had disappeared once the box had opened, and his mind struggled to comprehend what lay inside.

A weapon.

Django had quickly closed the lid and tucked the pistol back under the bed, trying to forget he had seen it. There had been enough surprises for one day.

But now he couldn't stop thinking about it.

Why did my parents have a weapon?

Ceiling panels stared down at him, his thoughts trying to drown him in waves of confusion and nostalgia, battling between the memories of his parents and his most recent discovery. A tug of war between the childhood he remembered and what the gun's presence might mean ensued, a wave of uncertainty crashing down on him until he wasn't sure which side was going to win.

Secrets his parents might have held now tainted the childhood memories that were embedded in every corner of his quarters.

The Christmas morning meals. The Sunday afternoon table games. The late-night tea and bedtime stories.

A weapon under the bed.

Their lumpy sofa poked and prodded at his backside. His father's impression had been worked into its surface and had created a dip in its cushion. Every night, he had sat in the same spot, usually with a book in hand. His mother would sit in the adjacent chair, humming to herself as the evenings passed, working on a new pair of socks for Nova, a sweater for himself, or whatever article of clothing was needed.

Why did they have a weapon?

And how would things play out from here? Would each memory be a void that he and Nova would desperately try to fill? Until she, too, inevitably moved out? Admin would force him to marry someone, and if it couldn't be Eventide, who would it be?

Surely nobody he could care for half as much.

Django's home had been filled with love and affection that so many of his peers had never known. Within its walls were love; respect; unconditional support.

He held no illusions that the shared quarters of the D-Ring held as much warmth. Abuse was common down here. So many of his peers had been beaten and battered, both literally and emotionally. They'd share stories of their scars in the classrooms before most of them were taken out to work the fields. Hard grunt work, not the analytical tasks Django had been assigned.

Life on the station wasn't always easy, but his parents had made it seem like it was. His upbringing had been a gift, and it was one Django had taken for granted far more than he should have.

And now, the affection of his parents, their laughter and determination, their fierce devotion to their family, to *Eclipse*, to restoring the tired planet below, was all gone.

Instead, there was only cold white metal and a digital display.

His mind drifted back to the pistol. There was no reason to be armed on the station. Security might have been assholes, but they were effective at clamping down on violence. There was no need for individual defense on the station, certainly not with a weapon.

Django suddenly realized he hadn't responded to his sister's apology.

"You don't have to be sorry," he said. "But you do need to sleep."

"I can't sleep," Nova replied. "I can't stop thinking about what Uncle Marvin said. What if I'm next?"

"Uncle Marvin was always full of wild ideas." Django pinched the bridge of his nose between his thumb and forefinger. "Remember when he said that Corielus seed was really a drug?"

"But this is different, Django!" Nova persisted. "He also said that *Eclipse* wasn't alone. And you *saw* more stations out there. *You* saw ships flying back and forth to Earth."

"Why would Marvin think that what we see every day was a lie? Why wouldn't the glitch be untrue? Wouldn't that make more sense? Ships flying to Earth is nothing new," he said. "How do you think we get our supplies to the surface? We're restoring the planet. Of course, some of us are transporting goods down there."

"But how come we don't know who any of them are?" Nova turned on her side so she could look at her brother. "Have you ever met anyone who flies one of the shuttles?"

"Uncle Marvin was a pilot, remember? Mom and Dad said the cosmic radiation affected him so he couldn't fly anymore. After flying through space for so long, I don't think many of them make it back alive. There are half a million people on the station, Nova. I've never met a lavender farmer either, and yet, Benson had a flower on his lapel. I've never met a bartender or a shoemaker, but I know they're here. *Eclipse* is bigger than what you see every day. Sometimes, when we don't understand what's happening, our mind makes up stories to fill in the gaps. Uncle Marvin did that a lot."

"But he said we weren't safe because you saw outside the viewport. Now, he's dead! Just like he said would happen!"

"That's enough, Nova! This has all been one sad coincidence. We don't have to worry about what Uncle Marvin said anymore. Get some sleep. And don't say anything else about it, especially when there are other people around."

Nova flopped back down on her bed in a huff, crossing her arms over her chest as she continued to stare at the ceiling.

There were too many unanswered questions, and none of them made any difference. Uncle Marvin might have been right about some things, but that didn't mean *everything* he said was true.

His death had just been a coincidence.

Besides, like Django had told Eventide, it wasn't like there was anything he could do about it even if it *was* true. His best course of action would be to keep his head down and to not attract further attention. As long as Officer Avery didn't make any waves, he'd be okay.

He sighed. The woman who, at first, had seemed so cold while relaying the news about his parents could barely contain her compassion the next day, as though the news about Marvin's death had a more significant impact on her.

The officer's actions were disjointed. She was an enigma, but Django wasn't sure if he cared enough to figure her out.

Whatever you decide.

But what did that even mean?

You're lucky I'm the one who found it.

The envelope.

Django had shoved it in his pocket as they'd entered their suite, eager to wash up and get food into their bellies. It had remained forgotten for the better part of the day.

He pulled it out and studied it. He recognized his uncle's penmanship gracing the front of the envelope.

Django.

The back of the envelope was sealed with a wax circle.

You're lucky I'm the one who found it.

Had Avery meant to say she had read it? Or would another guard not have delivered the envelope at all?

He pulled open the seal, opened the envelope, and removed a slip of paper, turning it over so he could read the characters scribbled on its back.

Thursday - Shuttle Bay 8

9:45 p.m. - The Black Swan

Django stared at the handwritten words, at first unsure of what he was looking at. He had half expected a fond note or instructions to receive an inheritance; some nugget of substance from the uncle who had always taken a liking to him.

Of course, that's not what it is.

"It's a ship!" he realized out loud. Instinctively, he looked at Nova, not wanting to discuss the revelation just yet. Sounds of snores bounced off the bunk beds. The girl was more tired than she'd realized.

He wanted to crumple the paper and toss it aside. He blew a steadying breath, incensed his uncle had held onto the ridiculous notion of leaving the station right until the end.

It was just a coincidence.

Instead, Django stared at the paper, struggling to process his uncle's last words.

He didn't just write it down. He wrote it down, folded it, put it into an envelope, and wrote my name on it.

Marvin had known he was going to die.

If he hadn't, he wouldn't have gone to the trouble. He wouldn't have sealed it with wax and left it for someone to find. But when did he write it? Was it while the alarms were sounding? Before?

Django wished he could talk to Eventide, but he wouldn't be able to see her until the next day at the earliest—if he was lucky. He had considered heading to her quarters again for the night, but after the incident with Benson's guard, he'd thought it would be better for them to stay in their own quarters. He was ready for any sense of normalcy he could get.

Normalcy. He sighed again and swallowed against the dryness in his throat. *Would things ever feel* normal *again?*

CHAPTER FIFTEEN

Django
Eclipse

IT WASN'T until the door's buzzer rang loudly that Django realized he had fallen asleep on the couch. His thoughts had kept him up well past curfew; well past when he would normally have fallen asleep.

8:00 a.m.—much later than he would ever normally sleep. It was fortunate he had the day off, though, he had to admit, he didn't know what he would do with himself without the distraction of work.

If it hadn't been for Nova, he might have gone to the fields anyway. Today, they would be transplanting bulbs, and though it was a tedious task, it would have provided him with a space to clear his head. There was a certain simplicity in moving the bulbs from their transport trays into the artificial soil that took up so much of the D-Ring's real estate.

The buzzer rang again.

"Hang on a moment!" Django called.

He shoved the blanket to the corner of the couch and set his bare feet down on the cold paneled floor, allowing the coolness to bring him to his senses. More than one vertebra cracked as he rotated his neck, then he reached up and allowed the same release further down his spine. He must have been more tired than he'd realized to have fallen asleep so soundly—the couch made for a lousy mattress.

Nova also stirred, now sitting on the edge of her bed, rubbing her eyes as the artificial lights hummed to life around her.

Django gave his temples one last rub before standing and crossing the room.

He fumbled for the access panel to open the door, his motor skills still not catching up to their suddenly wakened state.

I sure could use a cup of coffee, he thought. But he didn't have the credits to spend on such a luxury purchase.

One problem at a time.

He made a half-assed attempt to straighten his hair before he hit the last key to open the door, but it was a futile attempt. His reflection in the panel mocked him; wisps of his brown hair stuck out every which way in chaos. He gave up before finally allowing the door to their apartment to slide open.

Django groaned.

"Good morning to you, too," Avery greeted him as the doors parted. Light from the hall crawled over her features and reflected off her uniform, the blue luminescence giving her a sickly appearance. Behind her, Officer Isaacs stood silent, the red and yellow double hexagonal pattern on his chest glowing faintly as it sat in Avery's shadow. Though Isaacs didn't have bags under his eyes as Avery did, they were bloodshot and sunken, as though he hadn't gotten any sleep, either. The entire station was running sleep deprived.

Isaacs's hands rested on his hips, his fingers itching as though ready to draw the weapon from his belt at any moment.

Avery rested a hand on the doorframe to his quarters, her fingers drumming on the wall impatiently.

"What do *you* want?" Django said. "I'm all out of relatives to kill."

Avery stood still for a moment and blinked at the phrasing of his words. The tapping of her fingers stopped as she moved her hands to her sides, and a look crossed her face that appeared as if it could be sadness mixed with regret.

Django wasn't sure if the woman felt either of those emotions, though. Twice already, she had brought bad news. Twice, it had meant losing people close to him. He braced himself for what she might bring to his doorway this time.

The officer cleared her throat and the look quickly disappeared, replaced by the stoic, uncaring face Django had become familiar with.

"I'm here for Nova," she said. "Is she here?"

"Nova?" he asked concernedly. "What the hell do you want with her? She's only a child."

Avery let out a sigh as she pulled out her datapad, tapping on its screen. "Yes, that's *exactly* why I'm here."

"What do you mean?"

Nova emerged from the rear of their quarters, summoned by the calling of her name. "What do you want with me?" His sister, both confused and half-asleep, let out a yawn as she stretched her arms over her head. "I haven't done anything."

"Nobody's accusing you of anything," Avery replied. "You're being transferred to different quarters."

Bile churned in Django's stomach, threatening to make an appearance. Had he heard her correctly?

"I don't understand. Yesterday, you said we could stay here . . ."

"*You* are inheriting the quarters, Django Alexander. You'll be expected to marry and have a family of your own, sooner rather than later. Until then, your current position will not provide the resources or time needed to take care of both Nova and yourself.

The girl is too young to be left on her own. Admin will place her with new guardians capable of fostering her development until she, too, comes of age."

"You can't be serious!" Django protested.

"You will be permitted to visit each other as often as you'd like, and her new family will ensure she is enrolled in an appropriate training program."

"Don't we get a say in this? *I* can take care of her!"

"Your perception is irrelevant. You can't escape station regulations. This is out of your hands."

"You realize it hasn't even been *two days* since our parents died? Give us some time to grieve . . . To get used to this."

"Unnecessary," Avery replied indifferently, deactivating her datapad and clipping it to her belt. "And completely out of my control. Let's go, Nova—your new family awaits. You will return to pack your things later."

Officer Isaacs pushed his way into their quarters, his weapon now in hand.

What does he think he's going to need that for?

The more Django thought about it, though, the more appealing the idea of knocking the man out became.

The case under his parents' bed flashed through Django's thoughts. Perhaps his father had had a use for a weapon after all, not that it would help Django now. He'd have to get to it, unlock the case, and determine how to use the device, and by then, he'd likely be shot himself—though he'd never heard of a guard shooting a citizen before.

They'd shove them out of the airlocks first.

Uncle Marvin had messed with his thoughts, and now he was seeing conspiracy theories everywhere.

Django clenched his fists and forced himself to remain calm. Regardless of his feelings, he'd never held, never mind *fired*, a weapon before, and testing his luck on the two trained guards wouldn't be the place to start. Even if he dodged their grasp, there'd be nowhere for him to hide. The station was only so big.

Thursday - Shuttle Bay 8

9:45 p.m. - The Black Swan

Uncle Marvin had laid his bets on leaving this evening.

What am I thinking?

There was no telling what had been going through Uncle Marvin's mind when he'd jotted that note down. Heck, Django didn't even know for sure it *was* a ship. Or where it would be going.

"Let's move!" Isaacs barked from behind Nova. Her eyes widened with the order, but she scrambled to get her shoes on and picked up an armful of clothes that she could wear for the day.

"Don't talk to her like that!" Django argued, bridging the gap between him and the officer. Airlock be damned, he stood inches from the man's face. The officer smelled of licorice and burnt metal.

Isaacs didn't hesitate in shoving Django backward, causing him to stumble as he tripped over his own feet, sailing onto his backside.

"That's enough! Both of you!" Avery commanded. "There's no need to frighten the child, Geoffrey. She's not in trouble."

"D-Ringer *scum!*" Isaacs spat as he planted a kick into Django's ribs.

Django barely had the time to brace himself before the crushing blow landed on his side. He grunted but refused to yell out in pain.

If Avery noticed, she said nothing to admonish it.

"Come with us, Nova," Avery said. "Don't worry, we're not going to hurt you. Station regulations dictate that all youth must be properly provided for. You can't stay here anymore."

"You can't do this," Django persisted. "We're family!"

"You must understand, this is for her well-being. She will be well taken care of."

"She will be taken care of *here*." The jostle in his ribs prevented him from standing quickly, but Django pushed through the pain. "*Please*, don't do this."

A gentle weight rested on his arm. It took a moment before he realized it was Nova's small hand, gently offering a calming voice.

"It's okay, Django. I'll go."

Everything else faded except for Nova's brown eyes, trying so hard to be reassuring. Was she really trying to comfort *him*? He staggered as the station seemed to give way beneath him. He was losing the last family member he had left.

The last person close to him.

He was so blindsided that he couldn't say anything else in her defense. He stammered, but no coherent words left his mouth. His voice failed him as his lips moved without structure.

"We'll always be family," Nova continued. "No matter where I live. No matter where you are. That will never change."

She seemed to have worked something out that he hadn't.

That he *couldn't*.

There was a peace in her tone that he had yet to come to terms with; a reconciliation with the tragedy they had both endured. Perhaps she had lost so much over the last two days, that she had become numb.

He sure as hell was.

Perhaps she wasn't thinking clearly.

"It won't be that bad," Nova assured him. "I'll be back tonight to get my things."

She stood on her tiptoes to offer him a hug. He numbly returned the gesture, feeling his sister's coarse hair grazing his cheek.

"I'm stronger than you know," she whispered. "We're both stronger than you could ever imagine."

Django held on for dear life to the last semblance of family he had—only for a moment before she released the embrace and stepped out into the hall.

Avery's rigid expression melted for a moment as her eyes met his. What sinister plot had this woman devised to tear his family apart like this? And what purpose did it serve?

He might only be eighteen, but they would have managed. He knew how to take care of his sister.

"She will return later to pack," Avery repeated.

Isaacs pushed past him huffily, sending Django off balance once again. This time, he caught himself, his ribs still aching from the last tumble.

All he could do was watch as his sister followed the two guards out of their quarters and continued down the hall. As the door slid closed, Django sank to his knees, his frame sinking onto the blue carpet.

Tears streamed down his face; the last bit of his normal life gone.

He curled up against the door and wished away the nightmare he'd been living for the past forty-eight hours.

CHAPTER SIXTEEN

Mikka
Shackleton City

"CAN I HELP YOU?"

Masked in shadow, it was impossible to discern the features of the man who stood in front of Mikka. The silhouette of the jagged-topped edge of his helmet, however, was all she needed to identify whom he represented. Bulky shoulder pads provided the illusion of muscular development; without them, it was quite possible he was as frail as a moonjay. All the same, he carried himself as though he had earned his uniform, so there was likely enough muscle beneath it.

A red and yellow double hexagon pulsed from his chest, the yellow outline of a star in its center confirming the soldier's affiliation.

She gripped her Pulsar SC tight. The low-powered weapon would be no match for the firepower this Syndicate Front soldier would be sporting.

"Put the weapon down, ma'am." Confirming her thoughts, the officer lifted a full-barreled rifle—a two-handed, military issue high-powered weapon that Mikka wasn't familiar enough with to name. Lights on the weapon's side provided a glow that didn't extend past his hands, but it was enough to highlight his gray gloves. Maybe the officer wasn't used to the chill the subterranean world provided, but it was more likely he was avoiding having to touch its filth and disease.

As much as Mikka wanted to fault the man for his caution, he probably wasn't wrong. Even so, the blatant disdain for the world he was supposed to protect gnawed on Mikka's nerves like Lunar rats on the bones of the dead in the streets.

"This is my home," Mikka said, holstering her own weapon—there was no point in giving the guard a reason to shoot her. "Can I help you?" she repeated.

"That's her!" a mousy voice echoed. "That's the person who did this!"

Even in the dark, Mikka recognized the petite frame. Standing at barely five feet, the woman was well below the average height of those who lived on the Upper Rim. Lunar's artificial gravity helped with bone density and offset most of the height difference a low G environment provided. Still, the average height of a woman on Lunar was six feet, and Tabitha, her mother's caregiver, stood a foot shorter. Even the malnourished in the Tubes were closer to six feet tall.

"Tabitha? What are you talking about?" Mikka asked, confused.

"Don't pretend to be stupid. This has *your* handwriting all over it."

"Why would I break into *my own* house?"

Tabitha snorted. "You tell me, *pirate*. Why did you come back? Were you looking to finish her off?"

Pirate? How did . . .?

Before she had time to process the accusations, the guard had closed the distance between them, spun Mikka around, and had her face pressed against the wall. She could feel her pistol belt being removed as the guard's forearm pressed into her back.

"Jax Luana, you are under arrest . . ."

Mikka didn't hear the rest of the rights. Instead, she focused on two things: not choking on the layer of dust that clung to the wall as it came loose and entered her lungs, and the use of her old name.

The dust won out and sent her into a wild coughing fit. The Syndicate Front soldier only pushed harder against her, trying to prevent her limbs from shaking with the effort. Cold metal handcuffs clicked behind her, followed by the *beep* of their electronic lock.

"My mother!" Mikka cried between coughs. "She needs . . ."

"Your mother will be better off without you!" Tabitha spat. "*You're* the reason she's in this place."

It was true, she guessed, but . . .

The dust settled, and the coughing subsided enough for Mikka to look Tabitha in the eye.

"What is wrong with you? I pay my mother's rent, bring her medicine . . . I pay *your* fucking salary!"

"*Pfft!* You're just one of my clients—and a lousy paying one at that. You steal from her, and then leave her here to rot! How am I supposed to take care of her? Look at this place. Look at *her!* You've turned it upside down, no doubt trying to find something to sell. This is all *your* fault. Underground scum like the rest of them. Worse. Good-for-nothing *pirate.*"

Mikka flexed her wrists in the cuffs, but they tightened as she did so. She wanted to scream; to punch the sweet smile off Tabitha's rat face.

You tell me, pirate.

How did she find out?

Mikka had worked so hard to keep her past a secret.

Apparently, with enough digging, it was possible to uncover

her past. If you knew how to work the system, nothing was truly impossible to find, but Mikka had believed she'd done a good enough job of covering her tracks that it shouldn't have been an issue.

It had worked for seven years, and now, over the course of twenty-four hours, two different people from two wildly different backgrounds had learned her secret.

Something had changed.

But what? And who had let Tabitha in on it? There was no way the caregiver was bright enough to have figured it out on her own.

I can make this all go away.

If that slob of an Orbital Guard had felt embarrassed enough, he might very well have gone digging. But Argus was a buffoon. Abigail could have figured things out, sure; pirates had to be crafty in order to survive. But Argus? Not in a million years.

The SF soldier tossed her to the front of the house and out the door. After being in the cave of her mother's quarters, the street was bright by comparison. Mikka's eyes took a moment to adjust, though her nose made no such transition; the putrid scent of the alley hit her in waves.

"*Ugh,*" the guard grunted behind her. "How do you rats stand it down here? The stench of piss and shit all day long? Don't any of you clean up your filth?"

"We're too busy cleaning up yours," Mikka spat. Tremendous pain rocked the back of her head as the guard's baton connected with it. She resisted the reflex to cry out, not wanting to give him the satisfaction.

"Nobody ever taught you manners, either?"

"I guess I was too busy trying to feed myself." Mikka braced herself for another blow, but the guard responded with an amused grunt and shoved her toward the street.

A Syndicate Front vehicle awaited their arrival. Its wide tires were purpose-made for traversing the deeper tunnels and undeveloped surface terrain. The vehicle had to be kept within a controlled atmosphere, as it was not equipped to protect its passengers outside of the colony walls. The vehicle was a brushed silver, the lights mounted to the top of its frame dwarfing any other meager source of light within the Tubes. Children shielded their eyes from their intensity, their pupils unable to handle the sudden brightness.

The Front rarely ventured far into the residential areas of Shackleton City, and they certainly never came to the Lower Tubes.

Sure, her offenses as a pirate had been extensive, worthy of arrest, but these measures seemed more extreme than Mikka was worth. She'd always assumed she'd be found out by accident, not through an organized hunt.

This search had been targeted, and it wasn't initiated by Tabitha. So, the question was, who was after her?

And why bother with the ransacked house? The Syndicate Front dealt with high-scale crimes and notorious prisoners. Never in a million years would they care about a crime against a property in the Tube. Why steal her mother's furniture and leave a frail, sick woman bleeding on the floor?

Only one thing was certain: Mikka was sure she was about to find out.

CHAPTER SEVENTEEN

Mikka

Shackleton City

MIKKA TRACED the outlines of the cell's flooring tiles with her index finger. The guards had placed her in a chamber set apart from the other cells, down a long hallway and a further flight of stairs. Mikka suspected this cell was reserved for the most heinous of offenders, or those who had pissed the Front off the most.

Though it was dark and isolated, she knew it couldn't possibly be their *worst* cell—she still had all her fingers. She could still breathe, and she had been there for hours, so oxygen levels must have been at least somewhat close to normal.

At least they had the decency to take the handcuffs off.

There was no chair or bench to sit on, so Mikka had resigned herself to the floor. Even the Front's prison cells were more polished and in better condition than anything in the Tubes. And though she hadn't traveled extensively within its bounds, the facility was even more exquisite than anything she had seen in Shackleton's Upper Rim.

The headquarters of the Syndicate Front had been more impressive than Mikka had ever imagined it could be. On the way through the building and into the dungeon, she couldn't help but stare at the excessiveness of it all. There was gold everywhere, and where gold was not used, the Front had settled on a mix of iron and glass. And Mikka was sure they didn't haul prisoners through the most ornate parts of the facility.

Even the basement level felt as though it were a step up the ladder, though it was hardly a large step. The room was dark, but no more so than the underground streets. The room smelled of vinegar and sulfur, but it was more subtle than the stench below.

This cell would be a better place for my mother than the hell-hole she's in now.

If only the Tube's prisoners were granted such treatment. The Syndicate would send those strong enough to Psyche 16 to mine, and from the looks of SF HQ, their efforts went straight to the Syndicate coffers. Those who weren't fit to mine . . . well, there were pits in the Tubes deeper still that made the lower residences look like paradise.

None of it mattered to Mikka at the moment. Feeling the edges of the tile below her fingers was a way for her to focus her mind, the tactile reality keeping her mind from spiraling wildly out of control and going over the many ways the last twenty-four hours had gone spectacularly wrong over and over again.

Most of her problems had started when she'd picked up that damned space pirate.

All of my problems.

The pickup. The Orbital Guard. The fine. The raid on her mother's home. Tabitha. This prison cell.

If Mikka had ignored the call for help like Kiara had suggested, if she'd turned Abigail in when the Orbital Guard had boarded, if she'd turned the pirate in when they docked, would any of this have happened? She laughed, the sound echoing through the chamber, as a saying she had often said in a past life came back to her.

No good deed goes unpunished.

Except Mikka was used to being on the benefiting end of that sentiment. Perhaps her string of good luck had finally ended.

It was likely that, whether she had rescued Abigail or not, she would have found herself sitting where she was, wondering what deed had led her here. Turning her in would have left Mikka with the added guilt of sacrificing the woman for her own convenience; a woman whose path was probably not so different from her own. With the list of charges Abigail had on her head, she'd be begging to be sent to Psyche 16.

Begging for an airlock.

That was clear on the faces of the damned that hung at the port; skeletons locked in screams of agony for all eternity. That was the fate Abigail would have met.

The fate Mikka anticipated she would still have to face.

It had only been a matter of time before her old life had caught up with her, but Mikka had always assumed she'd be able to dodge it for a lot longer. She had, after all, avoided capture for half a decade as a criminal, and then another seven years as a law-abiding citizen with a past.

Bloody Syndicate!

She had committed the majority of her crimes trying to even the playing field, bringing hope to those who were hopeless and taking from those with everything, helping those with next to nothing.

Piracy wasn't all about bootlegged liquor and stolen seed. Sometimes, it was about making a difference.

Sure, Mikka had taken a sizable enough cut for herself, but a girl still had to eat.

But *how* had the Front found her? She didn't believe it was a coincidence. Couldn't believe they'd stumbled upon her because of a phony break-in. And there were only a handful of people who knew the truth.

Mikka's mother, of course, knew her past. Had she had a moment of coherence and let it slip? It wasn't as though Mikka had never stolen from her mother. But that had been a decade ago, before she was a pirate, when her mother had lived in the Upper Tubes and had things worth stealing. It was possible her mother had recounted a troubled memory and couldn't distinguish between the past and present . . . but still.

Kiara knew. She was the only crew member Mikka had ever trusted enough to share the truth with. It had been a calculated risk; given Kiara's affinity for research, she might have eventually figured it out for herself. But the navigator had been loyal to Mikka for years. There was no person alive Mikka trusted more with her life.

Though there's always the chance the allure of a ten thousand credit reward got the better of her . . .

Would she have outed Mikka in order to report Abigail and claim the reward?

That hardly seemed like Kiara's style, and she had no reason to throw Mikka out the airlock with the pirate.

And then there was Abigail. Somehow, she had known, but then again, pirates had a knack for finding their own. Hiding from a crafty pirate was damn near impossible, but there had hardly been time for the newcomer to have determined who Mikka's mother was, where she lived, and to have hired the goons to turn the place upside down—and then alert Tabitha and the Syndicate Front.

Then again, the fugitive had figured out who she was while her escape pod was falling apart, so she'd put nothing past the woman.

Mikka's fingers continued to follow the pattern in the floor. The grouted lines were grimy and likely covered in dried fluids Mikka didn't want to think too hard about. The only luxury she wished for was a bench so she could sit above the filth. But the repetitive action of tracing the tile kept her grounded, reminding Mikka there was substance beneath her. She could focus and convince herself that she was okay.

Nothing is okay.

She had a list of crimes stacked against her higher than her cell was tall, and it was likely the Syndicate hadn't killed her yet only because they were going to make an example of her.

It had been a while since the Syndicate had held a public execution, and Mikka figured she'd be the perfect candidate. Her corpse hanging from the rafters would be a call to all dissenters: *No matter how long it's been, we will find you.*

She shuddered. Abigail hadn't been far off when she'd said Jax had been the most notorious pirate the Syndicate had ever dealt with—at least, from their perspective. From hers, Mikka just had a knack for getting lucky; for finding holes in situations others would run away from.

Life by my own rules.

There was no doubt her execution would be broadcast to the entirety of the Syndicate's dominion: all the lunar colonies; the terraforming projects; Mars; Ceres; probably Psyche 16, even. Hell, Mikka wondered if even the FLOW stations would be able to watch—though, if rumors about the stations were true, their inhabitants believed they were the only ones left in the solar system. She didn't know how the Syndicate had managed that one, which was why it was widely dismissed as a conspiracy theory, but either way, there was a good chance she'd be part of the most widely watched public execution in human history.

"Get up!" a guard—a woman, judging from her voice, though Mikka couldn't see through the darkness—barked.

Mikka complied but took her time. She would not jump for these guards, but she wasn't hungry for a beating, either. She also wasn't eager to step inside a gibbet anytime soon, but that wasn't where this was leading. Not yet.

Whatever event the Syndicate would plan for her execution would take weeks to organize, days, at least. They had locked her in the cell overnight at most. They weren't leading her to her death.

Yet.

"Where are we going?"

Unless I've misjudged how much of a spectacle they'd make of my death? Maybe I'm not that important to them anymore.

"Shut up. No questions." The female guard was abrupt but didn't raise her voice. There was no need to in the empty cavern of the basement; her words echoed through the chasm, amplifying as they carried on.

Cold metal slapped against Mikka's wrists with a *beep*. Sharp edges of the electronic cuffs dug into her skin, peeling layers away one at a time. The more she struggled, the deeper they cut; an effective measure to convince prisoners to comply.

Two more guards fell into step as she left the cell; an escort of three armed guards to keep the shackled prisoner in line.

Mikka tripped up the stairs as the guard pushed her along. From there, they meandered down a series of halls and doorways, each room getting progressively brighter than the last.

Along the way, they passed additional holding cells, each strangely empty.

Through squinted eyes, Mikka had a hard time focusing on anything other than the next step in front of her. The passage was so white her eyes watered. Harsh white lights and institution-white walls, floors, and ceilings burned Mikka's retinas. She wondered how anyone who worked in such an environment didn't walk around with a persistent headache.

I think I'd rather be in the dank dungeon.

They passed through an oversized metal doorway, and the intensity of the lights diminished by several factors.

Mikka tried to shake off the tears that streamed down her face and dripped onto her jacket as she blinked to adjust to the new luminosity level once again.

The corridors and spaces past the threshold were more immaculate than the dungeon below. There was more iron, more bronze, more gold, and a blue reflective metal Mikka couldn't name, strung with fabrics of various degrees.

This new section buzzed with noise. Where the previous section had been filled with nothing but the hum of electricity, this area was teeming with life. Glass office walls separated desks and coworkers with their heads down and coffee cups steaming. Holo-screens danced, reporting numbers, figures, and charts in each of the respective cubicles.

Glimpses of the holos revealed the tasks of those operating them, images of faces, charts, and graphs that Mikka couldn't read as workers flicked through their displays.

More screens hung in the top corners of the ceilings, displaying news clips that were silent to her ears. But she didn't have to hear the newscasts to understand the topic.

The feeds projected the same images they always did: talking heads emphasizing that the almighty Syndicate was as popular as ever; images of festivals—that may or may not be happening somewhere in the system—marking their successful one hundred and fifty years of progress after the Climate Wars; anger against those who opposed Syndicate reign; the successful rehabilitation of humanity.

Successive images flashed of Syndicate success stories. The well-adorned Upper Rim of Shackleton City was alight with celebration. Monuments erected at Peary Crater on the north pole, infrastructure at Tranquility, and the solar arrays lining much of the south pole. Newly developed settlements on Mars and Ceres also got a nod, though they were aesthetically less pleasing. Besides these, there were clips of the megalithic sky cities on Earth. Mikka had only seen a few streams on their luxury, but like nearly everyone else born off-planet, she had never been allowed to see the Earth's surface. It was strictly inhabited only by the descendants of those who had been allowed to stay in the few remaining Terran cities while the rest of the planet was evacuated.

More images displayed lush green forests, waterfalls, lakes, mountains, and waterfalls that had all been saved from the deadly climate disasters from centuries before.

Though the disaster had been real, the Syndicate's presentation was complete bullshit.

One of her escorts prodded Mikka roughly from behind with a baton, causing her to realize she had slowed her stride to view the feeds. She didn't often watch them; she had no desire to. The Syndicate propaganda only made Earth and Upper Rim residents feel better about themselves and was a surefire way to stoke the embers of her anger, so she abstained.

They turned another corner and left the room of glass cubicles behind for a long hallway. Black stone tiles paved the floor, clicking beneath her boots and those of the guards behind her. To Mikka's right, several more glass-walled offices, more spacious than the cubicles in the previous room, were filled with swanky metal desks, holo-screens, and personal décor, though there wouldn't be any higher-ranking staff working at this hour.

To her left, a stretch of floor-to-ceiling windows overlooked the terraformed outskirts of the Shackleton City rim. The glass of the hallway stretched upward toward a ceiling nearly two stories above them.

Unlike the cratered stretch behind them, decades of workers had transformed the plains into a forest of trees. It stretched out among the glass-walled buildings and hovering transit cars that defied the hostile moon humankind had conquered. Lunar was a terraformed masterpiece that naysayers of centuries past had said couldn't be achieved.

The Syndicate had proven them wrong.

The hall's tinted windows dissolved much of the harsh sunlight, allowing the ghost of Earth to be visible in the sky above.

An office encased in glass sat at the end of the hall of windows. Holo-screens filled the room, but electrostatic blurs in the glass walls obscured their content; a security measure to prevent nosey onlookers.

A man stood in the center of the room, casually monitoring whatever data was being presented on the holographic displays. He lifted his hand to his mouth and held it up with his other arm as he studied whatever mysteries the data sets contained. The man's black uniform indicated he was a high-ranking member of the Front, perhaps a captain or a commander.

One of the guards pressed a finger to a touchscreen beside the entryway. "The pirate, sir."

The man turned to face the hall and Mikka's heart stopped.

David.

CHAPTER EIGHTEEN

Django
Eclipse

EVERYTHING HAD CHANGED.

The best Django could hope for now was to find some normalcy within the chaos; to find comfort among the confusion. He didn't know where else to turn, or who else he could go to, except his oldest friend.

The station he had grown up in was now alien. Empty. Even though there were dozens of people around, Django had never felt more alone. People he had grown up with his entire life brushed past him without a second glance. Section after section, the people he passed were in a hurry, but they had nowhere to go.

He cursed to himself as he made his way to the station's transport shuttle.

Mom. Dad. Marvin. Nova. Now Eventide.

The list of people now dead or forced out of his life began swirling through his thoughts. The ache of each name struck anew with each step, as though a bandage were being ripped off a congealed wound, tearing it open again and again.

His stomach churned and threatened to void its contents on

the station's floor. Django didn't care if it did. Maybe retching would clear his head, along with the immense pain and heartache inside.

Everything was unraveling around him. He had fought so hard to keep his life in order; to hold on to something familiar, to the life he had only days ago. But despite every straw he had grasped at, it had all slipped through his fingers.

Everything had changed.

He didn't know where else to go. Eventide wouldn't be able to change what had happened—she wouldn't be able to keep the Station Guard from moving Nova—but at least she would lend a sympathetic ear. She was the last remaining person on the station he could talk to and still feel as though he was being heard. His last bastion of familiarity.

Django's hand drifted to the side of his belt. Cold metal and plastic hugged his hip beneath his brown shirt. He didn't know why he had taken the energy weapon from under his parents' bed, but with the way things had gone down over the past forty-eight hours, something about arming himself had seemed right.

Django moved his hand to his neck, pressing his uncle's double-circle pendant against his skin. He now wore his father's weapon at his side and his uncle's most prized possession around his neck; pieces of those who had meant the most to him, of those who were no longer with him in the flesh but would never leave him in spirit.

Would they reveal their answers to him? Would they provide him with any sense of stillness? Or was he damned to spend his remaining days in chaos, desperately clinging to any shred of normalcy he could find?

As Django approached the InterRing shuttle, he could tell something wasn't right. A sea of people enveloped the lobby, pushing among themselves as though struggling to reach the turn-stiles that separated the Ring from the transit. Chatter buzzed at a high volume, their tone incensed, the anger in their mood palpable. Most of the crowd raised grease-stained hands from beneath heavy garments—salvagers eager to distribute their wares.

The only destination frequented by D-Ring citizens was the C-Ring, where raw materials could be traded for manufactured goods. The materials would be used to build furniture and other products, but sometimes antiques that had been brought up from the planet's surface could be repurposed for things they weren't able to build on board the station. Most of the items put together on the C-Ring were intended for future colonization of the planet and were shipped back down to the surface. The C-Ringers would also repair ancient relics, and what they couldn't repair was sent down to the D-Ring for scrapping. They usually did this through official channels, but residents would often board the train and make exchanges directly for items they could use personally. It was a way for both parties to conserve credits and gain access to amenities that would normally be outside their grasp.

Only today, it was clear they weren't headed anywhere.

White-uniformed guards blocked the gates, as though expecting a siege. Red and yellow hexagons glowed from the breasts of their sculpted uniforms. A wide barrier of open space separated the guards from the crowd, and Django could only imagine that they had ordered the crowd to stay back. He had only traveled aboard the tram twice, but neither time had he seen such a garrison on watch, nor a sea of people clamoring to get on board.

It was no simple task, but undeterred, Django wormed his way through the crowd, shielding himself from shouts in his ears, jabs to his sides, and the concentrated heat of bodies and sweat.

"Excuse me." Django approached the nearest guard, a man not much older than himself with a pale complexion, a pimpled face peering out from beneath his helmet. "Is something happening? I need to get on the shuttle."

The guard kept one hand on his weapon, the same issue as the one Isaacs had held earlier that day. The ache in Django's ribs burned anew, as if suddenly remembering the boot that had produced it. He refrained from rubbing his side.

"New policy," the guard grunted. His eyes warily surveyed the crowd without so much as a glance at Django. A white-gloved finger pointed to the digital bulletin board that sat next to the turnstile's entrance.

Effective Thursday, June 25, 12:00 p.m. and until further notice: for your safety, shuttle service between Rings will be restricted to official business only. Travel is prohibited to all other citizens.

"Restricted?" Django asked as he looked at the clock. It was 11:30 a.m. There would be enough time to get to Eventide before the cut-off time, but he wouldn't be able to get back. "For how long? Is there scheduled maintenance?"

The guard snickered. "No, kid. Benson ordered a travel ban. For good."

Django stood, blinking at the guard.

This was his one connection to Eventide; the one path to the only person he had left.

"But why?" Django asked, fighting the lump in his throat.

The guard scoffed again. "Too many of you dirty D-Ringers making their way to the upper levels where you don't belong. Have to ruin it for everyone. Traveling to the C-Ring to sell scraps is one thing, but there's been too many of you poking around the B-Ring."

Recent remarks against the D-Ring were boiling his blood. Where had this sudden resentment come from? Or had it always been there? His fingers twitched, but Django recalled his encounter with the last officer. He didn't want to kill any chance of being able to return, and he also didn't want to push his luck and end up out the airlock this time.

"A stupid kid who shouldn't have been there threw a punch at a guard yesterday," the officer continued. "Commander Benson wants to keep the Rings separate from now on to avoid *incidents*."

Django couldn't help but swallow. This was because of *him*?

"Only technicians, diplomats, and a handful of key workers will have the authority to cross between zones. Those selling their wares will need to use a licensed merchant."

Django knew enough about licensed merchants to know they took their own exorbitant cut. Many of them worked for the station and would send the little profit generated right to the A-Ring. That didn't bode well for the D-Ring merchants, who depended on their sales of raw goods to the C-Ring to get by.

But that wasn't Django's concern at the moment.

The shuttle pulled up behind the glass partitions that separated the station from the shuttle track, its structure grinding to a halt as its doors hissed open.

Django looked at the clock again.

Thirty minutes.

He took two steps toward the turnstiles before a hand landed on his chest, stopping him in his tracks.

"Whoa! Whoa!" the guard said. "Didn't you hear what I just said? Shuttle's closed to dirt-ringers."

Django's mouth fell open, his hands waving at the digital clock on the wall. "The notice says the ban starts at noon! I have thirty minutes!"

"That's not enough time to get there *and* back, smart-ass. Get on home to your barn. The upper decks are closed to you and your kind."

Heat burned through Django's veins.

His parents. *Dead.*

Uncle Marvin. *Dead.*

Nova. *Taken.*

Eventide. *Cut-off.*

Django's fists clenched so tightly he could feel his fingernails digging into his palms. It was all he could do to keep from slugging the guard.

But that, of course, was what had started this mess in the first place.

He had no way to argue that wouldn't end in disaster. He was only a few feet from the shuttle, yet lightyears away from the last person he could talk to about his problems.

The tighter he held on to his life, the more he seemed to lose. Every piece of him was stretched out, pulled to its limit, and Django feared he couldn't keep himself from reaching his breaking point for much longer.

What did he have left? Visits from Nova? The hope that Eventide would be authorized to make the journey to the D-Ring to see him? How much hope of that did he have now that she had B-Ring friends? Now that she had Faron. He'd quickly become a memory; somebody she used to know.

The only choice he had was to go back to his empty quarters and sit there alone, waiting to be let back into the fields; to go back to his job, to work day in and day out. If he didn't find a wife, Admin would arrange a marriage for him. There were certain expectations that had to be fulfilled to keep the station's numbers at a sustainable level. Administration wouldn't allow him to remain single in his quarters for long.

A life with Eventide was nothing more than a fantasy. A lost opportunity that he'd always wanted but had never acted on. A dream unfulfilled.

He took one last look at the patrol officer's gun, contemplated how far he could get if he rushed the officer, and took a deep breath as he let the fantasy fade. He didn't want to go home. He wanted to curl up on the floor and give up. There was nothing left for him.

Nodding absently, Django turned to leave.

"Let him through." The voice broke through his heavy heart

and defeated spirit. A hallucination? A figment of his imagination?

He recognized the voice but couldn't believe its source until he saw it. And even then, he thought he must have been dreaming. Standing at the entryway to the platform stood Avery Inglewood. The platform's blue lights reflected off her skin and glossy white uniform. The hair that hung down to her side shifted gently as air from the overhead vents blew against it, giving her an other-worldly quality. One that Django didn't believe she deserved.

"Ma'am?" the guard stammered, rifle still in hand. He looked confusedly between Django and the officer who had just given him the order to stand down.

"You heard me," she said. "The lines don't close for another thirty minutes. Let him through."

"He'll never make it back in time," the guard asserted. He lifted a hand to the back of his neck, letting his rifle fall to his side. Similarly, the rest of the guards holding the line between the plat-form and the crowd appeared stunned.

Django had to stop himself from rushing onto the platform in the guard's moment of uncertainty, but he couldn't help but gape at the woman coming to his defense. The same woman who had brought him nothing but bad news from the moment they'd met.

"That's his problem when he returns. He's aware of the policy. Let him deal with the fallout."

"Officer Inglewood." The sentry's eyes danced left and right, as though afraid to look Avery in the eye. "With all due respect, the commander was clear with his orders. With the increase in hull breaches, he wants to keep all citizens within their respective Rings. For their own safety."

For their own safety? So that's the official line?

How quickly the man's tune had changed when a superior officer was around. Safety had no role in this decision. Django's behavior on the B-Ring yesterday had stoked the coals of Benson's ire.

"And that order hasn't come into effect yet. Are you questioning my command?"

The officer lowered his gaze and straightened his posture. "No, ma'am."

"Good."

"But, ma'am," the guard asked, more cautiously this time, "what about the rest of them?" He motioned to the crowd behind the invisible line.

"They stay. Only let this one through."

The guard raised his eyes but only lifted his head slightly toward Django, his nose scrunched in a snarl. "*You* may proceed."

Django shot a questioning look at Avery. He wanted to know why she was helping him; why she, of all people, would stick her neck out on his behalf.

He froze. Was this a trick? A way to trap him?

He hesitated, shaking where he stood despite his best efforts.

"Well," Avery barked, "don't make me look like a fool. Go on."

Django swallowed, and he realized that no matter Avery's intention, it was too late to turn around now. There was no opportunity to question her motives. No matter her reasons, he did not want to make an enemy out of Officer Avery Inglewood.

If he hadn't already.

He wanted to offer a word of thanks, but he couldn't bring himself to speak, so instead he wordlessly sprinted to the turnstiles and boarded the shuttle.

"You owe me!" Avery called after him as he pushed through the metal bar that separated the platform from the concourse.

Django cringed as he stepped aboard the shuttle, the doors now closing. Of all the people he could think of owing a favor to, Officer Avery Inglewood had to be at the bottom of the list.

CHAPTER NINETEEN

Django
Eclipse

"WHAT ARE YOU *DOING* HERE?"

The accusation hit Django like a ton of bricks. The shuttle ride between the Rings had set his nerves on edge, and the only thing that had calmed them was knowing that Eventide would be happy to see him when he arrived. Her face suggested she was many things, but happy wasn't one of them.

Her eyes widened as she opened the door to her quarters, her breath quickening as her eyes darted fearfully down the hall.

"You're not supposed to be here! Geez! Well, come in before someone sees you. *Hurry!*"

"If you don't want me here, I'll just leave." The last of Django's will melted as he turned.

"Don't be an idiot." Eventide snatched him with both hands and dragged him into her quarters. She glanced once more down the hall in each direction before retreating and closing the door.

Django rubbed his shoulders, her fingers still embedded in the sinewy muscle.

"What the hell are you doing?" He realized he was cradling his shoulder and dropped his hand to his side.

"Sorry . . ." She leaned her back against the door and sank to the floor. "I've had a lot to process today. Everything's changed."

"Tell me about it," Django started. "Officer Inglewood showed up this morning and took Nova. Admin are putting her with a new family. They don't think I'm capable of taking care of her."

Eventide sighed. Only then did Django realize her eyes were moist and puffy. She shook her head silently, as though unable to offer the condolences he could see etched on her face.

"What's wrong?" Django took a seat on the floor beside her. Eventide shuffled closer so their shoulders were touching, the heat of her body pressed against his, leaning her head against his shoulder as she settled.

The move was so surprising that Django held his breath, as though the slightest movement would cause her to question the intimate action and pull away. A warmth built in his chest, and with it came a sense that a piece of him was being put into place.

For the first time in two days, he was home—on the floor of an oversized apartment, with a woman who had never shown romantic interest in him, in a part of the station he wasn't allowed to be in. Somehow, he was where he was supposed to be.

For a moment, everything that had happened over the past forty-eight hours melted away, and it was just him and Eventide— as it should be.

She shuddered sharply beside him, and he realized that as comforting a moment as this was for him, something was terribly wrong.

"What's going on?" He was suddenly no longer concerned if she would pull away or not; he wrapped an arm around her and pulled her in close. Eventide shuddered as she leaned in, and the shoulder of his shirt grew damp with her tears.

The top of her head smelled fresh, like cut marigolds. He

struggled to understand why her hair was also wet, but then Django realized he was crying, too. Everything that had transpired over the last two days, everything he had fought so hard to keep locked inside unraveled and was released in sobs.

Moments turned to minutes, which turned to hours. Django lost track of time until he felt Eventide rustle against him, pushing his arms down. He jumped and then realized he had fallen asleep. How long had he been there?

He looked at his watch. 7:45 p.m.

"I should get back home. You're going to have to come visit me from now on. I'm not allowed to be here anymore."

Eventide straightened her hooded sweatshirt, wiping the remnants of tears and running makeup on its sleeve.

"You don't understand. That's why . . ." Eventide steadied herself against her countertop as she rose to her feet. "I can't see you anymore. Admin won't let me visit you. I'm not allowed to associate with anyone who isn't a technician."

All air vacated Eventide's quarters. Django struggled to breathe as the weight of the space station crashed down around him. His abdomen struggled to lift, as though a piece of equipment now sat on his chest.

"I'm . . ." He couldn't find adequate words.

Defeated. Broken. Hopeless.

None of them were quite right. None of them were enough. Not being allowed to visit Eventide in the B-Ring was bad enough, but not being allowed to see her . . .

"They let us know today."

"But . . . Evie . . . *Why?*"

"To minimize the chance of us . . ." She sighed. "Today, the senior techs told us what we really do. We're not allowed to associate with others because . . . we keep the station running, but we also keep its greatest secret."

Django couldn't breathe. This couldn't be happening. "What *secret?*"

"Your Uncle Marvin was right about what we saw out of the viewport at Celeste's wedding . . . *Eclipse* isn't alone. There are other space stations. The Earth isn't as dead as they've told us. It's had time to heal, but it's still not ready to be inhabited, not yet. Admin don't want everyone to know because they don't think we'd accept staying on board. The technicians are sworn to secrecy, and they kill anyone who learns the truth. If I tell anyone, if I let the secret slip, even accidentally, they'll kill me, too."

The breath in his lungs caught, and Django inhaled deeply.

His uncle had died. His parents had died. Everyone at his sister's wedding reception had died. All because they'd learned the truth?

His mind was still for the first time in two days. No matter how hard he tried, no matter how much he wanted to live the simple life of a farmer, nothing would ever be the same again. Not ever.

And it was all based on a lie.

Everything you saw is real.

So, if Uncle Marvin had been right about the viewports, about Earth, about the murders . . .

Eventide. Nova. Himself . . . They weren't safe.

Unless he acted. Unless he did *something*.

Django reached into his pocket and pulled out a mangled piece of paper. He held it for a moment, weighing the words he knew had been written on its surface. There was no question in his mind now; for the first time in two days, he knew what needed to be done. His left hand grasped at the double-circle pendant that hung around his neck. Uncle Marvin *had* been right; there was only one path forward.

"Then we leave. Just like Marvin said."

"What's this?" Eventide squinted skeptically as Django passed her the note. "What's *'Black Swan?'*"

"I'm pretty sure it's the name of a ship. Officer Inglewood found this note addressed to me in a sealed envelope among Uncle Marvin's things."

Eventide pursed her lips and raised an eyebrow. "How do you know it's not a setup?"

"What do you mean?"

"Your parents weren't killed by accident. The viewport display failed, and they witnessed it. Marvin wasn't there, but the next day, he dies in a hull breach, too. What if Avery *wants* you to be at this location so they can kill you, too? Nova was the only member of your family who wasn't at the party, and they've already dealt with her."

"That doesn't make sense. Avery is the reason I'm here. She came to my defense at the transit station. If it wasn't for her, I wouldn't have been able to come see you. And it was almost as if she felt bad for delivering the news about Nova."

Eventide shook her head. "No, I don't buy it. Something's up."

She paused, grabbing a deck of cards from a hidden pocket in her sweater, and started absently shuffling as she pondered.

Django followed the movements, mesmerized, the cards clicking together as they flipped through her graceful fingers.

The cards stopped. Eventide's hands froze in midair as her deep blue eyes narrowed and landed on Django.

"It's not you they're after . . . It's me."

"What are you talking about?"

"I'm the reason. Commander Benson came to the wedding and specifically asked about me. Minutes after he leaves the party, there's a supposed hull breach."

"That's just a coincidence."

"The next day, he implements a policy where no D-Ringers can travel to the Upper Rings, *coincidentally* when I receive my full technician's training. He wanted to cut me off from those who care about me."

Django cleared his throat and winced. "I'm pretty sure he issued the ban because I punched a guard."

"You *what?*"

Django explained the details of the altercation. He also told her about the guard's words at the shuttle station on the way to her quarters.

"That probably just provided Benson with the justification," she reasoned after he was done. "I think he would have done it anyway."

Eventide shuffled the deck again, her hands moving over the cards as though they were guiding them without her even realizing what she was doing.

"At any rate, Avery then hands you a note with a time and place to be at and allows you to flout the rules to come find me. She knew full well you'd try to convince me to join you. With nothing else to lose, and having learned the truth for myself, she knew I'd go with you."

"But that doesn't tell me *why*. Why would Benson be after you? You're the first person from the D-Ring to become a technician. You should be hailed as a hero!"

Eventide shook her head. "I'm a risk to them. A risk to the order of this station. Admin can't let a D-Ringer move into this realm. It threatens their power structure. What happens if dozens of us decide to become technicians? Or engineers? Or security officers? It threatens everything."

Django bit his tongue, considering Eventide's words. They were damned if they stayed, and damned if they tried to leave.

"So, what now? We just roll over and let them hold us down?"

"I just think we need to be careful. We can't run headstrong into this."

"We can't afford to wait, either. This ship leaves tonight. We have no other options if we miss this chance."

Eventide smirked. "What happened to wanting to remain in the fields and live the simple life?"

"I think that shuttle has flown, don't you?"

"You're not thinking this through. You'll be walking right into Avery's trap."

"What choice do we have?" Django asked. He swallowed what he so badly wanted to say; the confession that would change everything between them. His stomach heaved at the thought of one more change; at the thought of one more dream being crushed. Instead, he would have to plead for reason. "And I hope you'll join me. If you're right, Benson and the rest of those A-Ring bastards are not going to stop trying to kill you. If I'm going to die, I'd like to know I did so trying to take the chance my uncle gave me."

Eventide nodded and, with a flick of her wrist, stacked the cards neatly in her hand and tucked them back into the sleeve of her sweater. A smile curled over her lips.

"Django Alexander, are *you* asking me to join you on an adventure?"

CHAPTER TWENTY

Mikka

Shackleton City

DAVID ARIES HAD CHANGED his appearance since the last time Mikka had seen him, but there was no doubt it was him. Even though it was clear he had received cosmetic surgery to fix a flaw in his jawline, the grin that formed over his face remained slightly crooked. His teeth, however, were as white as some of the cells in the prison facility below. They were difficult to look at, as though he'd had them bleached but had forgotten to take the solvent off for three days.

Annoyingly, he was as good-looking as ever.

"Jax Luana." The left side of David's crooked smile lifted, and his brown eyes sparkled with amusement. There was a small triangular tattoo that pointed downward below his left eye; it glowed yellow and appeared to be an attempt to cover a scar, possibly the result of a brawl but more likely to cover the work of a modification that had enhanced his vision.

The SF guards had pushed Mikka inside the cylindrical-shaped office. Its exterior walls were all glass, overlooking a newly developed part of the city. The rest opened onto the hallway where she had come from, as well as a large communal area where other guards and their administration milled about.

David chuckled and pulled a bottle of yellow-tinted alcohol from a compartment in his desk. He tugged at the oversized cork handle, giving it a few good pulls before it broke free.

Here was a man Mikka had never expected to see again. For one, she did her best to ignore the Front soldiers. If you weren't looking for trouble, encounters with them were rare. They sought targeted individuals—people deemed a threat against the Syndicate or their interests. Their ranks weren't widely publicized, and even if they had been, Mikka had more pressing matters to occupy her time.

Second, the last time she had seen the man, he was nothing more than a junkyard watchman.

Mikka kept her voice cold. "I no longer go by that name."

"You think I give a shit what you call yourself?" he replied. "You can change your name. You can change your hair. Hell, you've even changed your face. But even after all that, you can't escape your past."

Mikka had the urge to spit at the man, but the baton still wedged between her ribs forced her to reconsider. Instead, she remained silent. There wasn't anything she could say that wouldn't make her situation worse.

"Don't get me wrong, you've made a magnificent effort. I was rooting for you, I truly was." David poured two glasses of whatever alcoholic elixir he held, pushed one across the table toward Mikka, and nodded for her to take it.

"Canadian whisky," he said. "The finest from Nova Scotia. Or at least it was when Nova Scotia and Canada still existed."

"I thought a man of your caliber would possess something a little more antique," Mikka goaded him. "The old territories— Scotland, Ireland. I hear their whiskeys are what collectors seek.

You must have acquired a few bottles that were produced before the droughts killed the industry."

"What? Two hundred years not old enough for you? I have a couple older, finer vintages in my private collection, but one of those bottles would be worth more credits than you can imagine. I sure as hell won't waste a dram on you."

"Well, if that's the way you feel, I'd gladly take a bottle of this piss off your hands. Canada hasn't existed in more than a century; it's likely worth enough to the right buyer. And it seems like you might have an extra to spare."

The grin spread across David's face as he chuckled. "You always had a peculiar sense of humor."

"I'm serious. I have a large fine that I'd very much like to pay."

"Just drink the damn whisky."

"I'd love to, but . . ." Mikka lifted her hands, twisting as much as the guard behind her would allow to showcase the cuffs that still bound her.

"Remove them," he said to the guard before turning to Mikka. "But don't try anything funny."

Two guards had their weapons trained on her back, and security cameras targeted every angle of what was likely the largest Syndicate Front command center on Lunar's surface. Mikka had no illusions of going anywhere.

The woman behind her grunted but released the cuffs with a *beep* and a tug. Mikka didn't waste any time in picking up the glass, swirling it around as though she cared about its aesthetic. Though she wasn't in her first choice of locales, it had been far longer than she could remember since she'd last had a glass of anything decent. The cheap grain sludge the underground pubs called ale was barely fit to drink, but it got the job done. Even the poorly crafted spirits she stowed away aboard the *Redemption* were barely passable.

It was rare Mikka got the opportunity to sample an Earth

vintage. In her pirating days, she had smuggled a case of prewar Scottish single malt to a collector in the Sea of Tranquility. That single case of twenty-first century liquid had fetched her enough credits to sustain her and her crew for over a month.

"Yes," she said, sniffing the amber liquid and inhaling aromas of vanilla and oak. She lifted her glass in mock celebration. "A fine example of Earth snobbery and pretension." She took a sip, savoring the toasted flavors of orange, wood, and maple that coated her tongue before allowing the liquid to roll down her throat.

David's smile faded and his eyes darkened. "Enough games," he said. "Jax. Mikka. Whatever you call yourself, a few credits against your name are the least of your concerns. Your life hangs by a thread. I told you your crimes would catch up with you."

"I believe what you said was that I *had a pretty face.*" She batted her lashes in case it might still hold true. "If you didn't want to play games, then why am I here? Surely you didn't just want to flex your status that you've made Captain of the Front."

"I'm Commanding Officer of the Shackleton City colonies. Captain of the Front isn't a . . ." He dismissed the comment. "No, that's not why I brought you here."

Mikka grimaced. She knew what was coming.

"You still owe me a favor."

It had been seven years. He wasn't a captain then, not even close. She had no idea how the Syndicate Front ranked their officers, but a rise from a boneyard guard to captain showed the man had more drive than she'd ever imagined. Nevertheless, even then he'd been a cocky one, especially for someone watching a scrap heap.

She had her own set of rules about making deals when she didn't know what the stakes were. But seven years ago, she broke that rule; she had been young and desperate. And David Aries had seemed harmless enough.

Before her body modifications, the hair extensions, the adjustments that would make her unrecognizable, unscannable, she had had very few options. The best she'd hoped for was a guard either too stupid to notice or too lazy to care. She'd gotten neither.

Aries had been the one that had scanned the *Redemption* through the system. He had ignored the lack of serial numbers, the tampered code, and had ignored that the vessel was being absconded by a fugitive pirate. And made a deal with her that she had always feared would come back to bite her in the ass.

CHAPTER TWENTY-ONE

Mikka
The Boneyard, Orbital Junkyard 027
Seven years ago

"YOU GOT THIS WORKING BY YOURSELF?" asked the guard, who'd introduced himself as David. A nameplate that read "ARIES" was fixed to his chest, below the stitched intertwined double hexagonal Syndicate logo on his gray-brown uniform. "You can't expect me to believe someone left a working shuttle here. It's old, but it runs."

By myself? What the hell is that supposed to mean?

The Boneyard's on-duty guard had spent more time looking Mikka up and down than he had the ship. There weren't too many soldiers who wouldn't have recognized her on sight anymore, not after the heist at Space Dock Nineteen had gone horribly wrong. The Syndicate had touted her face on every holo-feed and channel between Earth and Psyche 16.

Mikka had known her face would be the weak link in her entire plan and had debated for weeks whether she should use the last of the credits she had tucked away to purchase a new ship or a new face. The Syndicate had confiscated most of her resources, but fortunately, she had leeched away a contingency fund in case everything suddenly went south.

Which is exactly what had happened.

Unfortunately, she didn't have enough credits saved for both a new identity and a new ship. She'd eventually decided that with a new ship, she could get a few backlist gigs in order to pay for the cosmetic surgery, but it would be hard to do the reverse. The prettiest face in the Loop wouldn't buy her a new ship.

Well, not through any endeavors she wanted to pursue.

The decision meant she would have to be careful; it would be worth more to turn her in than to have a shipment delivered. Or worse, someone could hire her to complete a job and then turn her in instead of paying. But Mikka didn't have much of a choice. She'd complete a few contracts with her new ship and use that money to change her features. She had enough saved for the ship, plus the few parts she had to scrounge together to make it fly again.

No ship meant no contracts, period, and her mother needed her now more than ever. She had become sick and then destitute, all because her daughter had abandoned her. Because *she* had abandoned her.

Mikka hadn't realized the lunar sickness had taken hold of her mother before she had left on her pirating adventures. She hadn't even checked in with her mother to find out if she was okay. If she had, she could have put away more funds to take care of her. She could have given her mother a better life. Instead, she squandered it and gave the rest away.

Mikka had debated sticking the life out a little longer. A few more bootlegged crates of whiskey, a few black-market sales of Corielus, and she could probably set aside enough money to give her mother a leg up for a year, maybe more, until she could secure a few more legitimate contracts. But Mikka couldn't afford to take the risk; the raid on Space Dock Nineteen had been a close call.

Too close. She had lost her ship and her crew, and she'd barely escaped with her life.

She needed to disappear. She needed legitimate contracts. She needed to find a steady, if meager, income.

To do that, she needed a ship.

David Aries stood in between Mikka and her redemption. He was the one man who could make any plan of supporting her mother disintegrate like a pebble against her ship's protective plating. These graveyards were full of treasure seekers and lawbreakers, and the guards were trained to look for criminals.

And David Aries had definitely recognized her.

The irony of these scrap heaps was that the poorest people, who could get the most use out of flipping parts, couldn't afford to access them. Any hopefuls would require a separate ship to get to the facility, plus the credits to buy the scrap. From there, one had to either sift through the material manually or scour through the inventory list of the larger pieces that sat suspended in the field surrounding the enormous cargo ship.

Mikka's instincts told her to go along with the guard's questions. It was a long shot, but as long as he didn't make a move to arrest her, she might still have a chance.

"You'd be surprised what some of the less experienced fliers will abandon," she said. "Some of these kids are second, even third generation owners. They inherited their parent's routes or older shuttles and have more money than brains. This shuttle only needed a few parts, a new solar panel, and some hydrogen cells. Whoever turned it in didn't know what they were doing. It still had its most rare and valuable parts installed."

"In my position, I see a lot of junk come and go. Nothing surprises me anymore . . ." David not so subtly eyed her up and down, almost as though he was more interested in her body than her bounty. "*Almost* nothing. Still, it's rare that a ship flies out of here. Especially for this price."

"She may be old, but with a little skill and a little love, these ships still work. She won't get me to Mars unless I want to spend a few months in open space, but she'll do for orbital loads. I got lucky."

"Is that what you're looking for from her?" he scoffed. "A little luck?"

"More than a little."

"She's not exactly a ship built for smuggling."

Mikka swallowed. This was it. She had to lay all her cards on the table if she had any hope of getting out of here without cuffs attached. "I'm not looking to smuggle, sir. The ship is my ticket to a new life. There's some bad karma I need to account for. I've made some connections and have lined up some private contracts. I plan on rum-running for the private sector. But those contracts hinge on my ability to obtain a shuttle."

David raised an eyebrow; her response was closer to a confession than he'd been expecting. He continued to make notes as they circled the ship.

"What designation would you like to give the vessel, Miss Lua—"

"Mikka." She cut him off before he could get her real name out. If she was going to leave her old life behind, her name had to go with it. Even if she made it out of the junkyard, she wouldn't make it more than a few miles from the Boneyard with the name Jax Luana attached to the ship. "My name is Mikka Jenax. I'd like to register the ship as the *Redemption*."

"Hmm, very well, Miss . . . Jenax. The *Redemption* it is. I don't think it's a secret that I shouldn't let you out of here with her, but you have a pretty face, and you've chosen a fitting name. I hope you find it."

"Thank you, sir."

"Don't thank me yet. You owe me a favor." A smile crossed his lips, and the blue of his eyes glinted in the light of the Boneyard's office. "You never know when I'll need a rum runner."

Mikka nodded slowly. Hesitantly.

As a rule, she never entered an arrangement with someone she didn't know. Someone she didn't trust. Especially when the stakes weren't laid out.

But Mikka was desperate, and this was her only shot. The next Boneyard guard probably wouldn't be as accommodating. Besides, if she could change her face and disappear off the Syndicate's radar, then this guard would likely forget about her.

What would a junkyard warden need as a favor, anyway?

Mikka lifted her finger to the holographic screen, pressing her finger to the biometric contract. Of course, it didn't feel like anything—it was all light and quantum sensors—but a chill ran through her body regardless, and she shivered at another form of energy coursing through her body. If someone was suspicious and willing to do some digging, they could have traced her bio-signature back to her true identity, but it would be difficult. The crux of being a pirate meant Mikka had never attached her biomarkers to a legal document before today.

"Excellent," David said, as though he didn't notice the weight of what had just transpired. "The *Redemption* is all yours. Just be advised, Miss Jenax—I always collect my debts."

Mikka should have felt relieved. Part of her actually did, the logical part of her brain reminding her that this was exactly what she had come here for, and she had done what was necessary.

But Mikka had a hard time ignoring the gnawing in her gut; the small but persistent voice screaming that the deal she had just made would come back to haunt her.

"One more thing." David swiped intently through a few more screens on the datapad. "You might want to get some mods. It's going to be hard leaving your old life behind with a face as stunning as yours."

CHAPTER TWENTY-TWO

Mikka

Shackleton City — Upper Rim

"WHY DID YOU DO IT?" Mikka asked. "Why did you let me go?"

"Why do you *think* I did it?" David lifted his glass of whisky to his face, pausing before taking a sip. "I didn't want to fill out the paperwork."

"I don't believe that for a second," Mikka replied. "Nobody goes from boneyard watch to Captain of Lunar in a handful of years if they're too lazy to follow protocol."

"As little as you might think of the Front," he said, "we're not monsters. Sometimes people deserve a chance to forge a fresh path."

"I doubt many of your associates would agree."

"I'm not here to defend my actions, or the actions of my peers. I brought you here to call in a favor. You've gone the past seven years without getting into trouble, which is commendable. Though you almost blew that record yesterday, didn't you?"

Did he mean Abigail? How could he possibly know about her?
Unless they had arrested her, too.

"The OG inspected my ship. They found nothing."

David snorted. "The OG wouldn't be able to find their own station without their navigation systems. We both know that. Regardless, I'm afraid your days as a rum runner are coming to an end."

Mikka studied the man. In a few short years, he had somehow maneuvered his way through the ranks to become some sort of leader of caliber. His station might not have been in the most prestigious of locations, but in comparison to junkyard monitor, David had come a long way. And it just so happened that the day she arrived at Shackleton City's port, the day she visited her mother, the day her house got ransacked and she got arrested, Commander David Aries was sitting in his office tower, waiting to call in a favor.

This definitely isn't a coincidence.

"Nobody ratted me out, did they?" Mikka asked. "You knew where I was and sent the Front in looking for me."

David sipped his drink, his eyes locked on Mikka, but said nothing in response.

"How was Tabitha involved, though? She thought she'd cracked some great caper in bringing the Front down to seize me."

"Simple minds," David said with a wave. "Don't worry about her. She was an unfortunate hire for you, but she had nothing to do with any of this."

"So, you've been tracking me? For seven years?"

"More like keeping tabs," he replied.

Mikka would have sat down if there had been a chair to do so. Instead, she leaned her weight against David's desk, but a rough hand soon pulled her away from the support.

"Guards," David said, "please wait outside. I'd like to talk to Miss Luana alone."

"But sir . . ." one guard protested but was quickly cut off.

"I assure you, I can handle an unarmed civilian."

"With all due respect," the guard's tone was slow and measured, "she's the most wanted pirate in the system, sir."

"What do you expect her to do?" David asked. "Knock me out? Kill me? Then what? The room is made of glass, for pity's sake. If you can't keep watch from the hall, perhaps I need to find someone more capable."

The guard opened his mouth to argue, but he either thought better of it or couldn't come up with a sufficient rebuttal. He grimaced and gave a curt bow. "Of course, sir. We'll position ourselves outside." The door closed behind them as the guards left, each giving the other questioning glances.

Mikka had to admit, it *was* a strange request. There had likely already been enough discussion in front of them to get the commander in trouble if the guards had reason to betray him.

Stars, he had all but admitted to aiding a pirate's escape.

Mikka wondered how long it would be before those guards disappeared.

David set his drink on his desk and turned to look out of the office window. The dark Lunar sky juxtaposed the harsh sunlight reflecting off the streets and buildings the residents of the Upper Rim of Shackleton City called their home. Located on the south pole, the sun almost never set on the Upper Rim. The long days allowed for solar reflectors to heat and utilize the water in the crater below. It also allowed for the entire city to be powered and heated with the sun's energy. The force field above Shackleton protected it from debris and cosmic radiation and maintained the city's temperature and atmosphere.

"I took a significant risk in letting you slip away," David said. "There was a good chance you were lying and were going to run off with that ship to perform your next heist. You can't blame me for keeping watch to make sure you hadn't pulled the wool over my eyes."

"Plus, you were holding this favor over my head."

"I didn't get where I am today without a little mutual back-scratching. You would do well to remember that's how the system works. Nobody gets ahead in life without calling in a few favors. Well, who knew I'd ever be calling in a pirate for help—but here we are. I need some assistance, and you're the only candidate who fits the bill."

"You're a commander with the Syndicate Front, and the only person you can enlist to your aid is a pirate-turned-rum-runner with a pile of bad debts and who'd rather be left alone?"

"That's *precisely* who I need."

"I'M ALMOST AFRAID TO ASK," Mikka ventured, "but what does a Syndicate Front commander need with an ex-pirate?"

"You keep doting on that title as if it's of great importance," David replied. "And while it may carry some weight with the moon's citizens, I assure you, within the Front, it's not that esteemed."

"I'm guessing it's important enough that you wouldn't want to be caught dealing with a pirate?"

David snorted. "No, I suppose not. But regardless, here we are. I need someone who can deliver something for me and do it under the radar."

Mikka furrowed her brow. "You want me to smuggle goods for you?"

"In a manner of speaking. Think of it more as a . . . *delivery*."

"Why?"

"The less you know, the better."

"Can I get a hint, at least? My hold, my rules—and I don't transport anything without knowing whether it's likely to go *boom* if I drop it."

David sighed. He crossed his arms, placing a butt cheek on the edge of his desk, the cloak he wore over his uniform spilling over its edge. He still faced the window toward the city, his back all but turned to Mikka.

All it would take would be a dagger between his ribs to end him. He wouldn't even see it coming. But Mikka had no dagger, of course, and even if she did, she didn't kill unless she was forced to. Clearly, whatever he was proposing weighed heavily on his mind, enough for him to momentarily forget that the woman standing four feet away from him was an incarcerated felon.

"Tensions are high between Earth and her colonies. The planet's relationship with Lunar hasn't exactly been bilateral."

"Tell me something I don't know. The elite shoved us off-planet a couple centuries ago. The Syndicate has built the entire orbital system based on imbalance."

"And the rest of us grow tired of it."

Mikka set her own drink down on the desk. It took little reading between the lines to now grasp what David was proposing.

"I hope you're not stupid enough to lead this charge yourself. You'll be shot out an airlock quicker than you can finish a dram."

David chuckled. "You let me worry about that. But I'll tell you this: a civil war *is* brewing, and it's not going to be pretty."

Civil war. That could only mean one thing: the Syndicate was fractured. Far worse than had been rumored. Almost nobody on Lunar truly knew the political situation on Earth, but if the tension had reached its top officials, it could only spell disaster for the Syndicate and everyone within their realm.

Mikka shrugged off the thought. What did it matter to her, some futile internal dispute within an organization that cared nothing for her or for its citizens? She thought it best to stick to the subject at hand.

"Will you at least tell me what the job is before I agree to it?"

David smiled. "I've got a package that needs to be delivered to the FLOW Station *Eclipse*. It needs to be handled by someone with a proficiency at avoiding checkpoints and red tape."

Something still didn't seem right. The task was too easy.

"So, that's all you need from me? Sneak one package aboard an orbital station? Surely, you're not going to burn your favor on a simple delivery."

The commander's smile widened. "No, I'm afraid not. *This* is just the beginning. If you can make this happen, then we'll talk about future projects."

"'Future projects?' Just how long do you expect me to run errands for you?"

"How long do you want to stay alive?"

Blackmail at its finest—a life of service or death. That was the deal he was laying down.

Mikka silently cursed as her mind scrambled to think of an out, but she didn't know what David had planned. Taking down the Syndicate wasn't something she was opposed to, in theory; she'd welcome it, in fact. But there was an entire spectrum of events and end results David could be implying to get there.

"What if I refuse?"

David shrugged. "I'm sure with your list of crimes, the courts will have you thrown out the airlock by the end of the day."

A setup.

"The courts? I'm being processed? How are you going to work out this deal if I'm already on the books?"

David lifted his glass. "I knew you were a smart one. One way or another, Jax Luana *will* be thrown out of an airlock in the afternoon. Whether Mikka Jenax is tossed out with her is up to you."

Mikka paused. A true end to her past life. With the official record showing Jax Luana having been executed, there'd be nothing to link her to her previous crimes. But she'd be in servitude, possibly lifelong, to the duplicitous shark that was David Aries.

Maybe. I've gotten myself out of stickier situations.

Mikka knew little about him. In years gone by, she had often fantasized about the man who had been her hero; the one who let her slip through the system with a wink and a nod. She had always assumed he had a soft spot for her 'pretty face.' He wasn't at all bad looking himself. She had imagined that perhaps there was a good man beneath that Syndicate uniform. Sometimes, she had imagined he truly thought people could change; that they deserved another shot at life after royally screwing up their existing one. A glimmer of hope standing within a system of vipers.

But that wasn't the man that stood before her at all. This man kept tally of his good deeds and held them as collateral to be cashed in at a future date. He likely also kept score of each offense against him. This man knew the weight of each person's actions, for and against him, and like a Lunar Anubis, he weighed each person's soul to determine whether they were worthy or not—down to those who blessed his sneezes.

"Then there's also the matter of your mother."

Mikka's heart stopped. How closely had he been watching her? How difficult would it have been to determine that her motivation seven years ago had little to do with the failure of Space Dock Nineteen, and everything to do with the ailing woman?

"What about her?"

"Well, without you around, she won't be able to pay her rent or her caretaker. It'd be a shame for her to lose you. To be forced out onto the street in her condition."

"You snake!" Aware of the guards still peering in from beyond the glass walls, Mikka had to stop herself from tackling the man. "Leave my mother out of this!"

"Now, now," David warned, as cool and collected as he'd been the entire meeting. "I'm not making threats. On the contrary. Without you, your mother has nobody to look after her. Right now, she is currently lying on her bed, in pain and alone, in the lowest part of the Tubes, long forgotten by any branch of the Syndicate. If you decide to take on this mission, I will make sure she is well looked after. We can move her to the Upper Rim. That will ease the lunar sickness somewhat, and part of your salary will go to providing for her. I will arrange an exclusive caregiver who will ensure she's getting the help she needs."

"Why would you do that?"

"I've already told you—I'm no monster. You have such disdain for the Front that you imagine us all as demons."

"I'm *sorry*," she sneered. "I guess I've leapt to conclusions based on personal experience."

"You may find it hard to believe, Mikka, but I'm not so different from you. I'm merely trying to get by."

Mikka's face twitched as she held back a snarl. *You have no idea of the struggles that occur beneath your feet. Beneath your glass walls and holo-screens.*

David didn't seem to notice and continued. "I would have thought I've proven myself benevolent enough in the past for you to trust me."

You've tracked me for seven years. Left me to struggle as my mother lay dying in this hellscape's underbelly. Then you set me up. Raided my mother's house and left her bleeding on the floor. All so you could bring me in here for this . . . opportunity.

Trust? No, I'll never trust *you.*

"I can see you're still hesitant," David continued. "I don't have to, but here's something that might sweeten the deal."

Mikka crossed her arms. She'd listen. What choice did she have? But that didn't mean she'd be eager to jump.

"Have you ever stopped to wonder why there's such disparity? Between the Upper Rim and the Tubes? Between the Earth and us?"

"Because the Syndicate's filled with greed? Because you use

hard labor and exploitative practices to mine and produce in order to send it to a planet we're forbidden to see? Because you've built an empire off our backs and then told us it's for our own good?"

"Precisely."

Mikka blinked at the unexpected confession. What was he getting at?

"You see the Syndicate as a single unit, but it's not. There's a hierarchy among the corporation. Status depends on whether you're on the planet, on Lunar, Mars, or even a despicable FLOW station. Our ranks are not all equal."

"As you've said, civil war is coming. But I don't give a shit about your political maneuvering. What does this have to do with *me*?"

"Imagine what Lunar would look like if we didn't send 80 percent of our wealth back to the planet? Imagine what we could achieve if we made our own policies? If we could control our own people? What if Lunar, Ceres, and Mars could join forces and unite against the planet that strips us bare and leaves us with breadcrumbs?"

"I'd say it's a long shot, at best. And likely a suicide mission."

"It *will* be a reality. And you can help make it happen. What would benefit you and your mother more? A 'united' Syndicate that robs its citizens, or a fractured orbit, with each part taking care of its own needs? Its own people?"

Mikka truly didn't care. She knew enough about the Climate Wars to know that the only people it hurt were those on the front lines; everyday citizens that had everything to lose and nothing to gain. Their commanders would sit on the sidelines, sending their people to their deaths. Only the desperate had fought in the Climate War; people who sought nothing more than water and a habitable place to live, each fighting the other for a scrap to cling on to. The survivors were rewarded with eviction from their planet, while the elite sat in the habitable zones, sipping champagne, and claiming it was unsustainable for the rest of humanity to stay behind.

Mikka had no desire of roping the inner solar system into a civil war, but she did need to help her mother—whatever the cost. With David promising to take care of her mother in exchange for her service, all Mikka would have to do was stay alive. If he was a man that kept tally of his debts and debtors, she believed he was also a man that kept his word.

Her head was spinning with potential outcomes and ways she could make the proposal work in her favor. Any way she looked at it, it would be dumb not to take David up on his offer.

But Mikka knew better than to place all her chips on a single bet. If she was going to be going to *Eclipse* anyway, then she might as well take advantage of the situation. If the choice was helping David or death, she didn't have much to lose in agreeing, but she still needed to watch her step. Even though it didn't seem to be his style, there was always the chance he'd dispose of her as soon as he was done with her, and it would be prudent to have a backup plan, just in case.

"I'll do it," she said, trying to hide the disdain in her voice. "But I choose my crew."

CHAPTER TWENTY-THREE

Mikka
Shackleton City — The Velvet Underground

MIKKA COULDN'T REMEMBER the last time she had stepped foot inside the Velvet Underground. She wanted to say it was another lifetime ago, except that lifetime didn't want to leave her alone.

Hell, this morning felt like another lifetime ago.

This bar was the last place she wanted to be—a cesspool of pirates, thieves, outlaws, and politicians.

Cheap ale left a fermented stench in the air that never quite dissipated. The bar wasn't teeming with patrons, but there were enough paying customers for their unshowered stench to hang in the air. Overall, it was better than the toxic odors of the Lower Tubes, but not by much.

Purple strip lighting along the bar's ceiling and floor bounced off wisps of smoke that lingered between customers' heads and the ceiling, giving the bar an otherworldly vibe. Otherwise, the interior was dimly lit, remaining dark enough to hide the scratches in the tables and the stains on the floor.

It was late afternoon, so the loud, thumping music the bar was known for had yet to begin. A stage at the back, meant for regular musicians, sat empty. Instead, synthesized music—some Martian political bullshit—flowed from speakers mounted on the walls. Even those beats were nearly drowned out by the voices of patrons speaking over it. Waves of volume assaulted Mikka as she scanned the room, and she couldn't help but shudder.

She didn't want to be in this place for two reasons—and she didn't know which she hated more. First, it was known to be a hangout for anti-Syndicate radicals. She understood the sentiment, but the Syndicate had always been quick to stomp out any rebellious activity before it got anywhere. The Front turned a blind eye to the Velvet's reputation, but Mikka had always assumed the bar's presence allowed them to keep track of those hostile to them. It made sense for the Syndicate to allow a place where all the main shit-stirrers congregated, instead of having them spread out across the city. And by planting spies, any word of dissent would get back to them before the anarchists started.

The whole setup made Mikka uneasy. If a Syndicate crony singled you out, it would be your word against theirs. Anyone in the bar could be made a target if they pissed off the wrong person.

Second, she had little interest in working with the pirate. Any pirate would be bad enough to team up with, but Abigail Monroe was a special case. She had proven herself to be savvy, and Mikka wouldn't doubt for a second that the woman would betray her if the situation warranted it.

Then again, that was the case for most pirates. They'd sell their own mother if it benefited them. Mikka would have done the same.

Until it was too late.

But Abigail was also far smarter than she let on. Anyone who uncovered Mikka's true identity in a matter of minutes had far more technical capabilities than the average pirate, let alone person.

Mikka sighed. That was only the beginning of her worries. She didn't want to return to her old ways. Didn't want to go back to illegally smuggling crates filled with food, weapons, plants, animals, people. Turning blind eyes to indecencies. Working with criminals who didn't have anyone's best interest in mind other than their own. Most pirates were just trying to get by, but there were others who were more intentionally devious. Some harbored a vendetta against a world that had abandoned them. Often, Mikka couldn't blame them, but those pirates were the ones to watch out for.

And she had yet to determine which camp Abigail fell into.

But what choice did she have? Mikka's past was dragging her back in. Fate had a stranglehold on her, and it was using two hands—one named Abigail and one named David—both gripping so tightly that they threatened the very air she breathed.

And if one hand was going to force her down, she might as well accept the second.

At least approaching Abigail provided her with an alternative if David double-crossed her.

A scan of the room confirmed most of the patrons weren't from the same streets and alleys that her mother lived on. Even within the Tubes, there was a hierarchy of the haves and have-nots. The Velvet's patrons were not nearly as well off as those on the Rim, for sure, but they could shuffle enough credits aside to quench their thirst.

Later, they'd be dancing, grinding, bumping to the music, spending their last few credits trying to forget. Now, most patrons sat while they drank, enjoying the company of others and an afternoon imbibement. Some stood, leaning on counters and tables, enjoying a bit of reprieve from whatever toils the day had brought forth. Others still, the saddest of the lot, were nose-deep in a mug, tucked in a corner, trying to waste away a day they wished had never come.

The rest of the patrons were of the same ilk as Abigail: pirates; thieves; politicians who would rather not be hounded for their anti-Syndicate positions, regardless of whether they platformed on those views. A rumor could land a political hopeful with a one-way trip to the mines or out an airlock, but hopefuls still existed. Mikka imagined they'd be the first to pick up arms in Commander Aries's envisioned civil war. They would be given the choice to do so. Those in the lower districts of the Tubes would join simply at the promise of a morsel to eat.

These customers were easy to pick out, as they didn't have the forlorn look of hopelessness painted across their faces. They were engaged in lively conversation, table games, and darts. Smiles crossed their faces, as though they had few cares, though, in many ways, their lot was sadder than the residents of the Tubes. These were the folks who didn't belong anywhere; outcasts wherever they went. Except perhaps this bar.

Connotations of drinking in the late afternoon didn't mean much to the dozens of shady travelers that filled the place. The Velvet's spacefaring customers would do their flying after standard hours, and regulars who had ventured down from the Upper Rim were likely hiding from some responsibility they had shirked off for the day.

Behind the rows of old metal tables and squirrelly patrons, there was no missing Abigail's slight figure and regal presence. She sat at a round table covered with a dingy, checkered tablecloth likely there to cover up the rust on the table beneath it. A handful of hopeful chancers sat with her, cards in hand and chips on the table; all men, each of them as ragtag as the next.

Mikka recognized the game they were playing as Martian poker. It was a pirate's go-to game of choice, and it was rarely played with outsiders. In addition to secured credits and bits of treasures, the stakes often included favors that only a pirate would feel obligated to be bound by. Crews, ships, even a week on the winner's craft, were all prizes Mikka had seen being bartered. The shame found in not honoring the win would, at best, be enough to ensure the person would never play again, or at worst, see them killed.

Martian poker required nine decks of cards instead of one, to discourage counters, which made shuffling a chore for all except the most proficient dealers. It was a reckless game, and one that Mikka had never entertained. It was far too risky to be indebted to another pirate—especially one whose moral code might not match her own.

She scoffed at the irony. She was indebted to someone even less scrupulous than a pirate, but she supposed that's what she got for breaking her own rules.

In the purple-tinted light of the bar, Abigail, too, appeared otherworldly, her eyes and bleach white hair reflecting the color in hypnotic fashion. The pirate sat as though she had no interest in the cards she held. Her white irises scanned the room but remained motionless, like an ancient statue.

Mikka had no doubt that Abigail's eccentricities were a front for her true intellect. It was how all the best pirates operated: leave your enemies, your colleagues, everyone around you, guessing, so that they either underestimate what you're capable of, or, if they realize what you're doing, they're still caught off guard when you switch.

It only took the pirate a moment to spot Mikka. She simply smiled and nodded, then made a gesture for her to take a seat next to her.

Mikka was in no mood to waste any time. "We need to talk. Alone."

"Can't you see I'm in the middle of a game, love? You can join us if you'd like." The empty chair slid out a few inches as Abigail pulled it with her foot.

Several groans and more than one whistle accompanied the

gesture. It didn't matter what position you held; it seemed that all men were pigs, whether they were guard or pirate. A shout and the sound of breaking glass echoed from a dark corner behind her. Mikka turned in time to witness the first punch of the fistfight, one that was quickly halted by bar staff and resulted in the participants being escorted out before Mikka had even fully processed what had been going on.

"I'll sit this one out," she said, her eyes still locked on the Velvet's security escort. "Come find me when you're done."

Rounds of "*Aww!*" circled the table, followed by raucous laughter and several crude comments that Mikka chose to ignore. She hoped she wasn't making a mistake.

She opted for a stool at the bar and made herself as comfortable as she could with a half dozen criminals leering at her. The cold metal seat didn't help matters.

"What'll you have?" A burly woman approached from behind the bar, slapping thick fingers on the counter. It was rare to see someone who didn't appear malnourished in the Tubes, and the server had enough muscle on her to account for the meals of three or four regular inhabitants.

"Do you have anything good?"

"Depends on your definition of 'good,'" the server replied. "But probably not."

Mikka chuckled. "Fine. Just bring me a glass of any mid-list whiskey."

It was the bartender's turn to chuckle. "Mid-list, eh? Sis, I don't know where you think you just climbed up into, but we're lucky we have *any* whiskey." She poured a glass without confirmation that the drink would be acceptable, but then held on to it with a second's hesitation, as though unsure if she should serve it. "It's an Armstrong blend."

"You're getting imports from other colonies down here?"

"*Hah!* Leftovers is more what it is. They can't get their own citizens to drink the stuff, so it gets shipped to anyone who'll take it. You new around here or something?"

"In a manner of speaking."

"I should have guessed from your outfit. Nobody down here wears a jacket like that."

"They should. It's freezing."

"The Syndicate likes to conserve heat for those on the Rim."

"Yeah, that much I know." Mikka had continually brought blankets to her mother over the years. It was hard to keep them from disappearing, but if rogues were going to steal anything, at least Mikka knew her goods were going to keep someone warm.

"I wonder if their plan is to eventually just let us freeze to death," the bartender commented. "It's not like they don't have enough power to go around."

"It's just mismanaged," Mikka said. "There's enough, but the Syndicate refuses to upgrade the grid that filters it down to the Tubes."

The bartender puffed a burst of air through her nose. "You talk like you know a thing or two about how things work. You're not from 'round here."

"You're one to talk."

The barkeep smirked and focused an eye on Mikka while squinting with the other. "You've got a good eye. I'm Leslie."

"Mikka. Who'd you piss off to end up stuck pouring the Velvet Underground?"

"*Hah!* No one." Leslie finally pushed the glass in Mikka's direction. "I choose to live down here. As hard as that is to believe, the patrons here are happier than the snooty businesspeople that frequent the bars on the Rim. And it's not as rough here as it is down-tube. As long as the *shadier* traders keep coming, the tips aren't half bad, either."

"But you're not from the Rim either, are you?"

"Grew up in the crater. Parents were ice miners. Expected me to carry on in their footsteps, but ice mining is a lonely business—and it's stressful. Hit a fissure and you're done for. Here, it might be dark, but as long as the Syndicate doesn't decide to cut off the airflow, it's safe."

"I hear ya. Sometimes, all the soul wants is a bit of the mundane so it can rest for a moment."

"Amen to that."

Mikka took a sip from her glass and nearly spat it back out. Compared to what David had offered her earlier, the Armstrong blend tasted like recycled sulfur. The sting of ash and butane burned her tongue and carried down her throat and into her stomach, causing her eyes to water.

Leslie chuckled. "You get used to it." She turned to tend to other patrons, leaving Mikka to nurse her drink alone.

"You need to ask for the rum," Abigail said as she pulled up a seat. "The whiskey here is trash."

Leslie shot a glare at them, but she was in the middle of taking an order and couldn't respond to the quip.

"So, what can I do for you, love? Looking for a drinking partner? I'm ace at drinking my troubles away."

"Earlier, you said something about a job I might be interested in."

"I did, and you said something about not working with a pirate."

"Things have changed."

Abigail championed a grin and twisted on her stool, facing the rest of the bar. "I believe you're familiar with Corielus seed?"

"Of course," Mikka replied. "Who isn't?"

"From what I understand, your mother has an acute case of lunar sickness. Which means you understand that Corielus seed is the only thing known to stop the pain."

Stars, does everyone know the details of my life?

"What about it?"

"There're pallets of the stuff sitting aboard the *Eclipse*. I've negotiated a contract to pick it up. There will be more than enough there for you to skim from the top, plus you'll get a fair lump of credits for successful resale of the merchandise."

Mikka scoffed. "That's your mission? Seed deliveries happens every day. I don't know how hard you hit your head when your ship was attacked, but even if we packed the *Redemption* full of the stuff, it wouldn't be that impressive a payload. Corielus is grown on all eleven stations, plus the new agricultural pods on Lunar's dark side. Finding a shipment isn't that difficult a task, though I guess only a pirate would consider skimming from the top."

It wasn't as though the thought hadn't previously crossed Mikka's mind, but buyers monitored their shipments closely. It'd be a substantial risk, and she had sworn not to do anything that would risk her getting arrested.

But, like she'd said, things had changed.

The edge of Abigail's lip curled, as though Mikka had said something amusing.

"Oh, I might have forgotten to mention one *teeny* important detail." She held up her thumb and forefinger to emphasize the 'teeny' part.

"And that is?"

"The crop is from the *Infinity*."

Mikka tried to hide the catching of her breath, but there was no way to contain the sudden flash of excitement in her eyes.

"*How* is that possible?"

It had been nearly seven years since the *Infinity* had mysteriously shut down. The station had been placed under a quarantine order, and within a year, it was sent hurtling to the Earth's surface. All that remained was a field of debris that ships still needed to navigate around to this day.

The Syndicate had never released the official reports of how many people had died in the accident, but it had to be tens of thousands. Any specifics about what happened on the station, including how many people it had housed, were shrouded in secrecy.

Infinity-grown Corielus seed had been a highly sought-after black-market item in the twelve months that followed the station's destruction, but eventually, even that had dried up, and it had been years since Mikka had seen the last batch. If Abigail was right and the *Eclipse* was host to a large consignment of the crop, it would be worth *millions* of credits. The commission alone would mean Mikka could both pay off her debts and help her mother.

They could also help a lot of people.

And if there was a way Mikka could acquire some of that Corielus for herself, it would be life changing.

"I can tell by the look on your face you're on board," Abigail observed.

"Not so fast. I have a few questions."

"Such as?"

"How did this shipment go under the scanner for so long? Who is hiring you to retrieve it, and how did they find out about it? And how did it end up on another station?"

"All I know is this." Abigail snapped her fingers in the air, and it took a moment for Mikka to realize she was trying to get Leslie's attention. "A double shot of rum here, Leslie. Please."

"*Please?* I don't know what you're trying to prove to this young lady, Monroe, but pretending to have manners won't get you nowhere." Leslie winked at Mikka.

"Monroe," Mikka cut in, trying not to think about what the bartender was implying. "*Focus.*"

"I need to be properly lubricated to tell you this, love."

Leslie set a glass filled with dark liquid before Abigail, who shot it back the moment it touched the bar.

"There was one shipment scheduled to leave the *Infinity*

moments before it went dark. The ship chartered for the transport was named *Double Circle* and is said to have been filled to the brim with Corielus seed, meant to be taken to one of Earth's orbital ports. But the *Circle* disappeared, and nobody has heard from it since."

Mikka's hope deflated. This wasn't a lead. This was a dead end.

"I've heard this tale," she groused. "The *Double Circle* is an urban legend—nothing more. That legend's been flying since the station went dark. If there ever was a ship with that name, it went down with the station. I've heard enough tales of merchants, pirates, and opportunists wasting their savings—and their lives—hunting for a treasure that doesn't exist."

"Are you calling me a liar?"

"I'm calling you misinformed."

"Love. I know it sounds fantastical; I didn't believe it at first, either. But I've made contact with the captain of the *Double Circle*. He's been living on the *Eclipse* for the past seven years and has agreed to split the profits from the seed."

"Now I *know* you're full of shit. Why would this missing captain contact *you*? What could you *possibly* have that someone aboard a station might need?"

A wide smile spread across Abigail's face. "Freedom."

CHAPTER TWENTY-FOUR

Mikka

Shackleton City — The Velvet Underground

MIKKA SHOT BACK the glass of rum Leslie had set down in front of her and coughed as it burned the back of her throat. Abigail was right: it was better than the whiskey, but barely. The drink tasted of molasses, with a hint of ash. Once she caught her breath, she carried on with her questioning.

"You're saying the pilot of the *Double Circle* escaped the *Infinity* with a hold full of Corielus seed, flew to the *Eclipse* undetected, boarded without being logged in their records, and has been living there for *seven* years? Yet, in that amount of time, he's never found a way to leave the station, but somehow got a hold of you—a pirate without a ship—begging you not only to help him leave, but in exchange, he'll give you a cut of one of the most highly sought-after products in the system."

Abigail pursed her lips and lifted her eyes, as though deep in thought, considering the breakdown Mikka had recited.

"Yes, love. That sounds about right."

Mikka put a hand to her temple and sighed. So much for a backup plan.

"Listen," she said, pinching the bridge of her nose between her thumb and forefinger. "It just so happens I've just secured another delivery to *Eclipse*. I had hoped to kill two birds with one stone. I don't think I need to tell you that I think this lead of yours is bogus, but I'm willing to take you there. If it turns out to be for real . . . jackpot! If not, no harm done, but I will expect some form of payment for transporting this crackpot of yours off the station."

"See? Nothing to lose! Come, we don't have much time." Abigail stood from her barstool. "Leslie, add this lovely lady's drink to my tab."

Leslie looked up from the drink she was mixing. "One of these days, you're going to have to clear that tab, Abi. Syndicate's been on my ass about rent, and I can't run this bar on charm and good-will for much longer."

"I'll have it covered by the end of the week, love. Mark my word."

Leslie gave her a two-fingered salute. "The word of a pirate. Not much to go on. Don't die on me, captain."

Abigail ignored the woman, dragging Mikka by the arm across the bar. "I assume your ship is ready to fly?"

Mikka stumbled over a crack in the floor between the bar and the tunnels outside. "What's the rush?"

"We need to be en route to the *Eclipse* by the rendezvous time the *Black Swan* had been scheduled to arrive. We've only got a few hours."

"*A few hours?* Even if we hurry, we'll barely be able to *launch* within a few hours. We've got to ensure the ship is loaded, perform pre-launch checks, print off a new manifest . . ."

"I'll just need to call ahead, love. I've got the paperwork for the pickup already. As long as we launch before the scheduled time, we can make arrangements."

Mikka sighed. Nothing today was going to be easy. "My ship is ready. But . . . we're going to need a navigator."

"Oh, love! Don't tell me you're going to convince that charming lass we came here with to fly with me again? You'll be lucky if she doesn't shove us both out the airlock for even suggesting it."

Mikka chuckled. "Don't worry about Ki; I'll handle her. She has her reasons for being wary. Good ones, too, if you ask me. But she'll be worth the headache. There are few people I trust with my life—and she's one of them."

SHACKLETON CITY — *Lunar Port A11*

"NO *BLOODY* WAY!"

Kiara stood, hands on hips, face-to-face with Mikka and Abigail, just off the loading docks of the Lunar port. "I'm not getting back on board with *her!*"

They were back at the docking bay where they had left the *Redemption.* Security guards stood watch from above, guarding the dozens of shuttles that lined the port. More ships whirred overhead as they came and went. Muffled shouts from ground crew teams and announcements over the port sound system echoed through the expansive terminal, bouncing off the infrastructure that extended skyward to the force field and beyond into the stars.

"What happened to 'not having to worry about it?' Do you remember saying that?"

How many lifetimes had Mikka gone through since those words came out of her mouth?

"Listen, Ki. A lot has changed."

"You two sort this out," Abigail said. "I'll make myself scarce for a jiffy. Just don't take too long."

Abigail produced another apple from within her cloak and took a bite as she swaggered down the terminal walkway, swinging her staff around rather than using it for the support it appeared she needed. The woman aimlessly watched passersby in the bay in the same way she'd scanned the Velvet Underground during her card game: discreetly, but with purpose.

"Is she drunk?" Kiara asked.

Mikka sighed. "Probably." To be honest, she was feeling the warmth of the rum filling her head as well, and she wondered for a moment if it was clouding her judgment. "But I am convinced at least some of it is for show. She's got more wits about her than she lets on."

Stars, I hope that's true.

"Seriously, Mikka, what the hell are you thinking?"

Mikka put her hands up defensively. "I know, I know. But how have the last twenty-four hours been for you? Because mine have been a total disaster."

She recounted everything that had transpired to her since they'd parted ways, from the break-in to finding her mother lying bleeding on the floor, to Tabitha bringing in the Syndicate Front and the meeting with David Aries.

"You weren't kidding." Kiara whistled. "Mikka, I'm so sorry!"

"Don't worry about it. There's nothing that can be done, and nothing that wasn't the result of the choices I've made. But I *need* to get help for my mother."

"So, why bring the pirate into this? That Front commander said he'd get your mother the help she needs."

"For starters," Mikka said, "have you ever met a SF officer you trust? Aries isn't telling me everything, and it's odd that after seven years, he's calling in this 'favor.' I don't like it."

"He needs something delivered off the books. What's the big deal?"

"It's too easy. He calls in a pirate he happened to meet at a scrapyard? He follows me for seven years to deliver a box to a space station?

"I can only think of three possible motives. One: he could be telling the truth. Doubtful—I'm sure there's more he's not telling me, but the basics, maybe. He might just simply need a privateer. If it's true that there's dissension growing within the Syndicate, it makes it more likely that he'd want someone to act covertly. It's possible he doesn't interact with enough people willing to work off the books. He saw an opportunity and seized it. If that's the case, then we get paid as a contractor—an unscrupulous one, maybe, but as long as we're hauling supplies and not killing people, I could probably live with that. In this case, David will probably keep my mother comfortable for as long as we're on his payroll. It's his incentive to keep me in line."

"But what if we get caught? He's not going to back you up. That'd be the whole point of hiring a rogue—deniability."

Mikka chuckled. "I didn't become the most elusive pirate in orbit for nothing."

"You might be willing to take that risk, hun, but I've got three kids. I don't know if I'm ready to live a life of constantly looking over my shoulder."

"I'd understand that, Ki. If this isn't what you want to sign up for, I won't hold a grudge if you want to walk away and have nothing to do with this."

"What are the other possibilities?" Kiara asked.

"Two: there's the possibility he's sending us on a suicide mission. Likely not this one—I can't see how a delivery to an orbital station is anything but a trial run. But there's a real chance he has a task lined up that will cost us our lives. He's rid of me, and he'll have no obligation to take care of my mother afterward."

Kiara nodded, considering. "A reasonable concern. What's the third?"

"Three: he's using me as bait. For what, I haven't quite worked out yet, but you don't climb from junkyard watchdog to commanding an SF lunar district in seven years without some level of ambition. I'm just a pawn in a bigger scheme of his, and it wouldn't surprise me if I'm being set up to serve as an out for a separate plan. Listen, I totally understand that this is a huge ask. If you want to walk away now, I won't blame you, but I could sure use your help. If this goes sideways, I'm going to need someone I can trust to be on my side."

Kiara continued to nod, rubbing her face with an open palm. "That doesn't answer the original question, though. What does *she* have to do with anything?"

"I needed a contingency plan. David's offering a way to help my mother, and I owe it to her to take it. But I don't trust him, and I don't want to be stuck without another way out. Monroe's quest likely won't amount to anything, but if she's right, I could provide for my mother for a very long time. I could give her access to the only medicine that has ever been effective, plus enough credits to live on the Rim. And it won't matter what Commander Aries has planned."

"So, you want to invite the pirate along, but you don't even know if she's telling the truth?"

"*She* believes it's the truth. She's convinced *Double Circle*'s Corielus shipment is on the *Eclipse*. But you know that's an urban legend. More than likely, someone's pulling a fast one on her."

"What are the chances *she's* being led into a trap?"

"Then the Syndicate take her, and you get your wish."

Kiara shook her head. "That's if it's the Syndicate after her. You don't know how many other enemies she's made. We've only just met her. I really don't like this."

"I know," Mikka said. "I'm not expecting you to. You're an excellent navigator. I'm sure you'll land another gig easily."

"'Easy' is a relative term." Kiara placed a hand on Mikka's shoulder. "You've stuck your neck out for me more times than I can count . . ." A thin grin curled upward on her lips. "This *is* a bad idea, but someone's got to save your ass when you land it in hot water."

The *Redemption* stood silent behind them, its cargo hatch open. A small pallet, bearing a plastic crate wrapped in another layer of protective plastic film, was being rolled inside.

"You have no idea what Commander Aries wants delivered?" Kiara asked. "I can't see anything of importance being shipped to one of the FLOW stations. They have no influence over the Syndicate. Trees, crops, recycled garbage . . . I don't see a motive there."

"I don't know, and I don't care. Let's just get it there and get paid."

"Have you two got it sorted yet?" Abigail strolled up the promenade, staff in hand, her cloak lifting behind her. "If so, destiny awaits."

Something still didn't sit right. Mikka was already regretting asking the pirate to tag along. This would either be one of the best, or one of the worst, decisions she had ever made.

CHAPTER TWENTY-FIVE

Django
Eclipse

ADVENTURE.

The word spun through Django's mind like a black hole, its gravity sucking in all other thoughts and leaving the rest of his mind void. He had never asked, nor wanted, to go on an adventure. Venturing to the B-Ring had been more excitement than he'd ever need. The thought of leaving the station made him sick. His place was in the Agricultural District—or so he'd thought. And even though it had been *his* suggestion to follow Uncle Marvin's instruction, his stomach roiled nonetheless.

The door to Eventide's quarters had barely hissed shut behind them when a pretentious voice grated against every one of Django's nerves.

"What's *he* doing here?" Faron stood ten feet away, arms crossed, a sneer of derision on his face. "We aren't supposed to be associating with *anyone*, never mind a D-Ringer."

Django tightened his jaw and clenched his fists, wondering if this was when he'd finally get to deck the technician. The only thing holding him back was knowing it wouldn't win him any points with Eventide, but it was a weak hold, and it wouldn't take much for that string to snap.

"Django came to see me before the shuttle closed," Eventide said calmly, with much more sweetness than Django cared for.

There's nothing between us.

"The shuttle closed hours ago," Faron said. "You can't bring Jancy to the party, and he sure as hell can't stay here."

The party. Django had forgotten all about the celebration Eventide had mentioned at his sister's wedding. She had invited him to come meet her work friends.

Probably all as charming as Faron.

"He didn't know the rules had changed. I'm escorting him back to the terminal."

"If they catch you . . ." Faron glanced at Django with concern. "You know what the consequences will be."

"There's a difference between escorting and fraternizing," Eventide reasoned. "It's not like we're sitting down to lunch."

"He's not even supposed to be in our Ring! InterRing travel has been restricted."

"As you've already pointed out. But nobody told him that until he got here," she lied. "I'm going to get him back home. Don't worry, I can meet you at the party afterward."

"We should hand him over to security," he said.

"There's security at the terminal, isn't there? Let's leave it up to them to decide what to do with him."

Faron shot Django an annoyed glance, but Eventide's response seemed to satisfy him.

"Very well," he said. "I suppose they will."

"Come on," Django whispered. "We've got to get going."

"Yes," Faron said. "We should get going. The longer he's here, the harder it will be to send him back."

"'We?'" Django said. "You're not coming with us."

"Listen, everybody knows you're both from the D-Ring.

Nobody's going to believe you're being escorted. I'm coming with you."

"Faron, that's not necessary," Eventide said. "Really, I've got this."

"It wasn't a suggestion," Faron replied tersely. "I'm not going to lose you because of a misunderstanding with another tech."

Django fought to maintain his composure. *Lose her? You don't have* her, *buddy.*

Eventide seemed to ponder the suggestion, her hands twitching around the arms of her sweater where her playing cards were held, as though mentally shuffling them.

"Fine."

"*Evie!*" Django hissed. There was nothing more he could do without saying too much. How were they going to get to the shuttle bay with Mr. Tagalong? Would Eventide still board the train with him? He wasn't going to leave her behind. Not for anything. And certainly not for *him.*

Eventide shot Django a glare that clearly told him to shut up.

"Faron's right," she said. "With two of us, it will be clearer that this is an escort."

Django's mind froze. He didn't know what to say to counter the idea, or what other solution he could have provided that could have changed things, other than landing a fist against the pretty boy's jawline.

And that likely wouldn't improve their situation.

Defeated, he followed Eventide, with Faron trailing behind them.

IT DIDN'T TAKE LONG to navigate the B-Ring halls to the InterRing shuttle. Unlike the station in the D-Ring, only three guards stood watch, but they didn't need more: their presence enveloped the space, creating a barrier before the transit's turnstiles. There was no crowd here clamoring to board. Nobody from the B-Ring was interested in traveling to the lower decks, and as far as Django knew, nobody traveled to the A-Ring who didn't live there.

"Let me do the talking," Eventide whispered, low enough so Faron wouldn't hear. "No matter how they act or what happens, don't say anything. Don't react. Don't even meet their gaze."

Django wrinkled his brow. The clock on the wall flashed 8:30 p.m. They had just over an hour to get to the cargo bay, and, somehow, they had to ditch Faron along the way. He only hoped Nova would be at their quarters, packing her belongings, as was promised. If not, it was going to be difficult to get her and then to the shuttle bay in time.

Then they had to figure out how to get onto the ship. From everything Marvin had told him, they needed special clearance to even get close to the shuttle bay. The restrictions were meant as a defense against contaminating the ships that were headed toward a still-healing Earth. Now though, Django realized the true reason must have been to mask what lay outside the cargo bay door.

One step at a time, he thought. *First, let's get out of the B-Ring in one piece.*

Eventide strode toward the guards as Django slunk behind her. He did his best to remain invisible—not a threat, not someone who should be noticed or even looked at. Someone in tow of an official.

Not content to be part of the background, Faron pushed past Django and joined Eventide in her march toward the guards.

"Hold up!" The nearest guard lifted a hand as they approached.

Monitors flashed the same warning they had earlier that afternoon:

FOR YOUR SAFETY - SHUTTLE TRANSPORT SERVICE

BETWEEN RINGS IS NOW RESTRICTED. THANK YOU FOR YOUR COOPERATION.

Django tried not to stare at the message; tried to look natural boarding the transport. But in reality, it was impossible not to stand out; his drab D-Ringer clothes and flat hair made sure of that. In the safety of Eventide's quarters, he had forgotten how the B-Ring made him feel.

But it was different this time.

Last night, the halls had made him feel dirty, as though he was unclean; a tainted stain standing in the presence of the manicured. Even earlier that day, he'd felt as though he was muddying the sanctity of the Upper Ring.

Now, the scent of disinfectant and sanitizer made his skin crawl in another way, as though it might infect him. The lies and deceit that flowed down from the nooks and crannies of the B-Ring's corridors and halls, the secrets that hid in the consoles and behind the façade presented on the viewports, were no longer hidden from him.

He smiled despite the feeling. Though many of the B-Ringers he passed oozed arrogance and derision toward himself and his home, they were just as deceived as he was. Other than the technicians, the residents of the B-Ring were just as blind to the reality outside the station as he had been.

Yesterday, when he'd caught a glimpse of what truly lay behind the viewport, what the Earth and its orbit truly were, Django didn't even have the capacity to believe it. He had been so programmed to follow the routine set up for him that he had completely overlooked it had all been part of the ruse. Everything he had ever done, or had ever known, had been based on a lie.

"Good evening, sir." Eventide's words, directed to the nearest guard, roused Django from his thoughts. The tone of her voice had changed, its pitch softening, her stride slowing, and she swayed slightly as she stepped closer to him.

"Identification, please." The guard looked Eventide up and down, lingering longer than he should have. He had to have been nearly twice Eventide's age; old enough to be her father. He brought a finger to his thick mustache, running his fingers over it. He could have been scratching an itch or, failing that, revealing a nervous tick. His bushy eyebrows matched the hair above his lip, nearly growing into the white uniform hat that had been perched a bit too low on his head.

"Of course." Eventide lifted her forearm, allowing the guard to scan it with a portable reader.

"Where are you headed?

"I'm escorting this rogue back to the D-Ring. He didn't hear the announcement. Luckily, I ran into him before he could do any damage."

The guard didn't even glance toward Django. "I commend your intentions, Miss Rossi, but I'm sorry—we have our orders. We're to take anyone without authorization into custody."

Faron's smug face turned up in an *I told you so* smirk.

Django's heart rate quickened, and he silently prayed that Eventide had something clever up her sleeve. If they missed the shuttle, he didn't know if they would get another chance.

"*I* have the authorization to travel, and I'm escorting him." Eventide stated. "It's just a quick shuttle ride and then he'll never venture this way again. I'll travel with him to supervise until he arrives at his destination."

Django could feel the eyes of the lead guard on him, sizing him up.

"You are free to travel between the B and D decks as much as you like, miss, but this D-Ringer will have to come with us. My hands are tied."

"Are you sure about that?" Eventide lowered her voice to a near whisper, just loud enough that Django could make it out. She reached out to the guard, her fingers tracing the muscles along his forearm, over his bicep, and to his shoulder before she leaned in and whispered something in his ear.

Django could tell she uttered a few sentences, but he was unable to hear them. The guard's eyes widened, and a devious smile emerged. Django was suddenly glad he hadn't heard what she'd said. His heart sank at the prospect of what those words likely were, and a pang seized his heart that she hadn't directed them toward him.

It's a ruse, you idiot. She doesn't mean it.

"You heard the man," Faron said with an open scoff. "The boy's to be brought into custody. For heaven's sake, Eventide, don't make a scene."

"Well, in that case . . ." the guard said, with a victorious glance toward Faron and a curl that likely wouldn't leave his lips anytime soon. "Let them through, boys."

"You can't be serious," Faron muttered. "Officer, you cannot let them through! She's playing you."

Eventide shot the other technician a wide-eyed glare.

"But, sir, our orders were clear . . ." a younger guard protested.

"Orders that were left open to interpretation. *I'm* the commanding officer, and you follow my lead. This scum is not supposed to be in the B-Ring. Since he's under the watch of a technician, we'll let them through *this* time."

The two lower-ranking guards gave each other an uncertain glance as they stood to the side, their hands never leaving their weapons, as though afraid Django and Eventide might use their leniency as an excuse to attack.

"That is not how this is supposed to work." Faron took a step forward, reaching for the guard as if he was going to physically assert his will on him. Without hesitation, the guards drew their weapons and aimed them at Faron's chest.

Faron halted, his hands flying skyward as he realized his error.

Django couldn't help but feel more than a smidge of satisfaction at the technician being put in his place.

"Technician or not, take one more step and we'll put you under arrest."

"I wasn't—" Faron began, but a stern look from the guard shut him up.

With the path now clear, Django and Eventide stepped past the stationed guards, whose weapons were still aimed at Faron. The tram pulled up as the front guard stepped back. Django breathed a sigh of relief.

I can't believe that worked! We're going to make it. And we get to leave the tagalong here.

The guard gave Eventide a final once-over, placing his hands on hips and grinning, pleased with himself.

Faron shifted his weight from foot to foot, as though itching to find a bathroom. His face grew more agitated by the second. "Listen, you *can't* let them through! D-Ringers are not allowed to be here. And she's a D-Ringer, just like that one."

"*She's* a technician, same as you," Django sneered.

"She'll never be the same as me," Faron retorted, a satisfied smirk on his face. "She's proven that here. She'll always be a dirty D-Ringer. Just like you."

Eventide gasped.

"I tried to give you a chance, Eventide. I even agreed to be your training partner. Do you know how much flak I get for sticking up for you? What a waste! I guess you can't take the dirt out of the dirt-ringer, after all."

Rage filled Django's bones. It took everything in his power not to attack the arrogant prick, though it helped that the guards' weapons were already trained on Faron.

The guard ignored the quips and kept waving a hand for them to carry on. "I look forward to seeing you back . . . Wait a minute . . ."

The guard's long-barreled energy weapon suddenly blocked Django's path, stopping him in his tracks. Django grimaced.

"You're the kid that assaulted Officer Harrison yesterday." It wasn't a question.

The hair on the back of Django's neck stood straight. The transport doors hissed open, only a few dozen yards away. They were so close.

Faron snickered, but the other guards' weapons didn't move.

"Look, lady," the guard said, "there's a lot I'd be willing to do to bring you back to my quarters, but if I let this kid go, I'll be sent out the airlock."

Django gave his head a shake. This wasn't the way this was going to end. Something in him snapped. For every lie Admin had fed him throughout his life, he owed it to himself, to Eventide and Nova, to see that they got off the station and learn the truth for themselves.

"Eventide." Django heard his own voice as though it came from someone else. It was distant, confident, and steady, as though the person who spoke believed their next move was the right one.

That certainly didn't sound like him.

"*Run!*"

Django threw his elbow into the guard's gut, disarming him. He took the gun and jammed the butt into the guard's forehead, knocking him down, then tossed the weapon to Eventide in one fluid movement.

Reaching to his hip and beneath his shirt, Django grabbed his father's pistol and raised it at one of the other two guards, who still had their weapons trained on Faron.

"What the hell do you think you're doing?" Faron took two steps in their direction before the pulse of a guard's weapon sent him to the ground, stunned.

Two down.

Django fired at the guard who'd just shot Faron, but the shot went wide.

Eventide fired two shots before either guard could react, taking them both out.

Django had to do a double take. The friend he had grown up with looked more confident with a weapon than he could ever have imagined. She suddenly seemed older, and much more experienced. And he was just a kid playing with a toy gun.

"We need to move," Eventide said.

"We're just going to leave the bodies like this?"

"The shuttle isn't going to sit there all night! *Let's go!*"

Out of the corner of his eye, Django caught movement. The sound of a weapon's discharge zipped beside him. Instinctively, he turned and pulled the trigger on his own weapon, praying that its energy beams would connect with his target.

Faron fell again, face-planting the floor, his weapon skidding across the tile.

He couldn't say the bastard didn't deserve it. *Did he?*

After a short second, the man's chest rhythmically moved up and down. So, he wasn't dead.

Eventide let out a cry of pain.

Django immediately turned. Eventide was on the floor, curled in a ball.

Shit. No!

He raced to her, but even before he got there, she was moving. She slumped as she attempted to push herself up, hissing and grunting.

"Easy! You're hurt!" Django reached his hand out to help her up.

Thank the stars she's alive.

As she grabbed hold, he saw her shoulder. The arm of her black zip-up sweatshirt had melted away. Smoke from the energy weapon's blast still rose from the singed edges of what was left.

Blood also coated the edge of the ripped fabric and dripped down the arm below a black and red bloody mess of a wound. The smell of charred meat was unmistakable.

Django thought he was going to be sick.

"I'll be okay," she grimaced. "But we need to get on that shuttle! Come on!"

Without waiting for a response, Eventide closed the gap between her and the transit, bolting for the door that was already closing.

She grabbed it with her good hand and stopped it from closing, taking advantage of the transit's built-in safety mechanisms.

Django glanced at the four men slumped on the floor.

Things had just gotten extremely complicated.

CHAPTER TWENTY-SIX

Django
Eclipse

DJANGO GRIPPED the bottom of the shuttle seat so tightly his knuckles turned white.

Three guards were either dead or unconscious because of him. Even though he hadn't been the one to pull the trigger on two of them, it was his actions that had led to their demise. It wasn't their deaths that bothered him as much as what it meant for him and Eventide. There was no going back now. Faron was alive, so there would be no doubt about who was to blame.

The two friends sat in silence across from each other as the shuttle moved between the B and C decks. Thankfully, they were the only passengers on the transport.

Eventide cradled her wound with one hand. Her sweater had been torn, her pink skin exposed, the red markings of the burn marring its surface. She stared at the floor; at the hexagonal metal plating lining its surface. Under the paneling, artificial gravity plates kept the transport's passengers upright, despite being outside of the Rings' gravitational pulls.

Django doubted gravity plating was what Eventide was concerned with.

"We're going to make it," Django stated, trying to feign confidence he didn't feel. "We have a plan. We've just got to see it through."

Eventide breathed deeply but didn't respond. For a moment, Django thought he spotted tears forming in her eyes, but she quickly blinked them back and straightened her posture.

She stared out the shuttle's viewports as the station's core axis passed them by. She shook her head and brought a hand to her mouth, biting on the purple nail of her forefinger.

"I thought he was my friend," she said flatly.

Django didn't know what to say. *"I could have told you he wasn't,"* didn't seem to be the appropriate response, and he didn't want to say *"I'm sorry"*—because he wasn't. Though he felt bad that Faron had hurt her, both physically and emotionally, the man had proven himself to be the tool Django always knew he'd been.

How deeply Eventide was hurt by that action, he'd likely never know, but one thing Django promised himself was that he'd never hurt his friend in that way—whether she would ever accept him as anything more or not.

He moved to place a hand on her knee to offer her comfort, but she shrugged it off with a shake of her head. She didn't meet his eye.

Eventide had never been the physical type, so the shrug off didn't bother Django. Knowing that he didn't know how to help affected him more. He didn't know what he could offer her that would provide the support she needed—other than to be the friend he had always been. Maybe that was enough.

Django's heart raced as they pulled into the C-Ring. The transit car stopped, and its doors opened to the station. He expected nothing less than a legion of guards to storm the car.

Through the shuttle's viewport, he could see the line of white uniforms preventing passengers from boarding.

Django sank into his seat, doing his best to avoid being seen through the glass. He didn't want to risk being spotted by either the guards or the crowd. All it would take was one shout of *"Why do they get to ride?"* or a guard turning in their direction to blow their cover.

Eventide's fingers fidgeted over the weapon she had held on to, moving over its clean white surface in a rhythmic pattern that was comforting to watch. Every once in a while, her fingers twitched toward the hidden pocket in her sleeve, as though she wanted to grab the deck of cards within but wouldn't allow herself. Her hands mesmerized Django as they passed over the weapon's surface. The same delicacy and skill she demonstrated when handling the cards seemed to transfer to shooting. He couldn't explain why, but somehow the dexterity made him even more attracted to her and, at the same time, made her seem that much more out of reach.

His father's pistol hung at his side; an antique when compared to the weapons the security guards held. So far, Django had fired a couple of rounds and had stunned Faron, but he didn't have the finesse Eventide did; he'd just been pointing wildly and pulling the trigger. As impressive as he may have looked, he might as well have been shooting finger guns. He prided himself on being responsible, on being mature. He had worked hard; had earned commendations in his trade. Heck, Admin had even offered him his parents' quarters in anticipation of his success. Yet, sitting next to Eventide, he had never felt more like a child in an adult's world.

The holo-screens within the transport were either dark or displayed the now-familiar travel restrictions, an intrusive reminder of their trespasses.

Moments passed before the train doors hissed closed once

again and the shuttle continued its journey to the bottom of the station.

Django's stomach still roiled. Something about the artificial gravity and magnetic fields of the shuttle system wasn't sitting well, but the anxiety did him no favors, either.

"What are we going to do when we get there?" he asked, breaking the silence that had formed between them since they'd boarded. "Even if the alarm doesn't sound, we're going to be faced with the same wall of guards I encountered when I left."

"Just follow me. I'll get us where we need to go."

"I hope it goes better than last time."

He hadn't meant to be snide and regretted the words as soon as he'd said them. It was true: Eventide's flirting hadn't been the solution they needed, but she was the only friend he had at the moment, and she was trying.

She shot him an annoyed glare. "If you have any brilliant ideas, *please* share them. Just remember, we're in this mess because *you've* developed a habit of attacking station guards."

"You're right," Django admitted. "I shouldn't have said that. I'm sorry."

"Just stay close and try not to draw attention. The guards are looking for reasons to be aggressive here, so we'll need to be extra cautious."

Eventide stood as the shuttle slowed to a halt. She motioned for Django to follow and put a finger to her lips.

As the doors hissed open, the sound of the angry mob flooded in.

Eventide didn't hesitate in stepping out onto the landing and skirting around to the back of the train. Django followed, one foot striking the cool metal platform, then the other. He was granted one final step before the sirens began to wail.

"*Shit*," Eventide hissed. "They found the guards. Move! *Now!*"

Red lights flashed as though there was another hull breach. The pitch of the sound was higher, but if he hadn't known what was happening, Django didn't think he would have noticed the difference.

The station guards on the concourse looked around, momentarily confused. The crowd beyond them went from agitated to irate, though their roar was immediately drowned out by the alarm.

Eventide pulled Django behind the train, down a few feet onto the tracks that fed the line. A final glance at an overhead monitor confirmed their reality.

Django's face stared back at him from the transit lobby display screens, tired and sullied. He recognized the image as his official identification photo, taken earlier that year. Beside his likeness were his name, a brief description, and more text that flashed too quickly for him to read.

The image then flashed to the face of Commander Benson.

Feeling sufficiently hidden behind a large pillar, both Django and Eventide paused.

"Citizens of the D-Ring, this is your station commander, Roy Benson. As though your Ring hasn't already been through enough this quarter, I am afraid I once again need to be the bearer of bad news. It has been many years since one of our citizens has been the victim of a homicide. However, today, that reassurance has come to an end. This evening, near the transit station located on the B-Ring, two security guards were shot and killed while performing their routine duties."

Django's face returned to the display.

"This man, Django Alexander, is a resident of the D-Ring. Perhaps you know him. He is wanted for illegally trespassing in the B-Ring, aggravated assault, kidnapping, and murder. We are seeking your assistance in finding this man. His target was another of your citizens; a woman who had shown great promise, having advanced her position to station technician."

Django's face faded from the display and was replaced by Eventide's. Even her wanted photo was gorgeous.

Something didn't add up, though. Somehow, Eventide wasn't being implicated in the attack on the guards. He'd gladly take the fall for her if that's what it took, but there was no way she'd managed to remain above reproach. Between Faron's presence and station security footage, Eventide was either being goaded into returning, or there was another nefarious reason for the claim.

"We believe Django Alexander to be armed and dangerous. Because of this, you should not attempt to approach him yourself. If you see either of these individuals, or have any information regarding their whereabouts, please contact station security immediately."

Eventide moved before the report finished. And, considering everyone else in the station was now likely glued to the displays, Django agreed it was an opportune time to keep moving.

Django didn't understand everything that was happening just yet, but he knew Commander Benson was behind it. He was behind the reported hull breaches, and he was choosing to keep the wider station in the dark about their situation. He just couldn't figure out why.

On the other side of the tracks, an unassuming gray door was barely visible in the shadows. A "RESTRICTED ACCESS" sign flashed on the door's keypad, but a quick scan of Eventide's forearm was all it took for the lock to click open.

"Won't they be able to tell you opened the door?" Django asked. "They'll know where we are."

Eventide nodded. "They will. That's why we've got to move fast. Lucky for us these tunnels are a maze. We'll hopefully be able to bide ourselves some time if we can keep moving."

The clamor of the shuttle platform disappeared as the metal

door closed behind them. Before them, a dark hallway, dimly illuminated only by computer panels and failing strip lighting, stretched endlessly.

"What is this place?" Django asked.

"Maintenance shafts."

"I thought that's what the lookout tunnels were for?" The two of them had explored the walkways and catwalks that crisscrossed the station as children. Django didn't recall seeing any passageway that resembled the space they were in now.

"That's part of it, but these are meant to hide us from public view. Technicians use these shafts to make repairs and carry out diagnostics without station citizens getting in the way." Eventide sighed. "They're also used to escort those who've seen the viewport malfunctions to the airlocks."

Mom. Dad. Uncle Marvin.

Django steeled his mind to the tragedies. He couldn't let their deaths slow them down. If anything, he needed to reach down and use the pain as motivation to get off the station.

But there was one thing he needed to know.

"Do they make the technicians . . . *murder* them?" He hesitated at the word, but there was no point; that was what had happened. They were murdered, their only crime seeing through the lies that Benson told them. Their punishment was death.

"There are people we call Coroners. They arrive on the scene before the technicians. We saw them escorting people out of the wedding. They do the dirty work."

Django cleared his throat and breathed a sigh of relief. He didn't know why, but it was reassuring to think that Eventide wouldn't ever have been the one to perform the heinous task.

"We're headed to Shuttle Bay Eight?" Eventide asked.

"Yes," Django replied, working to keep up with Eventide's hurried pace. "But first, we need to stop at my quarters to get Nova."

Eventide stopped so suddenly that Django nearly toppled over her. She flashed him a look of warning. "That's the first place the guards will look for you."

Django met Eventide's glare. He wasn't about to leave Eventide behind, but he couldn't forget about Nova.

"I have to try," he said. "I'm not leaving the station without her."

"How do you know she's even there?"

"She was scheduled to return to the quarters to pack up her things. With any luck, she'll still be there."

"With any luck, we won't get our asses handed to us." Eventide let out another sigh. "We don't have much room for error if that ship is supposed to leave at 9:45."

"We'll make it," he said. "We have to."

"We've got one shot at this, Django," she said. "Let's not screw it up."

CHAPTER TWENTY-SEVEN

Django
Eclipse

LIGHT from the main corridor streamed through a slit in the doorway. Django had his eye pressed to the space, monitoring the situation outside the maintenance halls. As Eventide had predicted, guards swarmed his quarters.

Patrols came and went, their arms loaded with his family's few possessions. Their datapads, electronics, and notebooks were the most prominent items. There were others, too, but what torqued Django's veins the hardest were the memories he knew he'd never be able to replace and would likely never see again. Whatever history his family had maintained after they'd left Earth was on a stash of hard drives now on their way to an unknown destination, likely to be processed, probably to be destroyed.

Django repeatedly flexed his fingers into fists, mentally letting go of another piece of normality he hadn't realized he had been about to lose. He was leaving this place, anyway; he had to let it go.

But where's Nova?

He hadn't been told who her adoptive family was, so if she wasn't here, he had no way of tracking her down.

"If she doesn't show up soon," he thought out loud, "we'll have to decide whether or not to leave without her."

"I know it'd be tough," Eventide ventured, "but the fact that they've bothered to put her with another family tells me they aren't going to kill her. The official record shows she wasn't near the initial accident. If she keeps quiet about what your uncle said, she might go on to live a normal life."

Normal.

"What's 'normal' anymore?" he asked absently. "Getting spat on by B-Ringer guards while growing their food and fueling the lies of the A-Ring?"

"You were content with it until a couple of days ago," she reasoned.

I was fine with it until this morning . . .

Until they took everything from me. Until I accepted it was all a lie.

"She's lost everything, the same as me."

Another group of sentries passed the doorway, and Django ducked back into the hall to avoid being seen. The longer he stood with his face peering through the crack, the more he risked being discovered. Four guards stood watch outside his quarters, but none were in direct line of sight of his hiding place.

The smaller frame of a youth rounded the corner. The teenager's dark hair and features stood in contrast to the blazing white uniforms of the guards. Django had to stop himself from rushing out and snatching her in his arms.

Nova walked independently, but close by her side was another familiar figure. He had hoped Officer Isaacs would be scouring the train terminal looking for him, but of course, security would want one of the only two officers who would recognize him on sight in the most likely spot of his appearance.

Django scanned the hall discreetly. Surely where Geoffrey Isaacs was, Officer Avery Inglewood wouldn't be far behind. But the woman was nowhere to be seen.

Nova appeared to be holding together well, considering the circumstances. She had loaded her arms with bags that Django could only guess contained her clothes and other belongings.

It's too bad she didn't grab the albums or hard drives.

There had to be some way to reach out to her, some way to grab her attention, but whatever he did risked attracting Issacs's attention. Somehow, he had to let her know their location.

Nova and Isaacs would pass by the doorway at any moment. If he was going to get her attention, it had to be quick. If only he had something he could use to attract her attention; something she would immediately recognize. Django did a quick search of his pockets for something that would be recognizable as his. He could throw down his ID card, but that was too much; it couldn't be anything so obvious.

His search came up short and he was about to give up on the idea until he looked at Eventide. The woman must have been more nervous than she'd let on; she'd unconsciously grabbed the deck of cards from the unburned sleeve of her hoodie. Silently, she shuffled with her good hand, and Django could practically see the thoughts spinning through her head with each pass of the deck.

"Quick, give me one of your cards," he said.

"What?" The shuffling stopped. "What for?"

"Trust me. Just hurry."

It was hard to judge her reaction in the dark, but Eventide offered a card in his direction.

Django grabbed the card and slid it through the doorway, leaving it faceup on the floor. The ace of spades.

Nova drew closer, only a few paces behind Isaacs. Django counted his lucky stars that his sister wasn't being closely monitored. This *had* to work.

He slid the door closed, minimizing the gap that would reveal their location, but not so much that the door would click shut. There were maintenance doors throughout the station, as Eventide had explained on their way through the corridors, but since most blended into the hallway walls, most people didn't realize they were there. The security guards might, though.

Django backed up a few feet and held his breath. There was always the possibility Isaacs would discover the card or that a guard would notice the door wasn't secure. His hand hovered over his weapon, just in case.

But with a half dozen guards several meters from their location, there was no way that a few rounds of blaster fire would go unnoticed.

The hall was insulated well enough that no sound from the main corridor leaked through. Only their own breathing made any noise.

"I hope you know what you're doing," Eventide whispered. "I want that card back."

Moments passed. It hadn't been long, but Nova should have passed their location by now She had only been steps away and should have found the card.

Django bit his tongue as he realized that the longer they waited, the greater the chance the card became a liability instead of an asset. If Nova didn't pick it up, someone else was bound to, and if they noticed the door wasn't sealed, they'd be discovered.

The metallic taste of blood coated Django's tongue, and only then did he realize he had bitten it in nervous anticipation.

His hand landed on his father's blaster as the door creaked open. Eventide didn't waste time in aiming her weapon at the door, precisely at the height where Isaacs's head would appear.

The figure who emerged, however, was a solid foot shorter. Big, unsure eyes landed on the weapon, and Nova froze as she assessed what she had walked into. She held a card in her hand, the ace of spades, and it sat in the air in front of her as though she wasn't sure if she should drop it and run or use it as a shield. Eventide holstered her gun and ran to Nova with outstretched arms.

The tension in Nova's body immediately released as Eventide grabbed her in a bear hug while simultaneously shutting the door behind her.

"What are you guys doing here?" Nova whispered. "Everyone's looking for you. The bulletins are saying you've been kidnapped!"

"I haven't been kidnapped," Eventide said. "But I'm sure security couldn't imagine any other reason why a technician would be accompanying a D-Ringer."

Nova flinched at the term. The answer seemed to satisfy her for the moment, but the look she gave Django was hesitant and fearful.

"Hey! Don't be like that," he said. "It's me!"

"Is it true you killed someone?"

Straight to the point—and to the gut.

Django hadn't had much time to process his feelings about the man who had died by his hand, but the uncertain look from his sister twisted a knife deep into his belly.

"You punched a guard when I was with you, and now you've *murdered* one, too?"

Stab. Twist.

"We have to move." He motioned to Eventide, who nodded.

"Can I have my card back?" Eventide reached out and plucked the ace of spades from Nova's hand, almost before the girl let go of it, and shuffled it back into the deck before, once again, making the cards disappear into her sleeve.

HEAVY FOOTSTEPS on the metal walkways pounded furiously as the trio jogged through the maintenance corridors. Echoes in the distant halls warned they weren't alone. Despite Eventide's assurances, patrols had discovered their location and were now in pursuit.

But Eventide still insisted that the maintenance network was expansive, weaving throughout the Ring in a maze of arteries feeding the station. It would take several teams of patrols hours to track them down. Fortunately, there were no cameras installed— almost as if Admin didn't want a record of the misdeeds that occurred within them.

Django fought the urge to constantly check his watch, but it was difficult. His sense of direction had been eradicated through the twists and turns of their journey, and there was no way to know how much further they had to go without badgering Eventide every few minutes. So, he trusted she was taking them on the most expedient route; trusted that they were moving away from the shouts and footsteps of the guards, who sounded as if they were behind every turn and intersection.

Nova had stopped asking questions and seemed to accept that her older brother was trying to help—though he still caught the occasional sidelong glance from her, surveying him as though he were a stranger. As if she were trying to figure out what to believe.

Is it true you killed someone?

How had so much changed in forty-eight hours?

After countless turns and thousands of steps, they finally came to a halt in front of a metal door. Nothing about this door appeared any different from the countless others they had passed along the way.

"This is it," Eventide said as she inspected the door's frame. She hesitated, as though momentarily uncertain. "Shuttle Bay Eight."

"'Shuttle bay?'" Nova asked. "What's going on? What are we doing?"

"We're leaving the station," Django said.

"We're . . . Wait . . . What?"

"Listen, Nova. It's a lot to explain, and we don't really have time. But the Station Guard are trying to kill me and Eventide. Uncle Marvin was right. We need to leave."

"But what about me?" Nova protested. "I don't want to leave."

"We don't have a choice," Django said. "They're trying to kill us."

"You *did* kill a guard, didn't you?" The accusation in her eyes left Django cold. "I'm not going anywhere with you! *My* life isn't in danger, and yours wouldn't be, either, if you'd control your temper!"

Django was about to argue, to explain it was self-defense, but Eventide put up a hand to stop him.

"*Shh!*" she whispered. "There's someone on the other side of this—"

Before she could finish, the door slid open. Bright light silhouetted the armored figure.

Django reached for his weapon.

"I wouldn't," a familiar voice warned.

CHAPTER TWENTY-EIGHT

Mikka
Eclipse

"I DON'T CARE who you say sent it! I don't have a scheduled delivery coming from a ship called the *Redemption*." The cargo bay worker swiped furiously at his datapad as though he might find their information by going through the inventory list faster. "I don't know who Commander Aries is, but Commander *Benson* has left no instructions for us about any arriving supplies."

Mikka knew she shouldn't have bothered to pull the Aries card—he wanted nothing to do with the shipment—but she at least thought he would have made arrangements.

"Like I said, we're here instead of the *Black Swan*. Look, I've got the delivery instructions, the ship's manifest, and an import code right here. You just have to scan it."

The crewman sighed. "I have an outgoing shipment for the *Black Swan*. There's nothing *incoming*. From anywhere."

The worker was young, but all station crew were. Rarely had Mikka seen a worker older than thirty on any of the eleven FLOW stations. Despite his age, his dark hair was already thinning, and the pockmarked skin on his scalp appeared infected and picked at.

The station workers were always short and scrawny, too. Their hollowed-out eyes reminded Mikka of laborers in the lava tunnels, except that FLOW station workers at least had a purpose about them.

"You have to realize, we don't *receive* any shipments from the surface. We ship *out*. What comes back are *empty* containers. Look, I shouldn't even be talking to you pilots. You know the drill: you dock, we load the goods, you take off, and repeat. No contact."

The guard was right. Mikka realized this was the first time she had actually been outside of her ship while in the station's shuttle bay, and she was only in the cargo hold. The *Redemption* sat waiting for the station's crew to load the Corielus crates meant for the *Swan* through a giant bay door. Before launch, the team would seal the cargo bay off, with them on the other side.

"Right, love," Abigail intervened. "It's the same this time. We're just unloading this pallet first, then taking the rest. After that, we'll be out of your hair."

The worker shook his head as he swiped the screen on his datapad a few more times, letting out an exasperated breath. "*Fine*. I'll get my crew to wheel it in. But I'm not going to have it clogging up my cargo bay! If it's not claimed within thirty days, I'm dumping it."

"Frankly, I don't care what you do with it," Mikka said breezily. "I was only paid to deliver it. That's where my concern ends."

"What about the goods we were supposed to pick up?" Abigail asked.

"Well, the order was for the *Black Swan*." The man sighed again. "Always at the end of my shift . . . This was Marvin's paperwork. I've never had a request to swap craft like this."

"As I told you earlier," Abigail persisted, "I'm the captain of the *Swan*. But we had an unfortunate accident. I'm sure if you bring Marvin here, he'll clear the whole matter up. I organized the collection with him directly."

The man sighed a third time and clipped his datapad to his belt, his face stiffening. "That's part of the problem. Marvin's dead."

"Dead?" Abigail asked. "I just talked to him two days ago. I was in contact with him while the *Black Swan* was going down."

"Hull breach. This meteoroid cluster's been a real bitch. We've had a half dozen ruptures in the last few weeks. Listen, this stuff has been sitting in the back for a long, *long* time. I'll be happy to have it out of here. Marvin was pretty adamant that we don't dispose of it since, you know, it's vital to rebuilding the atmosphere, apparently. But I'm surprised it finally hit your scanner. Since you were dealing with the big guy directly, I'll get the order loaded up for you. You should probably get back on board your ship, though. You two *really* shouldn't be out here."

The man unclipped his datapad once again as he turned and shouted orders at a few of his colleagues.

"So, now what?" Mikka asked, lowering her voice. "Your contact's dead. What do we do?"

Abigail's eyes lit up. "We take the seed and run."

"Don't get too excited." A man approached the women from behind. "I'm not dead yet."

THE MAN who stood before them was tall compared to the rest of the men Mikka had seen on the station. He seemed to be older than the cargo bay worker, but his hair was full, his skin smooth, and he had a boyish glint behind his tired eyes.

Mikka wasn't sure what she had expected, but it hadn't been the charming man she saw before her. She didn't know why, but she had imagined the man behind the legend of the *Double Circle* and its cargo to be less gallant.

The man introduced himself as Marvin Alejandro. Abigail took it all in her stride, but it was a lot for Mikka to digest.

"That worker just said you died in a hull breach?" Mikka asked.

"Let's get on board the ship, and I'll explain what I can." Marvin glanced over his shoulder nervously. "I don't want anyone seeing me."

The three of them—the ex-pirate, the pirate, and a dead man walking—boarded the *Redemption* and joined Kiara, who was waiting on the shuttle's bridge, hands behind her head and her feet resting on a console.

"That took long enough," Kiara said as the three boarded. "I was starting to wonder if they'd shoved you out the airlock. What took so long?"

"We were resurrecting the dead, it seems," Mikka snarked. She sealed the door between the cockpit and the cargo hold, closing the screen between the two.

"You want to explain to us how you survived a hull breach, love?" Abigail asked, a playful smile on her face. "That's a trick that could come in handy one day."

"*Hull breach*," Marvin scoffed. "There's never been a single damn hull breach on this station. We've been hitting some extra debris the last few weeks, but nothing the shields can't handle. The station Admin cry 'hull breach' every time they want to off someone."

Kiara's mouth was agape. "You mean they're *killing* people?"

"Standard station policy," Marvin replied. "Anyone who finds out the station's not alone, or that the Syndicate still lives planet-side, are sent out the airlock for a final look."

"So, the rumors are true . . ." Mikka's voice was hardly louder than a whisper. "Why do the people put up with it?"

"They don't know any better. They think they're still sending trees, seed, and animals down to Earth's surface to rebuild. It's likely their ancestors set up the ruse. Their viewports are all projecting a fake image of an Earth that's been dead for two hundred years. In the meantime, nobody's bothered to tell them the restoration work was completed decades ago."

"What purpose would the Syndicate have for keeping them in the dark?" Mikka asked.

"Why does the Syndicate do anything? Listen, we don't have time to get into the politics here; we can chat about that later. Right now, I just want to get out of here."

"What about everyone else? You've been here, what—seven years? There must be people here you care about."

"I've tried to keep quiet. Anyone who finds out the truth is killed. These are good people; I'd rather come back aboard with a strategy."

Marvin paused, lifting his eyes as though reconsidering the question. "There's one family I've considered my own. Most of them died two days ago. I tried to convince the survivors to join me, but, well . . . they didn't want to hear it. And I can't wait for them to come around. It might never happen. I was hoping to see them here, but I guess once people are set in their beliefs, it's hard to convince them they're wrong."

"Surely there's a way to let everyone on board know what's happening?" Kiara pressed. "Some way to let everyone see what's out there?"

Marvin scoffed. "What do you think happened to the *Infinity*? There was no malfunction there, either. The Syndicate killed power to the station, and everyone on board suffocated. Then they blew it out of the sky to hide the evidence. I was lucky enough to escape with my life, but then I got stuck here."

The bridge went silent as the three women looked at each

other. Abigail still maintained a smug look on her face, but Kiara's horrified reaction reflected Mikka's.

Blew it out of the sky.

Mikka's breath caught in her chest. The Syndicate was no friend of hers, but . . .

"There had to be *thousands* of people on board that station . . ." She voiced the thought out loud, not directing it at anyone, the implications mystifying her.

"*Hundreds* of thousands," Marvin corrected.

Mikka struggled to breathe, oxygen refusing to enter her lungs, as though the shuttle bay doors had already opened to the vacuum of space. She swallowed, her stomach swirling at the thought of their presence on the *Eclipse*.

How could it possibly be so many?

"Seven years?" Mikka pressed. She had to learn more about this man. "In *seven years*, you couldn't find another way off the station?"

"You know the penalty for harboring a stowaway. How much more of a risk would it have been to take someone from a FLOW station? I'm no angel, but even I wouldn't have taken that risk for anyone. Plus, every person I told was a risk. Without even meaning to, they could have exposed me to the station Admin. I would've been killed, along with anyone else who discovered who I really was. I needed to find a pirate; someone with nothing to lose. And those people aren't exactly broadcasting their presence to the rest of the Loop. It was a miracle I was able to connect with Abigail here, and even then, it took a lot of persuading to convince her I was the real deal. Being marooned on a station is not exactly a common occurrence."

"But *how* did you get here? What happened to the *Double Circle*? Why couldn't you fly off with your own ship?"

"That's a story for another day. What's the holdup? Why are we taking so long to get loaded up?"

"Red tape, love," Abigail replied. "Apparently, your death hasn't gone unnoticed around here."

"We brought in a delivery," Mikka said. "It took some convincing to get clearance."

"'Delivery?'" Marvin asked. "What kind of delivery would you be making *to* a FLOW station?"

"That's not your concern," Mikka said. "No offense, but I've only just met you. I've got client confidentiality to think about. You understand."

Marvin nodded, but he wasn't satisfied.

"Something smells off. In seven years, we've never *received* a shipment."

"Sorry, friend. That's all I can tell you."

"Sometimes, the less we know, the better," Abigail offered.

"You can say that again," Mikka replied, shaking her head.

All she wanted was to get off the station and take her mother some of the seed.

CHAPTER TWENTY-NINE

Django
Eclipse

THE NOTE. *Of course.*

Avery had known all along where Django would be and at what time. Now that he thought about it, that explained why she wasn't with Isaacs while Nova had been collecting her things. She didn't have to *look* for him; she just had to wait for him to come to her.

And he had brought Eventide and Nova with him.

Django cursed under his breath. He had known there was a risk of getting caught, but what with everything else that had happened over the past few hours, he had forgotten who had given him the note. He had forgotten Eventide's warning.

How do you know it's not a setup?

Avery had been working for Benson this entire time, following Django's every move. Each time she had rung their doorbell, he should have realized she had been keeping tabs on them, waiting for the opportunity to finally bring him in.

The trio stood frozen. There was nowhere to run and no way they could hope to overtake Avery. They were at her mercy.

"Your sister's right." Avery nodded toward Nova. "Her life isn't at risk. She wasn't in the lounge when the viewport went down. She could go on to live a long and healthy life with her new family."

"What kind of life would she have here?" Django asked.

At the same time, Eventide chimed in with, "How do you know about the viewports?"

"There's no time to answer either of those questions," Avery answered. "Come with me."

She waved them into the light of the cargo bay. Tension filled every ounce of Django's body. There was nothing he could do now but follow Avery and come up with a means of escape later.

Avery was an easy target for his anger, but she was as much a pawn in this game as he was. Commander Benson was the real source of all this. That man understood the truth. He was their leader, and he had lied to them. And now he was seeking to end not just Django's life but Eventide's, too. For whatever reason, Benson had drawn a target on his back.

The cargo bay wasn't anything like Django had imagined. He had pictured a large luxurious chamber with dozens of men and women running around, hauling supplies, and feeding them into multiple crafts. Instead, the room was lackluster. A shuttle sat in its center, on legs that lifted the base of its frame eight feet off the ground. A conveyor belt loaded with crates ran from the large storage warehouse behind the shuttle bay to the base of the craft. The pilots had backed the shuttle toward a large cargo bay door that led to the same warehouse.

Django could see a few men and women loading pallets through the ship's hatch. Their muffled voices echoed throughout the cavernous space; instructions without form, commands without meaning.

Piles of cargo, storage containers, and equipment lay scattered about the room. Boxes marked with red, large-blocked lettering that read "BLACK SWAN" and "SC17" were piled next to the shuttle.

The bay smelled of fertilizer, dirt, metal, and a burnt aroma that faintly resembled food.

It took Django a moment to process the craft that sat dormant before them. He had never seen a spaceship up close before. Its frame had seen better days, and the hull was banged up in various places, black scuff marks marring its surface, and its painted features had faded and were peeling off the craft's side.

"The *Black Swan*," he said, unable to contain his awe.

A wave of sadness washed over him. He had made it so close, yet he'd likely never see the inside of the craft. Instead, Avery would probably kill them. She wouldn't even have to do anything; just leave them in the bay long enough for the shuttle door to open and allow the vacuum to take them.

"No," Avery said. "The *Black Swan* was destroyed."

Django tensed. He could feel Eventide straighten beside him.

Just how far did Benson go to stop me from leaving? Would he have destroyed a shuttle?

He supposed it didn't matter now. Whatever means Benson had used to stop Django from leaving had worked. He had stopped an escape that, until a few hours ago, Django didn't even know he wanted.

But now there was nothing else he wanted more.

"So, . . . it's gone now. This was all a waste."

Avery must have been getting a good laugh. He had been running around the station all day, attempting to bring his two allies to a place of escape. That shuttle was supposed to be their safety net; a chance to avert death.

It was all for nothing.

"This is the *Redemption*," Avery said. "It's taking over the *Black Swan*'s shipment. Those two attendants," Avery nodded to a man and a woman who were loading crates onto a conveyor belt that led into the belly of the ship, "will finish loading the ship's manifest soon. Once they're done, you'll only have a minute or two to get to the ship, crawl up into its cargo hold, and find a place to hide yourselves. Don't come out until you've reached the ship's destination, no matter what happens. There isn't a ship's captain out there who will want to be caught bringing a stowaway into port. They won't hesitate to eject you into orbit. Or that's what I was told, at least."

"Wait." He voiced the thought out loud, pausing as he tried to sort out what she had just finished saying. "What do you mean? Are you . . . *helping* us?"

Django didn't know what to believe anymore. This woman had done a fine job of riding the fence between good and evil, and he wondered if she even knew if she was going to help them or send them out the airlock.

"There's only so much I can do without raising suspicions," Avery replied. "But if you can get onto that shuttle before anyone sees you with me, I can report that I was unable to find you after my extensive search."

"But why?" Django asked. "What business does a station patrol have helping a bunch of 'dirty D-Ringers?'"

Eventide cleared her throat.

Avery's face darkened, and she averted her eyes from Django's. "I . . . I owed your Uncle Marvin. We had gotten to know each other over the last few years."

"Is that how you know about the outside?" Eventide asked. "Patrols shouldn't know that there's more going on out there."

"Marvin told me a few things—more than he should have, maybe more than he wanted to. After that, I was curious and did some searching on my own, but there isn't much information on the systems I have access to. Most of what's there is encrypted. I know there are more people out there than we've been led to believe. I know Benson and the A-Ringers have access to that knowledge. And I know this shuttle can take you someplace else; maybe somewhere you'll be able to make a life for yourselves. But if you stay here, you won't have that option. They'll kill both of you."

"What about me?" Nova's eyes scanned the facility wildly, taking in the wonder that few had ever seen. "You said they won't kill me. Can I stay here?"

"Nova!" Django admonished.

"If you wish to stay," Avery said, "I can take you back to the Jamesons' quarters. I'm sure I can explain your disappearance to Isaacs. They won't kill you as long as you never tell a soul about any of this."

"Maybe you can explain it here." Geoffrey Isaacs stepped out of the maintenance corridor; a large, one-handed energy blaster rested against his right shoulder.

Avery didn't miss a beat; the warmth in her demeanor fell away, and the cold soldier returned. "I was just telling Nova that you'd understand her brother had kidnapped her from right under your nose. I thought you were supposed to be watching her. If I hadn't found them, they'd be trying to stowaway on that ship right now."

Isaacs's eyes narrowed as they focused on Django. "This one has been trouble."

"His family was all killed in a hull breach . . ." Eventide offered.

Isaacs snorted. "And you. I knew you weren't *kidnapped*. Once a dirt-ringer, always a dirt-ringer! I thought the Academy would've taught you some sense in that training of yours."

Django's blood boiled. He could pull his father's gun out and fire, but likely not before Isaacs got a shot off, and Django didn't doubt the guard had substantially better aim than he did.

He wouldn't draw his weapon, but he had one chance to do *something*. And if he succeeded or failed rested wholly on whether Avery was trying to pull the wool over his eyes or Isaacs's.

Without another thought, he launched himself at the guard, squatting so that his shoulder connected with Isaacs's ribs between the ceramic panels of his uniform and maneuvering his elbow so that it plowed into his gut. The plated armor scraped against Django's skin, but his arms were thin enough to connect with the soft fabric areas that lacked protection. The clang of Isaacs's weapon hitting the metal floor followed.

Django's momentum pushed the guard over and pulled him on top of the man. The officer's head smacked the metal-ridged floor with a *thunk* and a wide-eyed look of surprise.

His knuckles connected with Isaacs's face before Django realized he had thrown a punch; the impact set the officer's head against the metal one final time.

Arms wrapped around Django and pulled him up, away from the man who now lay unconscious on the floor.

Django lunged forward, instinct taking hold, dying to land another hit on the officer's jawline, but the hold on him was firm. Nothing but the sound of his own pulse flooded Django's ears.

His hands were pulled behind his back, and when he tried to move them, he realized they were in cuffs.

"You idiot," Avery admonished behind him.

His adrenaline slowly settled as the world around him came into focus once again.

Dozens of eyes all rested on Django. Workers stood at the edge of the cargo bay with their mouths open in amazement, some curled up in a grin that seemed to say, "*stupid kid*."

"All right, folks," Avery called out. "Show's over. Back to work."

The crowd murmured as most of them returned to whatever task they had been doing. Some lingered, using the distraction to get out of working for a few extra moments before the whistles of supervisors sent them scrambling, too.

"So much for not drawing attention to yourselves," she muttered.

"So what?" Django said. "Isaacs gets what he deserves, and we mosey on our way. What's with the cuffs?"

"Well, dumbass," Avery said, "a couple dozen people saw you kick the shit out of him. What do you think would happen if I just let you stand up and walk out of here? I'll be sent out the airlock right beside you."

"Airlock? I thought we were getting on that shuttle . . ."

"Yeah, well, you've made *that* a lot more complicated. Not to mention when Isaacs wakes up, he's going to wonder what happened and why I didn't shoot you. Which, to be honest, I'm starting to wonder myself."

"So, your solution is to send us out the airlock?"

"Not exactly the sharpest plow in the field, are you?" Avery turned her attention to Eventide. "I don't know why you've thrown your lot in with this one. Being a technician is one of the most privileged professions on the station. Sure you want to throw that away?"

"It turns out the other technicians would never have accepted me, anyway."

Django squirmed, tensing his arms to test his bonds. The cold metal cuffs were a gentle reminder that, no matter what, he wouldn't break through steel.

"Calm down," Avery said. "Nobody's getting sent out the airlock. But I've got to make it look believable, or this will come to bite me in the ass later."

"But how are you going to explain this to Isaacs?" Django asked. "The entire hold just saw you cuff me."

"Don't worry about me. We just have to make sure you get on that ship."

"How are we going to do that now? Everyone's watching."

"They won't be in a minute. The cargo bay door is scheduled to open, so everyone's going to get out of here. Nobody is allowed to be here when that happens."

"So, we're going to have to try and board while the bay depressurizes?"

Django's mind raced. There had to be another way. The ship was only a few dozen feet away, but despite that, he didn't think they'd have enough time to jump on board with the air being sucked out of the hold.

"You sure are quick to panic," Avery commented.

"I think I've got reason—"

"The crew hasn't boarded yet. You'll have to jump into the hold, but you'll have a minute or two before they come round to do their pre-flight checks. Plan is the same as before; you'll just have to jump a little."

"And what about him?" Django nodded to Isaacs. "Can you just leave him out here until the shuttle leaves?"

"I wish—but, unfortunately, no. I'll carry him into the maintenance corridor and find someone to help take him to the Med Lab. I'll tell him you overpowered both of us, and we barely made it out alive. We'll get shit from Benson, but we'll be okay."

"*Benson,*" Django scoffed. "I wish I could give that asshat a piece of what I gave to Isaacs. I hate leaving here knowing that he'll still be in charge."

"You think getting rid of Benson would change things? Boy, you sure have a lot to learn."

"Things would be a lot better off. I've got unfinished business here, and I'll do everything in my power to make sure he meets his end. He needs to pay for keeping us in the dark. For killing my family."

"Don't make any brash decisions," Avery warned. "The complexity of these things might surprise you."

"Oh yeah? And what do you know of it?"

"As much as Marvin was willing to tell me, which wasn't much. But enough to know priorities change when you consider things from another point of view."

The wall separating the loading dock from the rear of the shuttle moved, interrupting their exchange. The divider was closing, isolating the bay from the rest of the station as the loading team scrambled to push the last couple of crates off their carts.

"Are you ladies ready?" Django asked.

"No," Nova said. "I told you, I'm not going!"

"But Nova . . ." So much had gone wrong. There were only two people left alive who he couldn't stand to lose. Nova *couldn't* stay here. He couldn't accept losing her, too.

His heart pounded. They were so close to their goal. His mind raced, trying to form a compelling argument to convince his sister —and struggling to comprehend why he had to.

"Do you realize what staying here means? Even if you're safe, we might *never* see each other again. This is our one shot to leave —*together*. If we don't, they'll kill me—and Eventide, too. And once I go, I might never be able to come back." He thought he had successfully hidden the emotion in his voice, but Eventide lifted a consoling hand to his shoulder.

He ignored the waves of warmth that radiated from her touch.

"Please come with us."

"I don't want to leave," Nova said. "Everything else has changed, but at least I have friends here. And you don't know that we'll never see each other again. You don't know the future."

Nova offered a smile. Apparently, Django's sister had a thicker skin than he gave her credit for.

A thicker skin than him.

Eventide offered him a pitying glance. "You can't choose for her," she said. "That's what everyone's been doing for you—for all of us—our whole lives."

Django couldn't ignore the logic, but he hadn't known any better. *They* hadn't known better. He had believed the choice had been his, but he had only followed the grooves that had been dug for him.

And he had only seen that once Benson had taken everything from him.

Now, Nova stood at the same crossroads—and she still wanted to stay. Everything in his being wanted to grab her; to carry her to the shuttle and toss her inside.

She would thank him one day.

Avery reached over and, with a *beep*, unlocked the cuffs that bound him. Without hesitation, he opened his arms and embraced Nova in the most encompassing hug he had ever given.

At the end of the day, Uncle Marvin had shown him the respect to make his own decisions and had provided the path for him to escape. He still didn't know what that meant, and he imagined that even his uncle hadn't been clear on the details. But he'd still allowed Django to come to his own conclusions.

And he'd have to do the same for Nova.

Nova's words from earlier that day struck him, and he couldn't help but repeat them with a heavy heart. "We'll always be family. No matter where I live. No matter where you are. That will never change." He lifted a hand to her face. "One day, when you're ready, I'll come back for you. Just try to avoid any hull breaches."

Besides, I still have a score to settle with Benson.

He grabbed Nova's chin between his thumb and finger, studying his sister's face. He wanted to say something more, something inspiring, but words failed him. There was nothing more to say.

Behind him, the wall hissed as it sealed off the rest of the station from the cargo bay. If they didn't want to get caught by the ship's crew, they were going to have to move.

"I'll make sure she's looked after," Avery promised. "But you're out of time! *Go!*"

Django shared a quick look with Eventide and then the two friends sprinted toward the ship.

CHAPTER THIRTY

Mikka
The *Redemption*

THE *ECLIPSE* FADED in the *Redemption*'s wake. Lunar lay ahead of them, brightly reflecting the sun's glow, the darkness of space threatening to swallow it.

Tonight, orbital traffic was clear. Mikka shuddered at the eerie calm. Despite the ease of their passage, she always felt vulnerable. There was less traffic to get lost in; fewer ships to blend in with. She didn't run too many late-night deliveries anymore; legitimate jobs all took place during the day.

But she supposed those days were behind her.

Abigail sat on a lounge seat to the side of the bridge, with Marvin beside her. The two whispered to each other, and Mikka surmised the two of them shared a past. Not romantic, perhaps, but intimate in other ways. Perhaps they'd flown together, once upon a distant past.

Maybe Mikka would learn what that past had been, but she didn't see a need to continue dealing with the pirate once they completed this job. It wouldn't be hard to find a buyer for the

Infinity crop, even in so large a quantity. A bidding war over the seed was more likely. She imagined she'd be parting ways with the pirate sooner rather than later.

Kiara had the controls, allowing Mikka to move through the ship. She slipped through the door leading into the cargo hold. The hum of the *Redemption* sang to her, more alive than it had felt in ages.

Over the years, Mikka had learned to read her ship; learned to understand it was a living vessel. And right now, the *Redemption* itched for adventure; itched to be more than a delivery shuttle between the Earth ports and Lunar. Mikka wasn't sure what kind of adventure it sought or what kind it would get—but she was certain it'd receive it.

Hundreds of thousands.

The number continued to haunt her. Men. Women. Children. All dead.

Her skin crawled, itching with the ramifications of what that meant. The Syndicate had killed before. Why did this feel so much different? Why was this the tipping point? Was killing hundreds of thousands worse than killing tens of thousands? Or thousands? How many lives lost would have been acceptable?

It was that thought which bothered her the most because, in her heart, she knew the number was greater than one. A handful? A dozen? These numbers she could have shrugged off. People died every day.

But this was murder. Large-scale, megalomaniac-scale murder.

And yet . . .

How many died every day in the Lunar Underground from malnutrition, lunar sickness, and neglect?

More deaths. Murders? Perhaps.

Hundreds of thousands.

How far did that number stretch when it included the untold

number of forgotten corpses hidden by the corporation that had damned them? How many had suffered an unnecessarily cruel fate? Millions? More?

Mikka hadn't planned on inspecting their inventory, but her body moved toward one of their loaded crates on instinct, and she was beside it before she realized where she had walked. She had to know; had to be sure that this shipment was legitimate before she would get her hopes up about what it could mean for her and her mother.

Not that they aren't sky-high already. But Infinity *Corielus? Could it really be true?*

She ran her finger over the wooden container. It was rare enough to see shipping material made of wood. Trees weren't rare, per se, but they also weren't being chopped down like they had been a couple of hundred years ago. Reforestation was a necessary step to terraforming Earth—and, more recently, Mars. The greenery on the Earth's surface had remained untouched, as far as she knew. At the very least, it didn't *leave* the surface. Supplies and materials were transported *to* Earth, not the other way around.

A civil war is brewing.

David's words wouldn't let her go. As much as Mikka didn't want to admit they would affect her, she knew what the ramifications of a war would be. And she knew her new role meant she'd be in the thick of it. Even if the pallets before her were filled to the brim with *Infinity* Corielus, her fate was still tied to David Aries and to whatever plan for war he was devising.

Hundreds of thousands.

Did knowing what had happened to *Infinity* change how invested she'd be in the war ahead? How could she ignore that?

Mikka shuddered.

Aries was holding her past over her head. How much did he

know? There were crimes she'd rather not revisit; secrets she dared not even admit to herself. What if they came to light?

War was coming. Hours ago, she hadn't cared. Now, she pondered what role she'd play. Would David's side be the winning side? Was it the right side? A side that would willingly sacrifice hundreds of thousands of lives certainly wasn't.

Perhaps there was merit to his posturing.

She pushed the thoughts down deep. There was nothing that could be done about them. Not yet.

The wood of the crate felt rough against her fingers. She dragged them across its surface, savoring the uncommon texture of raw timber. Its contents, if nothing else, would decide her mother's fate.

She walked around the box and stopped short, frozen at the sight of the black ink printed on the box. It had faded with age, but the word was more than legible.

"I told you, love." Abigail stood in the doorway to the cockpit, arms crossed, leaning against her staff. "It's exactly as I said."

Stamped on the crate's side, in big, block letters, was the word "INFINITY."

All of it was true.

Django
The *Redemption*

"I SWEAR IT WAS HIM," Django whispered.

The storage space had descended into darkness as soon as the ship's hatch closed. It was so dark Django couldn't even make out his own hand when he held it to his face.

He sat as close to Eventide as he thought she'd allow, ensuring their shoulders touched so that they had some sense of where the other was in the foreign hold. Eventide pressed her body against his, surprising him, as she cuddled into the crook of his arm, wrapping herself around him. Apparently, she wasn't a fan of the dark, either.

The ship above them creaked and groaned. Django tried not to let the noises unsettle him, but there was no way to push down the unease he felt at its complaints. He had no idea where the ship was going. He didn't even know where there was to go. The only clue he had received from his now-dead uncle was that they were simply going "away."

His dead uncle, whose voice Django swore he had heard.

"It's not him, Django," Eventide said softly. "It can't be."

"I know," he said. "Sorry. Just wishful thinking."

"It's okay to miss him," Eventide said. "You've been through so much this week. It's perfectly understandable that you're hearing things."

Django, for the moment, was grateful for the darkness the storage unit provided. Eventide wouldn't be able to see his tears, at least.

Life changes fast and in ways you don't expect.

Django couldn't have known how foretelling his uncle's words would have been. Forty-eight hours ago, if someone had told him even half of what would later transpire, he wouldn't have believed them. Now, he sat in the cargo hold of a shuttle, leaving his home for good.

He couldn't respond to Eventide's attempt at comfort. If he did, he knew he'd break down, and today wasn't about that. It wasn't about everything he'd lost. It wasn't about the sister he'd left behind with a security officer with questionable allegiances or the dead uncle whose voice he swore he'd heard.

Django felt around in the darkness for Eventide's hand and found it, squeezing it in a comforting gesture, though he had no doubt he was comforting himself more than her.

Whatever lay ahead, no matter their destination, he knew only one thing for certain: his life would never be the same.

AFTERWORD

Thank you for reading Eclipse and joining Django and Mikka on their journey.

As an independent author, reviews are really important. They help other readers—like you—discover my work.

If you liked the book, and have a couple of minutes to spare, it would be great if you could leave a short, honest review on Amazon, Goodreads, your bookish blog, social media or of course, on the book's retail page.

Thank you!

Watch for the second instalment of *The Fractured Orbit*, available in 2023.

ACKNOWLEDGMENTS

Writing can be a lonely process. You're sitting at a desk (or coffee shop, etc.) for hours and hours on end, drafting, editing, reading and marketing. It doesn't have to be though, and I am fortunate to have a team of individuals surrounding me and I greatly appreciate those who I've had the privilege of interacting with during the drafting of Eclipse. The more time I spend writing, the more I find myself surrounded by wonderful people.

I'd like to thank each and every one of you who have been part of this journey. I am sure to miss somebody though, but please know you are appreciated.

Shane Millar who gave this book an initial manuscript assessment and helped encourage me when imposter syndrome set in. And even without knowing it, your interview with Jeff Elkins was responsible for the inclusion of Faron and the ramped up tension Django felt in his longing for Eventide.

I'd like to thank Pete Smith from Novel Approach Manuscript Services for providing it with a copy edit, and assisting with details and phrasings that I was at a loss for.

To Aime Sund at Red Leaf Word Services for the final proofread and catching my Canadian-isms before the book hit the shelves.

Covers by Christian who outdid himself in the creation of this cover. I couldn't be happier with it.

I want to thank all of my author friends from my various writing circles who have provided feedback and encouragement.

The group at Dystopian Ink who created *The Dystopian Guide to the Galaxy*, if it wasn't for that anthology and my short story *Infinity, Eclipse* wouldn't exist. To the Rebel Author Slack group, thank you for your encouragement and motivation to set goals and stick to them. To my friends in the Dystopian Author League who are always willing to promote and lift each other up. All of the others who have offered a word of support and encouragement along the way.

And as always to my lovely wife Nettie, who understands my early mornings, late evenings, and weekends at the keyboard. It is truly a blessing to have someone so supportive behind me.

ABOUT THE AUTHOR

Herman Steuernagel is a science fiction and fantasy author. His internationally best-selling debut Lies the Guardians Tell reached the top of the science fiction charts in multiple countries.

Herman grew up with a love of story and science fiction, watching Star Trek, The Next Generation with his father. As a teenager he fell in love with The Sword of Shannara by Terry Brooks, and The Wheel of Time series by Robert Jordan.

His currently published works are dystopian science fiction that highlight the struggle between humanity and the technology we keep, as well as the motivations that keep us fighting with each other.

Herman currently lives in British Columbia, Canada, While he's not working on a new book he can be found cycling, running and dreaming up new worlds.

ALSO BY HERMAN STEUERNAGEL

Lies of the Guardians

Lies the Guardians Tell

Secrets of the Sphere

Sins of the Ancients

—

The Terre Hoffman Chronicles

The Guardian Program

Artificial Insurgence

Artificial Insurrection

CPSIA information can be obtained
at www.ICGtesting.com
Printed in the USA
LVHW101038190223
739874LV00017B/1024/J